EVENING THE ODDS

"Damn it to hell—Summers and the woman are getting away!"

Langler ran to the side door and threw it open. Realizing his mistake too late, he flung himself to one side as Grayson's and Fallon's rifles exploded in the dark from their two separate positions. Bullets sliced past him. One clipped him in his forearm; another swiped his hat from his head.

"Don't shoot. It's me!" he bellowed between rifle fire.

"Cole?" Grayson shouted toward the open side door.

"Yes, me, damn it!" Langler replied.

"Where's Cherry and the horse trader?" Fallon shouted, looking all around in the dark.

"I'm right here," Will Summers said in a firm voice, less than ten feet behind him.

Fallon shrieked in surprise; he swung around with his smoking rifle cocked and ready. But all he saw was the blinding flash of Summers' shot. . . .

D0028081

INCIDENT AT GUNN POINT

Ralph Cotton

A SIGNET BOOK

SIGNET
Published by New American Library, a division of
Penguin Group (USA) Inc., 375 Hudson Street,
New York, New York 10014, USA
Penguin Group (Canada), 90 Eglinton Avenue East, Suite 700, Toronto,
Ontario M4P 2Y3, Canada (a division of Pearson Penguin Canada Inc.)
Penguin Books Ltd., 80 Strand, London WC2R 0RL, England
Penguin Ireland, 25 St. Stephen's Green, Dublin 2,
Ireland (a division of Penguin Books Ltd.)
Penguin Group (Australia), 250 Camberwell Road, Camberwell, Victoria 3124,
Australia (a division of Pearson Australia Group Pty. Ltd.)
Penguin Books India Pvt. Ltd., 11 Community Centre, Panchsheel Park,
New Delhi - 110 017, India
Penguin Group (NZ), 67 Apollo Drive, Rosedale, Auckland 0632,
New Zealand (a division of Pearson New Zealand Ltd.)
Penguin Books (South Africa) (Pty.) Ltd., 24 Sturdee Avenue,
Rosebank, Johannesburg 2196, South Africa

Penguin Books Ltd., Registered Offices:
80 Strand, London WC2R 0RL, England

First published by Signet, an imprint of New American Library,
a division of Penguin Group (USA) Inc.

First Printing, February 2012
10 9 8 7 6 5 4 3 2

For Mary Lynn . . . *of course*

PART 1

Chapter 1

―――――

Will Summers had heard the sudden blasts of rifle and pistol fire echo out to him along the rocky hills far to his left. He'd stopped his dapple gray and pulled his four-horse string up alongside him. He listened intently as the gunfire raged for only a matter of seconds before falling away as quickly as it had started.

What was that about . . . ?

Summers scanned the black roofline of Gunn Point above the thin fresh layer of snow lying between him and the small town. His first thought was that the shooting could've been a couple of range hands who'd awakened surly and hungover in the rooms above Caster Stems' Maplethorpe Saloon, and crossed each other's paths on the way to their horses. He'd known it to happen just that way, he reminded himself.

But no, that wasn't it. Not cowhands . . . too many guns involved.

He watched wood smoke curl upward from tin stove-pipes and stone chimneys and drift away on the crisp morning air. Beside him steam billowed and swirled in the breaths of the four-horse string. Their backs glistened, half frosted, half wet—more steam wafting in the heat of their bodies.

Beneath him his dapple gray chuffed and snorted, and now that they had come to a halt, the big barb scraped a forehoof on the snow-covered ground, revealing a patch of dried wild grass.

"Pay attention here," Summers said quietly to the dapple gray, "you'll get your breakfast." He tucked up the reins to keep the barb from dipping his head. The dapple shook out his mane and blew out a steamy breath.

As Summers continued scanning the distant rooflines, shooting broke out again, this time on the trail leading out of Gunn Point in his direction. *All right, whatever it is . . .* , he told himself, he didn't want to be sitting midtrail on the open flatlands when the trouble arrived.

Summers levered a round into the Winchester's chamber and kept the rifle in his gloved right hand, the same hand holding the lead rope to his horse string. Like the dapple gray, the four horses had also begun scraping their forehooves and dipping their heads. He gave a tug on the lead rope as he tapped his heels to the dapple's side.

"Sorry, fellows, not yet," he murmured to the string. "Let's clear out of here."

Looking all around as he led the horses away from the trail and across the snow-streaked ground, Summers told himself the shooting must have been a robbery—a raid of some sort. That would have been his first thought had he been able to think of any business in Gunn Point worth robbing. But it had been over a year since he'd last been in town. Change came quickly in this rocky hill country, especially if there were any traces of ore in the ground.

But that was neither here nor there, he reminded himself, scanning the barren flatlands. What mattered now was cover—a safe spot for him and his horses. Whatever was coming would be here soon enough, and he would deal with it. But given a choice, he'd rather deal with it with his shoulder against a rock and his horses somewhere out of sight behind him.

No cover . . . , he thought as he slowed the dapple and the string almost to a halt. "Now what?" he heard himself say aloud. His breath steamed off on a cold breeze. He looked toward Gunn Point as he heard heavy firing coming from closer to town, followed by a few shots farther along on the trail.

"Yep, a robbery of some sort," he concluded to himself and the dapple gray. He could picture it now, a band of thieves leaving town in a hurry, a sheriff and a group of hastily gathered townsmen in hot pursuit. That was it, he told himself, looking toward the sound of the gunfire as two black dots rode into sight at the head of a white trail of swirling snow.

Out of the white swirl two more black dots came into sight, riding hard to catch up to their partners. *There's the thieves. . . .*

Summers turned his gray and jerked the string along beside him. Farther back along the trail, he saw another rise of swirling snow. *And there's the sheriff and his posse.*

He felt a little better knowing what to expect. But knowing didn't provide much comfort, not when he and his animals were still out in the open, standing in a swirl of their own steam, about to be caught up in the midst of the fighting.

"What a spot to be on," he said, still searching back and forth for any cover large enough to stop a bullet. There were times to pitch in and help the law, and there were times it was better to drop back out of the way and let the law do its job.

He considered quickly how this could all look to an angry posse—him out here on the flats with four horses, just the right number of mounts to have waiting. As he thought about it, he heard the shots firing back and forth along the trail, drawing closer every second.

This was not the time or place to get in the law's way. In the swirl of snow, their bullets had no way of knowing which side he was on. This was the time to lie back, let the thieves get past him—offer them no resistance, and wait for the posse. With any luck the sheriff and his posse would believe he had nothing to do with whatever the four riders were running away from.

All right, it wasn't the best idea he'd ever had, he told himself, turning the dapple gray, but it would have to do. He loped farther away from the trail, at an easy pace, leading his string, trying to raise no more powdery snow than he had to. He wondered if Turner Goss was still the sheriff in Gunn Point. He hoped so, he thought, looking back over his shoulder at the second cloud of snow rising and swirling along the trail.

Three miles back along the trail, riding sightless in the billowing snow raised by the fleeing gunmen, Deputy Parley Stiles stopped firing and raised a gloved hand.

"Stop shooting!" he called out over his shoulder. He

carefully slowed his horse down gradually until he realized the men following him did as they were told. As he slowed to a halt, the deputy could see the wake of powdery snow raised by the gunmen's horses already beginning to clear a little.

"Why are we stopping, Parley?" a townsman called out a few feet behind him. "We can't stop now! Not while we've got them in our gun sights. Let's ride them down!"

"Settle down, Dewitt," said the young deputy. "We're not stopping any longer than it takes to clear the air some."

"But damn it, Deputy—!" the mining engineer named Horace Dewitt cursed before the deputy cut him off.

"Strike that language from your mouth, Dewitt," the young deputy demanded. "Else you won't ride another step with this posse."

"I meant nothing by it, Parley," Dewitt said, fuming, but keeping his temper in check. "I'm speaking for all of us! We need to stay right down their shirts until we—"

"Don't call me Parley again," the young deputy snapped, once more cutting the miner short.

"It is your name!" the engineer countered. "What the hell—I mean heck—are we being so formal about?"

"I'm Deputy Stiles to every one of you," the deputy said, loud enough for all to hear. "Especially while I'm leading this posse." He looked around in turn from one face to the next through the steaming breath of men and animals.

"We understand, Deputy," said a meek voice among the townsmen. "But why are we stopping? Shouldn't we—?"

"To keep from breaking our necks and ruining some good horses," the deputy said with authority before the timid apothecary clerk could finish his words.

"Our deputy is right," said a gambler named Herbert Long. "As long as they've got a clear trail and we're stuck with riding in their wake, they've got the odds working in their favor."

Dewitt grumbled something cross under his breath, spit and looked away. "This ain't no poker game, Herbert," he said sorely, settling a little, but still clearly not happy about following the young deputy's orders.

"Oh, but I beg to differ with you, my ore-craving friend," Long replied with a hint of disdain lying beneath a rich Southern accent. "It's all poker." He passed a slight knowing smile around to the others. "We've only just been dealt this hand. Now we need to study our cards closely before we commit to any—"

"Anybody needs to step down and relieve himself, this might the best chance for a while," said Deputy Stiles, cutting the gambler off as readily as he had the others.

The gambler gave a toss of his gloved hand as if in submission. He swung down from his saddle and stepped away reins length from his horse. Four more of the seven riders followed suit. Deputy Stiles stayed in his saddle, staring straight ahead into the settling crystalline veil. To his left, Horace Dewitt stayed in his saddle, as did Martin Heintz, the town druggist.

As the splatter of the four dismounted men's urine set new rises of steam curling up from the cold ground, Dewitt shook his head in disgust and turned away.

Noting Dewitt's gesture, the gambler grinned, shook himself off and said, "I don't suppose any of you gentlemen had the foresight to bring along a bottle of whiskey, perchance."

"There will be no drinking, and no talk of drinking, in this posse," Stiles called out before anyone could respond in any manner.

"There you have it," Long murmured to himself, buttoning the fly on his frayed and faded pin-striped trousers. He put on his right glove and closed the front of his wool overcoat. "The voice of the law has spoken."

Leading the thieves, Jackie Warren spotted Summers and his four-horse string sitting a hundred yards off the trail. With no warning to the three other speeding horsemen behind him, the young outlaw jerked his horse to a reckless halt.

"What the hell!" shouted Henry Grayson, almost thrown from his saddle as his horse veered to keep from slamming into Warren's horse and tumbling end over end. The other two also veered and reined down. When all three horses had stumbled and slid to a stop, their riders glared at Jackie Warren as their horses settled.

"What's wrong with you, Little Jackie?" Grayson shouted behind his bandanna mask. He circled in close.

"Not a damn thing, Henry!" the young outlaw shouted in reply. He jerked his bandanna down from across the bridge of his nose and nodded toward the lone rider and the four horses sitting staring at them across the snowy flatlands. "Take a look at this." He gave a grin. "Are those our horses?"

The other three masked riders looked out at Summers, who sat with his Winchester resting propped up from his thigh—his warning for the four of them to ride on.

"Hell no," Henry Grayson said. He stared for a second, then said to Warren and the others, "All right, let's get going. We still got the law on our rumps." But before he could slap his reins to his horse and bat his boots to its sides, young Jackie reached out and grabbed his horse by its bridle.

"What's your hurry, Henry?" he said. "That posse has quit us. This is all going our way."

"Like hell they've quit us," said Lewis Fallon, a young Texas outlaw out of Waco. He looked back warily toward the swirl of white still adrift on their back trail.

"You don't hear any shooting, do you?" Jackie said.

"That doesn't mean they've turned back," said Avrial Rochenbach, known to the others as a former Pinkerton detective turned bandit.

"What about this one?" Jackie said, nodding at the single figure looking back at them from a hundred yards out.

"What about him?" said Grayson.

"He's got horses," Jackie Warren said, a Spencer rifle in his gloved hand. "We ought to take them just in case ours wear out. Especially mine." Behind his saddle his saddlebags bulged with stolen money.

"We've got horses waiting. We don't need his," Grayson said. "We don't need nothing he's got."

"But he might have seen our faces," Jackie said, searching for any reason to create mayhem.

"Not ours, he hasn't" said Grayson. "We kept our masks on like we all agreed to do." He jerked his horse away from Jackie's hand and slapped his reins to its withers. "This thing is set up perfect. Stick to our plans. Let's ride!" he shouted.

The other two outlaws booted their horses along

behind him. But before turning his horse, Jackie threw his rifle to his shoulder and shouted, "Yi-hiiii!" out across the flatlands. He fired wildly.

Summers saw the bullet strike the ground ten feet in front of him. Instinctively he raised his rifle. Yet he held his fire, hoping the outlaw was only giving him a warning.

"That's it, ride on," Summers murmured. "We've both got better things to do than shoot each other."

He saw the first three horses already pulling away. The fourth was ready to bat his horse's sides to catch up with them. But before the last outlaw left, he pulled off one more wild shot.

From the string beside him, Summers heard one of the horses whinny in pain. He caught a sidelong glance as the horse half rose on its hind legs and toppled to the ground in a spray of blood and snow.

At the head of the riders, Henry Grayson looked around at the sound of Jackie Warren's rifle shot. On the flatlands he heard the dying horse and looked at it in time to see it fall.

"Damn it, Jackie!" He shouted. "Why did you do that?"

Jackie came riding up fast, laughing, holding his smoking rifle.

"I'm as surprised as you are, Henry!" he called out.

But no sooner had he spoken his words than Grayson and the others heard a return shot and saw the young outlaw fly out of his saddle as a blast of thick blood exploded from his side.

"Holy—!" shouted Grayson, seeing Jackie Warren hit the cold ground in a puff of snow.

"Get his horse, Henry!" shouted Rochenbach, jerking

his bandanna mask down from his face, seeing Jackie's spooked horse turn to take off across the flatlands.

Grayson made a grab for the horse's bridle but missed. Another shot exploded from Summers' Winchester. The shot whistled past Grayson's head.

"Shoot that bastard before he kills us all!" Grayson shouted.

"I'll get the money!" Rochenbach shouted, taking off after Warren's horse, seeing the heavily loaded saddlebags bouncing on the animal's back.

As soon as the bullet had hit one of his string horses, Summers had leaped out of his saddle and slapped his dapple gray's rump. He hurriedly cut the rope holding the three live string horses to the dead one and sent them racing out behind his gray. He hadn't wanted a fight; he hadn't wanted to lose a horse. But now that he had a horse down, he threw himself behind the body and laid his Winchester out across its side.

Kill my horse . . . ! He jerked a fresh round up into the rifle chamber. Steam curled from the gaping bullet hole in the dead horse's neck. He was in the fight now, whether he wanted it or not.

Chapter 2

Avrial Rochenbach fired three quick loose shots in Summers' direction with his big Remington revolver as he chased Jackie Warren's fleeing horse across the snowy flatlands. His shots were wild and unaimed, meant to threaten Summers, keep him down while he caught up to the horse and the saddlebags full of money. But Summers would have none of it. They had killed one of his horses. He wasn't about to lie still and let them ride away without a few bullets in them.

He took close aim on Rochenbach as the outlaw's Remington belched fire and lead in his direction. He squeezed the Winchester's trigger as the Remington's bullets whistled overhead.

Grayson and Lewis Fallon saw Rochenbach fly up from his saddle in a spray of blood, turn a backflip midair and land sprawled on his back in a puff of white powder. The Remington flew from Rochenbach's hand, spun in the air and exploded once more as it struck the hard, cold ground.

"Who does this *jake* think he is?" Henry Grayson

shouted in rage, seeing Rochenbach down and the horse with the money still galloping fast across the flatlands.

"Get that horse!" Lewis Fallon shouted, firing his big Colt toward Summers. The two raced across the flatlands.

"You get it," Grayson shouted, "whilst I kill this sumbitch!"

Summers saw the two masked outlaws split up, one riding after the loose horse, the other charging straight toward him. He took close aim as the outlaw leveled his Colt and fired at him. As Summers squeezed the Winchester's trigger, a bullet thumped into the dead horse and threw his aim a fraction off target. The bullet sliced along the side of Grayson's jaw and ripped his right ear away in a mist of blood.

Grayson bellowed and cursed and swung his horse away; his hat flew away. His right hand, gun and all, went up and cupped the side of his bloody head. He screamed loud and long as Summers watched him make a complete turn around and ride straightaway.

Taking aim on the fleeing outlaw's back, Summers knew he had him cold. But he held his shot and swung the Winchester toward the other outlaw chasing the spooked horse. He took careful aim, knowing he had all the time he needed to make the shot count.

"Jesus, Henry!" Fallon cried out, seeing Grayson ride away screaming with his hat gone and his hand to the side of his head. "What about the money?"

"Get it, bring it! I'm shot!" Grayson screamed back at him without turning in his saddle. He'd never seen anything set up this good turn so sour *this fast* in his life. *Damn, Jackie!* he cursed to himself.

Fallon had jerked his horse to a halt, unsure of what to do next. He looked toward the dead horse where rifle smoke wafted in the cold air. Whoever was there was deadly with a repeating rifle. He looked toward the running horse, seeing it do as most any frightened horse would do, given a chance. The animal had spotted Summers' dapple gray and the three string horses loping along across the snowy flatlands.

Looking back and forth quickly between the deadly rifle and the loose horse running away with the stolen money, Fallon made a decision, just as Summers started to squeeze the trigger.

"To hell with this!" Fallon said aloud. He batted his boots to his horse's sides, swung a sharp turn and raced away in the same direction Grayson had taken.

Seeing him turn to leave, Summers let his finger relax on the trigger. He lowered the Winchester an inch and watched both outlaws' horses pound away toward the white-streaked hills five miles in the distance.

All right, it's over. . . .

He started to lower his rifle more, but he snapped it back to his shoulder when he saw one of the downed outlaws struggle onto his knees and scrape his battered derby up and put it on his head.

"Grayson . . . wait . . . for me . . . ," Avrial Rochenbach rasped, his left arm hanging limp at his side, his long black riding duster hanging from his shoulders and spread on the ground around him like a shroud. He wobbled unsteadily in place for a second, then pitched forward onto his face.

Summers stood up behind the dead horse and looked to his left where the horses had run themselves out and were standing with their muzzles down, scraping and pulling wild grass. The dead outlaw's horse had joined them, settled and taken his place among his own kind. Rochenbach's horse ran toward the grazing animal at an easy gait.

The horses were good for now, Summers told himself. He let the hammer down on his Winchester and stepped from behind the dead horse. To his right he saw the rise of snow behind the posse growing closer. He knew they'd heard the shooting; they'd be here in another ten minutes.

Walking to the outlaw lying facedown on the ground, Summers nudged him with the toe of his boot.

"What are you doing alive?" he asked flatly. "I had you dead to rights." As he spoke he nudged the downed outlaw over onto his back. Rochenbach moaned, batted his blurry eyes and stared up the barrel of Summers' Winchester.

"I—I don't . . . know," the outlaw stammered. He tried to look at the bullet hole in his coat lying dangerously close to his heart. A wide circle of blood lay around the hole, and around the blood a wider circle of what had to be whiskey, Summers thought, judging from the smell of it. "I—I think . . . this flask must have . . . saved my life."

He started to reach his weak right hand under the lapel of his coat. But the tip of Summers' rifle barrel nudged his hand away, then flipped the lapel open. Summers saw the top of a metal whiskey flask sticking up from the outlaw's shirt pocket. In the bottom right corner of the pocket, he saw the bullet hole.

Summers stooped and stood up holding the dripping flask, seeing where the bullet had pierced it. Yet, inspecting the punctured flask, he saw how the bullet had deflected away from Rochenbach's heart and sliced its way deep into his left shoulder.

"You might be right," Summers said. He dropped the empty flask on the outlaw's stomach and said, "Here, you can hold on to this till they haul you off to jail."

The downed outlaw looked off toward the rise of snow as the posse rode closer. He shook his head slowly, then dropped it back to the ground. His derby flipped off and lay upside down in the snow.

"Finish me . . . *Winchester*," he pleaded, raising his hand and touching his fingertip to the middle of his forehead. "I can't . . . go to prison." He gulped a breath of cold air. "I put . . . too many men there. They'll kill me . . . sure enough."

"Who are you?" Summers asked, searching the pained face for any recognition.

"Avrial Rochenbach," the wounded man said. "You've got to let me go."

Summers gave a short nod and said, "Rochenbach . . . You used to be a detective for Allen Pinkerton."

"That's me," Rochenbach said with regret. "Now let me go. Nobody has to know."

"You're not going anywhere, except to jail," Summers said. "Do you want some water?" He gazed off toward his dapple gray and the other horses. Then he reached over with the tip of his rifle barrel, opened the man's riding duster and coat and probed his vest pocket, searching for a hideout gun, finding nothing there.

"I'm clean," said Rochenbach. "If I had a hideout I already would have gone for it."

"All right, you're not armed," Summers said. "Do you want some water?" he repeated.

Rochenbach nodded.

Summers turned facing the horses and let out a sharp loud whistle. The gray jerked his head up from grazing, looked toward him, then came pounding across the flatlands, loose stirrups flopping and bouncing at its sides. Behind the gray the other horses fell in and followed him as if on command.

"Damn," Rochenbach said. "I always wished I could whistle a horse that way."

"You'll have time to practice the whistling," Summers said flatly.

"That's real funny," Rochenbach said with a bitter twist. He paused; then watching Jackie Warren's horse lope along with its bulging saddlebags, he said, "What if I told you there's close to . . . a hundred thousand dollars on that horse's rump?"

"From where?" Summers asked.

"The new bank . . . in Gunn Point," the outlaw said.

"New bank?" Summers said.

"Yeah, it just . . . opened last month." He nodded toward the body of Jackie Warren lying dead in the snow. "His father owns it. What do you think of that?" He raised his head slightly from the ground

Summers just stared for a moment, wondering if that could possibly be true.

"I think you're lying," he finally said.

The wounded man managed a dark chuckle and shook his head. "My whole life has been too crazy to believe." He nodded toward the horse approaching and said, "I'll split the money with you . . . you just get me up, let me ride away from here."

"Why would I split it with you?" Summers said, gazing off toward the coming posse. "If I killed you, I'd have it all."

"Oh," said Rochenbach, "so if money's involved, you would *shoot an unarmed man*?"

Summers didn't answer. He turned to the dapple gray as the horse trotted up and stopped beside him. He took down his canteen and opened it and turned back to Rochenbach.

The outlaw straightened up a little and reached his hand for the canteen. "What if I . . . told you this is my job . . . I'm working undercover?" he said.

"I'd say, *nice try*, but save it for the posse," Summers replied. "I'm the man who shot you, not one of the ones you have to answer to."

"All because Little Jackie shot your horse?" Rochenbach asked reflectively, as if knowing would make any difference now.

"That's right," said Summers, "all because your partner killed one of my horses. Had he left me and my horses alone, you'd be on your way right now."

"*Jesus. . . .*" Rochenbach held the open canteen and looked back toward Jackie Warren's body. He let out a sigh of regret.

"Not to speak ill of the dead, but Little Jackie Warren was the stupidest son of a bitch I ever met," he said quietly.

"And you rode with him," Summers said with a flat stare.

The wounded outlaw looked offended. But then he considered his circumstances and sighed.

"You didn't have to say that," he replied.

By the time Deputy Stiles and his six-man posse arrived, Summers had loosened and removed the wounded outlaw's broad-striped necktie from around his neck. Rochenbach watched him fold it and stick it under his shirt onto his bloody chest.

"Keep your hand pressed on it," Summers said, laying Rochenbach's good right hand on top of the makeshift bandage. While the outlaw watched with regret, Summers loosened the bulging saddlebags from behind Jackie Warren's saddle and pitched them on the ground.

"Aren't you going to even look inside?" Rochenbach asked. "Maybe the sight of that money will jar some sense into you."

Summers didn't answer. He stood with his rifle hanging from his right hand as the posse slowed their horses from a fast pace to walk and spread out abreast, rifles out and ready.

"Pitch your rifle away," the young deputy demanded, nudging his horse forward slowly.

But instead of carelessly throwing his Winchester onto the rocky snow-covered ground, Summers stooped and laid it across the snow a few inches in front of his boots. Then he straightened and raised his hands chest high, his right glove off and stuck down in his belt.

"Watch this one, he's a cool customer," Dewitt said under his breath. He had sidled in closer on the deputy's right.

"Keep quiet, Dewitt," said Stiles. "I'm not blind." He called out to Summers, "Keep your hands where they are, till we see what's going on here. Don't make any sudden moves."

"I won't," Summers said as the seven men stepped their horses forward. He didn't want to do anything to set a group of nervous trigger fingers into action. "I heard the shooting from town. When they come through here, one of them killed one of my horses. I returned fire."

Deputy Stiles looked over at the wounded outlaw lying on the ground—at the body of the other outlaw lying dead, facedown in the snow. With a look of stunned surprise, the deputy stared back at Summers as he stopped his horse again only a few feet from him.

"And you shot these two?" Stiles asked.

"I did," said Summers. "This one says he's Avrial Rochenbach." He gestured a nod toward the body. "Says that one's name is Little Jackie Warren."

"Little Jackie Warren?" said Dewitt. "Holy Moses." He and the others looked back and forth at one another; Stiles kept his eyes on Summers.

"Go over and see if it's Little Jackie," he said to Heintz the druggist. To Summers he said flatly, "There were two others in on it."

"They got away," Summers said. He jerked his head toward the tracks leading off across the snow. "One of them is short an ear." He nodded down at the bulging saddlebags. "I took these off the dead one's horse."

"Short an ear?" Dewitt chuckled grimly. "Good enough for the thieving bastard."

"Did you look inside the saddlebags?" the deputy asked Summers.

"Nope, it's none of my business," said Summers. "I took it off the horse and pitched it here, Sheriff. I wanted you to see it on the ground, knowing that my intentions weren't to cut out with it." He paused and then asked, "Is Turner Goss still sheriff here?"

"Yes, he is. I'm his deputy," Stiles said.

"I'm glad to hear that," Summers said with relief.

"I'm Will Summers. I'm a horse trader who comes through here now and then. Sheriff Goss will vouch for me."

"He might," said the deputy, stone-faced, "if he's still alive." He nodded at Rochenbach and said, "These poltroons shot him down in the street when they robbed our bank."

"I'll vouch for who he is," said an old teamster named Joe Leffert. He sat atop his horse at the end of the line on Stiles' left. "He's a horse trader, just like he says."

"I'll second that," said Long, the gambler. "I've seen him around. He is *indeed* a horse trader."

Summers gave Leffert and Long a slight nod of thanks.

"Not that it cuts any ice," Dewitt butted in, staring menacingly at Summers. "In my book *horse trading* never stacked much higher than a thief anyway."

Summers didn't reply, but he returned the engineer's stare.

From the body lying twenty yards away, Heintz called out in an excited voice, "It's Little Jackie, sure as shooting, Deputy Stiles."

"Damn," said Stiles, "this thing is shaping up worse by the minute."

"Don't feel you need to thank me for saving your money, Deputy," Summers said a little sorely, bringing attention to having his hands still raised chest-high.

"Keep them raised until we say otherwise," Dewitt barked before the deputy could reply for himself.

"Shut up, Dewitt," said Stiles, glancing at the horses standing a foot behind Summers. "This man's telling the truth. Why would he be standing here waiting for us if he was one of them?"

"I don't know," said Dewitt. "But then I never heard of an idiot robbing his own daddy's bank either."

Stiles ignored Dewitt and said to Summers, "Lower you hands. We'll see what Sheriff Goss has to say when we get back to town, provided he's still breathing."

"Back to town?" Dewitt protested. "What about catching the other two?"

"You ride on and catch them, Dewitt," said Stiles without turning toward him.

"*Me?*" said Dewitt. "By myself?"

"We've got two of them," said Stiles. "We've got the bank money back."

"So we're letting them get away with it?" said Dewitt.

"We're riding back to see about Sheriff Goss," said Stiles. "If he says go after the other two, we will."

"What if Goss is dead?" Dewitt persisted. When the deputy ignored him, Dewitt said, "Hell's fire. For two cents I *would* go on after them by myself."

Stiles ignored him and swung down from his saddle and walked toward Summers. He said back to the men over his shoulder, "Fellows, throw this one on a horse—Little Jackie too. Let's get the money and get back to town."

"What's Jackie's pa going to say about all this?" Joe Leffert said to Richard Woods, the town mercantile owner, as the men swung down from their saddles.

"I don't even want to think about that yet," Jason Jones, a land surveyor, replied. "They best tie him down before they tell him."

Chapter 3

———

On the trail back to Gunn Point, Summers and the deputy rode a few feet ahead of the posse. Summers led his three-horse string; Deputy Stiles had tied the saddlebags of money behind his saddle and led the wounded Rochenbach and Jackie Warren's body on their horses beside him. Avrial Rochenbach rode slumped and half conscious from his loss of blood. His good hand held the bandanna up against his bloody shoulder. He still reeked of whiskey from the punctured flask.

Beside him, Jackie Warren's body lay across his saddle, both arms dangling toward the ground. Stiles had pulled the dead man's bandanna back over the bridge of his nose, hiding his face. Summers had watched him cover Warren's face, but he didn't ask why.

"Things must have changed fast since my last trip through Gunn Point," Summers said as they rode along the snow-streaked trail.

"*Too* fast, according to some," Stiles replied. "I shouldn't complain, though—the town has grown so quick the past year it's caused Sheriff Goss to hire me on as his second star."

"All owing to this Warren fellow opening a bank and buying into mining operations," Summers commented, based on everything the deputy had told him along the trail.

"Yep, for the most part, that's what made it happen," said Stiles. "They say that Latimer Gunn wanted a bank here from the time he founded this town near twenty years ago. Jack Warren made it happen. He owns everything he can buy his way into. Cattle, mining, banking. You name it, he owns it. He's a powerful force."

"Why would a man rob his own father's bank?" Summers asked.

Stiles gave a shrug, saying, "They don't get along, I'm told. They've had some run-ins, but nothing like this that I know of. Old man Warren has bought Jackie out of trouble before. No matter what Little Jackie done, I reckon old man Warren figured he's still his only son."

"And I just killed his *only* son . . . ," Summers reflected grimly.

Stiles looked at him and said, "While he was robbing his own father's bank, don't forget. And don't forget, Little Jackie had already fired on you—killed one of your horses, right?"

"That's right, he did," Summers said firmly, realizing the deputy was scrutinizing everything he said to see if his story changed any.

Stiles nodded and said, "Don't mind me, Summers. I've been wearing this badge a few months now. It makes me question everything and everybody. Sheriff Goss has taught me well. I'm not about to let him down."

Summers nodded and said, "Goss is a straight shooter. I've always admired him for it."

"*Admire* him?" said Stiles. "I love the man. He's been like a father to me. He's done more for me than I can ever thank him for. If he's dead, I won't rest until I hang the men who killed him. See why I take all the questioning so serious?"

"I understand, Deputy," Summers said. "But you can question me till we're both blue in the face. My story won't change any. I happened on to the wrong place at the wrong time. That's not a hanging offense."

"Look at it from our position, mine and my posse's," said Stiles. "What if we let you go and found out later you really were one of the robbers? Say we found out you decided to turn against the others—keep all that money for yourself?"

"Then why would I stick around here?" Summers said. "Why didn't I take the money and get my knees in the wind before you showed up?"

"I haven't figured that out yet," said Stiles, "but I'm thinking on it. I'll put it all together, if it's true."

"It'll take some strange thinking to put that story together, Deputy," Summers said. "But I can see how you might get there." He glanced at the three-horse string. "Any thieves with any sense usually plant some fresh horses somewhere along their trail."

"Exactly," Stiles said. Before he could offer any more on the matter, Horace Dewitt came galloping up beside him from a few yards back.

"Parley—I mean, Deputy Stiles," the engineer said, correcting himself, "if you need me to, I can keep watch on this one and the other piece of trash while you rest some."

"Obliged, Dewitt, but I'm all right," Stiles said.

Other piece of trash . . . ? Summers stared at him.

Dewitt returned his stare for a second, then turned back to the deputy.

"If you're worried about me handling the job," he said, "I can promise you, either one tries to make a break for it, I'll put a bullet through his spine quicker than a cat can kill its dinner." He turned his gaze back to Summers for a second. "This man is not the only one who knows how to fire a rifle."

"Drop back, Dewitt," said Stiles. "I've got everything under control."

"All right, Deputy. I'm just saying, is all," Dewitt replied. He jerked his horse's reins around and batted it back toward the other posse men.

"I suppose Sheriff Goss would frown on me bending a rifle barrel over that man's jaw," Summers said evenly.

"Probably so," Stiles said. He looked away and scanned the distance hills for any sign of the other two robbers as he spoke. "The damn fool doesn't mean any harm. He's just strung up tighter than fence wire—all of them are. It's not every day they get shot at, get their bank robbed."

"I can understand that," said Summers. "But I'm just an innocent passerby. I've lost a horse, been shot at myself, saved your bank's money and dropped two of the men who stole it. Yet I get the feeling I'm looked at like a suspect."

"You're not," said Stiles. "Put it out of your mind. We just need to get to town, get everybody settled down and see what Sheriff Goss has to say."

"That sounds like a suspect to me," Summers said.

"You're not," said Stiles. "I can't help how it sounds to you."

Summers looked closer at him.

"So, if I want to," he said, "I can just turn my horse and my string and ride away? Go on about my business?"

"I wish you wouldn't," Stiles said, staring straight ahead.

Summers only nodded, getting the picture. All right, he told himself. They were only a couple more miles from town. He could go along with whatever he had to. Sheriff Goss would straighten everything out, he was certain.

They rode on.

Five miles away, in the shelter of the rocky snow-streaked hills, a gunman named Cole Langler sat hunkered down beside his horse and the four saddled horses standing beside it. He warmed his gloved hands over a low smokeless fire while he waited, looking off in the direction the gunfire had come from ten minutes earlier. He watched the flatlands as the two fleeing gunmen rode into sight. After a moment, realizing the other two weren't coming, he shook his head in disgust.

"Damned idiots," he growled to himself. "Sister Betsy could've robbed that bank."

He took a tin of tobacco from inside his long overcoat, opened it, pinched out a measured wad and stuck it inside his jaw. He didn't bother to stand when the two finally rode in close and stopped only a few feet away.

"We got jackpotted something awful back there," Grayson said, sounding as winded as his horse. He held a cupped hand and wadded-up bandanna to the side of his bloody head where his ear used to be. Fallon halted his horse beside him looking back warily over his shoulder, his rifle in hand.

"I heard it," Langler said, sounding unmoved by Grayson's excited tone of voice. He spit a stream into the low fire and stared at the spot where it hit and sizzled in a bed of glowing embers. "Are you shot in the head?" he asked without looking up at the wounded outlaw.

"No, but my ear is gone," said Grayson, "most of it anyway." He lowered the wadded bandanna, examined it and put it back to the side of his head.

"Losing an ear's nothing," said Langler with no sympathy in his voice.

Grayson smoldered in anger, but he managed to clench his teeth and keep himself in check.

"I thought much the same way myself," he said, "back when I had *two* of them."

"So losing one has changed your outlook on the world around you?" Langler said.

"*Jesus . . . ,*" Grayson said under his breath, casting Fallon a look, and replied, "All's I'm saying is, we could have used some help over there."

"It sounded like it," Langler said unmoved. He spit again, still looking into the flames.

"It got a little *hair-raising,* is what he's saying," Fallon put in.

Grayson glared at him.

"He knows what I'm saying. I don't need you restating a damn thing on my behalf."

"I didn't mean to say—" Fallon started to explain himself, but Langler cut him off impatiently.

"Where's the Rock?" he asked without looking up at the two outlaws.

"Dead," Grayson said with finality.

"Little Jackie?" Langler asked.

"Dead," Grayson repeated.

"The money?" Langler asked.

"Gone," said Grayson.

Langler chuffed, shook his head and spit into the fire.

"I mighta known," he said. "Were they shot in the back, or the front?" he asked.

"The hell kind of question is that?" Grayson asked, getting more and more irritated. "What difference does it make? They are both dead!"

"Makes all the difference in the world to me," said Langler. "The way we had this planned, I can't figure how a posse got so close to you fellows so soon." He stood up slowly. But when he turned facing them, a big Walker Colt appeared in his right hand and leveled up toward them, at arm's length. "Maybe you best explain."

"Damn, Cole!" said Grayson, talking fast, his hand still cupped to the side of his head. "You heard all the shooting! We got hit by surprise!"

"By what you call an *interloper*!" Fallon put in quickly.

"A *what*?" said Langler, cocking his head with a curious look.

Grayson also stared curiously. Fallon looked to him as if for permission to continue speaking. Grayson gestured with a nod toward Langler.

"By all means, tell him, son," he said to Fallon, not as easily offended now by the younger outlaw explaining on his behalf.

"An *interloper*," Fallon said, "somebody who butts in when things are—"

He stopped short, seeing Langler cock the big Colt and home it in on his chest.

"It was no posse shot Little Jackie and the Rock," Fallon said, talking fast, hoping not to get himself killed.

"That's what I figured," Langler said tightly. His hand tightened on the gun butt.

"Wait, listen!" said Fallon, speaking even faster now. "It was a man leading a string of horses! Little Jackie killed one of his horses. He shot hell out of us!"

"One man? Not the sheriff's posse?" Langler asked, eying him closely.

"One man," said Fallon, "that's the gospel."

"What was this *interloper* man riding?" Langler asked. His hand on the Walker Colt appeared to ease a little—but only a little.

Fallon had to consider it quickly. "A big gray. A dapple maybe," he said.

Langler let out a breath and lowered the Colt a little. He eased the hammer down with his thumb.

"I saw that man yesterday, coming up a trail across the valley from me," he said. "Looked like a horse swapper by the name of Will Summers to me."

"Might be," said Grayson, looking relieved. "Anyways, he killed them both." He gave a tired sigh and looked at the low flames flickering sidelong on a cold breeze.

Fallon watched them both, noting that Langler's Walker Colt was down at his side, but not back beneath his long brown overcoat.

"I can sure use some fire . . . some coffee too, far as that goes," said Grayson.

"I was just getting ready to boil some," Langler said. "I can cook you eggs—gravy too if you're hungry."

"Hungry? Lord yes!" said Grayson, starting to swing down from his saddle. "Eggs sounds wonderfu—"

"Stay your ass in that saddle, fool!" Langler growled, cutting him off, cocking the big Colt all over again.

These two . . . , Fallon said to himself, watching.

"What?" Grayson said, bewildered, his hands going chest high at the sight of the big Colt pointing up at him.

"You come in here, two men dead . . . the money gone. You want me to cook you a nice sit-down meal! You're lucky I don't empty your heads all over your horse's rumps!"

"I'm not hungry," Fallon said quietly.

"Good for you, Mr. *Interloper*," said Langler. He turned enough to grab the lead rope to the four fresh horses and jerked the string over to Fallon. "Here, make yourself *more* useful, *less* informational."

"Where we going?" Grayson asked.

"After *our* money, damn it!" said Langler.

"But the posse," said Grayson. "They're there by now, already seen what went on and got back onto our trail. We'll run dead into them, going back."

"And you wanted to stop and eat?" said Langler in disgust.

Grayson had no reply.

Langler said, "We're not riding back the same way you came. We're swinging wide, going around."

"Why are we going there at all?" said Grayson. "Whoever that was shot Little Jackie and the Rock is gone by now, money and all."

"His tracks are still there, fool," said Langler, once

again lowering the big Walker Colt. "We get on his trail and ride him down. He's got our money and gone with it. You can bet your wool drawers on that. I'm not risking prison just to have somebody ride away with my money, are you?"

Grayson and Fallon looked at each other for a moment.

"Are you going to tell?" Fallon said finally.

"Tell me *what*?" Langler insisted, getting impatient again. He had started to put the big Colt back beneath his overcoat. But he thought better of it, looking back and forth between them.

"Little Jackie killed the sheriff in the street," said Grayson.

"Shot him down like a dog," Fallon added. "So it's not about prison now. This is a hemp waltz we're looking at."

Langler stood stunned, staring in bemused silence for a moment. Grayson winced and looked away in shame.

"*Good God!*" Langler raged, finally. "This was supposed to be easy. Didn't you idiots do anything right?"

"Damn it to hell, we got out *alive*!" Grayson said, getting more than his fill of Langler's bullying, superior attitude.

"Not *yet*, you haven't!" Langler countered. "Now turn your horses and stay in front of me!" He wagged the big Colt at his side. "If you hear this gun go off, count yourself *dead*."

The two outlaws gave each other a guarded look. When Langler half turned from them, stamping and rubbing the fire out with his boot, Fallon let his hand tighten around his rifle. His finger went inside the trigger guard. His thumb eased over the hammer to cock it.

But catching a warning gesture from Grayson, he let his thumb ease off the hammer and slipped his finger from the trigger.

When Langler had put out the fire and pulled his gloves on, he stepped up into his saddle and motioned the two ahead of him. In the distance he saw no sign of the posse raising snow in their wake. Either they had given up the chase or they were riding awfully slow, he told himself. Either way was fine by him. He nudged his horse along behind the two outlaws.

"Swing south," he said, shoving his big Walker Colt down into a brace of leather holsters draped across the pommel of his saddle.

"How far south?" Grayson asked without looking back.

"Until we've got past whatever other mess you two jakes left behind you," Langler said.

"This son of a bitch . . . ," Grayson whispered to himself.

They rode south along the hill line for nearly an hour before cutting back across the flatlands to the spot where the shoot-out had occurred. Once they were there, Langler rode around slowly taking in the prints of many horses in the trampled snow until he finally looked in the direction of Gunn Point.

"I don't believe this," he said, gesturing the other two over beside him. "Looks like the damn fool rode back with the posse." He gave a dark chuckle. "Wonder what young Deputy Parley Stiles thought about that."

"Jesus . . . ," said Grayson, "all that money, gone."

"Watch your language," said Langler. "Money is never gone. It's just been misdirected. We play our cards right, maybe we get it back. Maybe we kill this sumbitch who messed everything up for us. Either way we're not folding—we're staying in the game."

Chapter 4

It was later in the afternoon when Summers, Deputy Stiles and the six-man posse rode onto the main dirt street running through the town. Instead of running straight from one end to the other, the main street took a forty-five-degree turn out in front of a large sprawling clapboard building with a large ornately painted sign that read CASTER STEMS' MAPLETHORPE SALOON.

Heads turned toward the riders as soon as they entered town. Seeing one dead outlaw hanging over his saddle and another sitting slumped forward almost onto his horse's neck, a townsman named Philbert Clancy stepped out in front of the rest of a gathering crowd of onlookers. He stood staring for a moment with his fists clenched at his sides.

"Get a rope," he said aloud to anyone listening.

"Dang, Phil!" said a telegraph clerk named Charlie Stuart. "We can't hang them if they're already dead."

"The hell we can't!" said Clancy, turning enough to give the clerk a hard stare.

"Looks like one is still barely alive," said another townsman. "We can hang him, if we hurry."

"Who's that riding beside the deputy?" a young saloon girl named Cherry Atmore asked.

"He's not one of the robbers," said a townsman as the gathering crowd shifted onto the street, drawing closer to the riders as they turned toward the hitch rail out in front of the sheriff's office.

"What makes you say so?" Cherry Atmore asked. She wore a long wool coat over a short gaudy saloon dress. She held the coat closed at the throat with one hand. In her other hand a freshly rolled cigarette stood in the scissors of her fingers.

"Because he's got no holes in him, little darling!" Clancy said with a laugh, walking across the street toward the sheriff's office, as if leading the rest of the men and women.

"Oh, I get it," Cherry said, smiling, after looking puzzled for a second.

"Sit tight for a second, Summers," Stiles said. He handed Summers the reins to Rochenbach's horse as the rest of the posse men gathered at the hitch rail and stepped down from their saddles.

Summers looked around and saw the wounded Rochenbach swaying slowly in his saddle beside him.

"We . . . there . . . yet?" Rochenbach asked weakly, barely conscious.

"Keep quiet," Summers warned him.

Swinging down from his saddle, rifle in hand, Stiles stepped into the street, meeting the coming crowd and stopping them in their tracks.

"Everybody stop right there," he said firmly. He held

his rifle in both hands across his chest like a barricade rail.

"Get the hell out of the way, Parley," Clancy said. He grinned confidently and kept coming. The crowd pressed forward more cautiously behind him.

"Don't use that language with me again," Stiles warned him.

"Language? Who the hell are you kidding, Parley?" he said to Stiles. "Damned if you're stopping us. Come on, folks, let's take a look-see at these thieving poltroons—"

Before the words left his lips, Stiles' Winchester rifle made a vicious swipe across his face. The rifle butt sent blood flying from his nose and mouth. The impact of the blow spun him almost a full circle and hurled him to the ground, knocked cold.

"He's killed him!" a hushed voice said.

The women in the crowd gasped; the men winced. But they all stopped in their tracks as if met by barbed wire. Summers sat half turned in his saddle, watching closely, seeing how the deputy handled himself.

A little harsh? Summers asked himself. The crowd stood with looks of terror on their faces.

"Clancy was the first to fall," Stiles said. "Anybody wants to be next, step forward."

Yep, harsh, Summers decided. But he had to admit, it got the job done. It seemed all right with the rest of the townsfolk.

"No takers, huh?" said Stiles after a moment of pause. "All right, then, let's all conduct ourselves in an orderly manner. No more profane language, from any of you. You're all better people than that."

"What happened out there, Deputy?" a man called out from the middle of the crowd.

"First things first," said Stiles. He looked at two men standing in front of the crowd. "Fellows, drag Clancy somewhere and throw some cold water in his face. When he wakes up tell him I'm sorry I had to hit him."

"I bet he watches his mouth from now on," a townsman said under his breath.

The two men hurried in, grabbed Clancy by his feet and dragged him away facedown in the dirt, his mouth agape. His bloody cheek bounced across the cold rough dirt.

"Stuart, how is the sheriff doing?" he called out to the telegraph clerk.

Charlie Stuart stepped forward. The rest of the town stayed back and listened along with Stiles. Eric Holt, owner of the *Gunn Point Weekly Press*, stood back with a pencil and paper in his hands, making notes.

"Doc Meadows says it's fifty-fifty whether he makes it, Deputy," said Stuart.

"I'll get right over there," said Stiles. He turned toward the saddlebags behind his saddle. "We got the money back, thanks to this man, Will Summers."

The townsmen all looked at Summers, some of them recognizing him from past trips through town.

"God bless you, Will Summers," said an elderly man with a long white beard who stood leaning on a walking cane.

"Hear, hear!" said another townsmen, leading the group in a round of applause.

"What's going . . . on back there?" Rochenbach asked Summers in a raspy voice, hearing the townsfolk cheer and clip.

"Keep quiet," Summers replied in a lowered tone. "I think he's keeping their minds off lynching you."

"Where's Bob Harper?" Stiles asked, looking all around the crowded street.

"Over here, Deputy," a man in a black suit called out, hurrying along the boardwalk from the direction of a clapboard and stone bank building down the street. "I saw you riding in. I had to lock up the bank first." His left eye was swollen and turning purple where Jackie Warren had smacked him with a pistol barrel. "Pardon me for not moving at full gait today, Deputy."

Stiles nodded, turned and stepped back to the horses and took down the bulging saddlebags. Without looking up at Summers, he said to him and the posse, "Soon as I hand this money over, you men take him inside and lock him in a cell. Carry Jackie inside too. We've still got *that* matter to deal with."

The posse men nodded as one.

"I—I need a doctor," Rochenbach rasped.

"If you don't do as you're told, you won't," Stiles warned him under his breath. To the men he said, "Some of you stay inside and watch things while I go see the sheriff."

"I've got it covered, Deputy," said Long, the gambler.

"Me too," said Leffert, the teamster. "Nobody is going to take him without your say-so."

"Obliged," said Stiles.

Walking back to the middle of the crowded street, the deputy handed the saddlebags over to the bank manager.

"Check it out good, Mr. Harper," Stiles said, loud enough for everyone to hear.

"Yes, sir, Deputy," the thin bank manager said. He took the heavy saddlebags and quickly set them in the dirt and opened them. He took out two banded stacks of bills and raised them for the town to see. "It'll need a full and close counting, but it looks to all be here," he announced.

The crowd cheered again.

Without a word, Summers and the posse men gathered around the two outlaws' horses. Lowering Rochenbach, Summers and Herbert Long looped his arms across their shoulders, walked him onto the boardwalk and through the door to the sheriff's office. As they led him back toward two empty cells, three other men carried Jackie Warren's body inside and laid it on a wooden bench against a wall.

Summers walked back out front. Seeing him, Stiles gave him a nod and said, "Walk to the doctor's with me, Summers. Let's go see how the sheriff is doing."

On their way past the front of Caster Stems' Maplethorpe Saloon, Stiles saw the owner gazing out across the top of the batwing doors.

"Good work, Deputy," the heavyset Stems said, a cigar hanging between his thick pink fingers.

"Thank Summers here," Stiles said. "He's the one who stopped them and got the money back."

"I mean good work keeping them from swinging the wounded outlaw from my overhang rafter," Stems said, turning his eyes toward the open rafters above the boardwalk. He looked Summers up and down.

"Howdy, Caster," Summers said.

"Howdy, Summers," Stems said. "Seems like every time I see you, there's some kind of commotion stirring."

"You two know each other, then," said Stiles.

"I know him," said, Stems. "He once led a posse out of Rileyville with a deputy named Abner Webb. They killed off a gang of guerrilla riders who thought the war was still going on."

"The Peltry brothers . . . ," said Stiles, looking surprised. He shook his head. "I feel foolish that I didn't recognize your name right off. Why didn't you say something?"

"He don't like to brag," Stems said on Summers' behalf. He blew a stream of smoke. "Do you, Will Summers?"

"It was a long time ago, and best forgotten," Summers said quietly.

Stems grinned and jerked his head toward Summers.

"See what I mean, Deputy?" he said.

"That explains how he dropped those two outlaws and sent the others running like scalded cats," said Stiles.

"See, you learn something every day, Deputy," said Caster Stems. He nodded toward the crowd in the street as many of them followed Harper toward the bank with the bulging saddlebags. "Want me to offer everybody a drink on the house, get them thinned out some—drinkers and *nondrinkers*?"

"Obliged, Stems," said Stiles. "Keep the conversation away from hanging."

"At your service, Deputy," Stems said. He looked back over his shoulder and called out to his bartender, "Bernard, go tell these folks they've got a drink coming, on the house, owing to the town getting its money back."

"Sure thing, boss," the bartender called back to him from within the saloon.

"Let's get on to Doc Meadows' office—see about

Sheriff Goss," Stiles said to Summers as the bartender stepped out through the batwing doors and walked toward the townsfolk still standing in the street.

At the doctor's office, Summers and Deputy Stiles followed a thin, gangly young man with a tangle of red hair down a hallway to a recovery room. Inside the room the doctor took a short cigar from his mouth and let out a stream of smoke.

"Sheriff," he said quietly, "do you feel like some company? Deputy Stiles is back off the trail."

Across the room, a pale, drawn face rose from a pillow and looked over at the three men standing at the door.

The wounded lawman gave a slight nod, then lowered his head back down onto his pillow. A wide bloodstained bandage covered most of his gray hairy chest.

The young doctor took a draw on his cigar and said to the deputy barely above a whisper, "Don't wear him out. He's lost a lot of blood."

Stiles whispered in reply, "Is he going to live, Dr. Meadows?"

The doctor gave him a look that revealed nothing. "He's tough. . . . We'll see."

Stiles and Summer took off their hats and crossed the floor to the bed as the doctor turned and slipped back out the door. Summers stood back a step as Stiles looked at the sheriff.

The sheriff raised his head an inch from the pillow and looked Stiles up and down.

"Did you . . . catch them?" he asked in a pained and shallow voice.

"Two of them, Sheriff," Stiles said, "one dead and one wounded. Two of them are still running loose. We got the money back."

"Good work," the sheriff whispered, relieved by the news.

"I can't take credit, Sheriff," Stiles said. "Will Summers here shot them both." He took a short step to the side and gestured Summers forward.

"Will Summers . . . ?" Sheriff Goss said, straining to keep his head raised slightly.

"Howdy, Sheriff Goss," Summers said, looking down at him.

Goss looked Summers up and down as if uncertain he was actually seeing him.

"Will . . . ? You shot them?" he said.

"I happened upon them on my way here, Sheriff," said Summers. "The one called Little Jackie shot one of my horses. I returned fire."

"Little Jackie . . . ?" Sheriff Goss looked at Stiles in disbelief.

"I'm afraid it's true, Sheriff," he said. "I dread telling you, but Little Jackie's the one he killed."

"My, my," the sheriff said. He let his head relax back onto the pillow. "Does his pa know yet?"

"Not yet," Stiles said. "I'll have to ride out and tell him everything. I've kept it quiet so far. The townsfolk were more interested in hanging the one who's still alive. I directed their attention toward getting their money back. But they'll be wanting to know."

"And rightly . . . they should," the sheriff said, staring up at the ceiling. "This is not time for me to be . . . laid up with a bullet run through my chest." He turned his eyes to Summers. "Do you know who you've shot, Will?"

"Yep," Summers replied.

"I told him, Sheriff," said Stiles.

"He shot at me, Sheriff Goss," said Summers. "He killed my horse, but he could have just as likely killed me."

"I understand, Will," said the wounded sheriff. "Any man would have returned fire. But Big Jack Warren won't see it that way." He sighed and fell silent, exhausted from even a short amount of talking.

"Sheriff," Summers said, "if it'll help, I'll keep riding, get out of here before Deputy Stiles tells Big Jack."

"Send you *running*?" Stiles said. "That's a hell of a reward, after you keeping this town from losing its money."

"I didn't do it for *reward*," Summers replied. "I did it to protect myself and my animals. Besides, it's not like you're running me out of town. It's my own idea. I was only passing through anyway—taking on supplies."

Stiles started to say more, but the sheriff raised a tired hand toward the two of them.

"Will . . . ride on," he said weakly. "When I'm back on my feet . . . we'll thank you properly."

"This leaves a bad taste in my mouth," Stiles said.

"Live with it," said Goss.

"It's for the best, Deputy," Summers added. "This hand was dealt me out of the blue. It feels right playing it this way."

Stiles considered things for a second, then said, "All right. But go draw what supplies you need and have them billed to the sheriff's office. It's the least we can do, right, Sheriff?"

Goss just looked up at him, too weary to talk any further on the matter.

"Obliged," Summers said to Stiles, "but I'll foot my own bill."

"I meant no offense," Stiles said.

"None was taken," Summers said. He nodded at the wounded sheriff, then at the deputy as he put his hat on. "I hope to see you both under more peaceful circumstances." He turned, walked out the door and closed it behind himself.

"Give him an hour head start . . . before you ride out to Warren's spread," Goss said.

"I will," said Stiles. He considered that matter and gave a look of dread. "This won't ride right with Big Jack, no matter how I stack it."

"It's his son, Deputy," said Goss, "his *only* son."

"Yeah," said Stiles, "and Jack Warren thinks he's bigger than God to begin with."

Chapter 5

On his way to the mercantile store to gather supplies and grain for his horses, Summers saw Horace Dewitt leave Stems' Maplethorpe Saloon with a bottle of rye tucked under each arm. Before Summers turned into the mercantile store, he watched Dewitt slip along the boardwalk and turn into the door of the sheriff's office.

Good luck, Deputy, Summers thought, imagining how difficult things could get, Stiles trying to keep the peace here on his own until the wounded sheriff recovered. *If* he recovered, Summers reminded himself. But he knew there was nothing he could do about it. Staying here, facing Big Jack Warren once he heard that the man who killed his son was in Gunn Point, would only make matters worse.

"Well, now, how can I help you, sir?" said a thin, bald clerk as he stepped around from behind a long wooden counter. But before Summers could reply, the clerk recognized him from the street and said, "Oh my! You're Will Summers, the one who stopped those outlaws and retrieved our money."

"Word travels fast," Summers said.

"Indeed, like wildfire," the clerk said eagerly. "Allow me to introduce myself. I'm Joseph Woods. My father is Richard Woods. He rode with the posse. He's at the sheriff's office right now. I can't wait to hear him tell what happened out there."

Summers only nodded politely.

Before the young clerk could continue, they both turned their faces in the direction of the saloon as a round of laughter and applause swelled above the street.

"Please forgive all the revelry," the clerk said. "But this town needed something to feel good about. We all owe you a great debt of gratitude."

"I only did what any man would do," Summers said.

"I understand, sir," said the clerk, "but most of us merchants in Gunn Point are forced to keep our operating capital in Warren and Sutters Trust Bank. We could have been ruined were it not for you. I just can't thank you enough."

"You already have," Summers said, feeling a little embarrassed.

"Yes, of course," said the young man, realizing Summers' reluctance to talk about it. "How may I assist you today?"

"Two ten-pound sacks of feed oats, saddle-tied," Summers said. "A pound of coffee, some airtight beans. Some jerked shank." He stopped as it struck him what the clerk had said a moment earlier.

"Yes, sir," said the clerk. "Anything else?"

"What did you mean, the merchants are *forced* to keep their operating capital in Warren's bank?"

"Oh, I apologize! *Forced* is not the correct word," the

young clerk said. "I should say we feel obligated to keep our money there. Mr. Warren and Mr. Sutters both explained how crucial our financial support of the bank would be if they agreed to open it here."

"Makes sense," said Summers. He dismissed the matter and looked all around at the shelves full of cans, bottles and tins of food and notions.

"Anything else?" Joseph Woods asked as he went about gathering Summers' items and laying them on the wooden countertop.

"I suppose that's all I'll need for the trail," Summers replied. "That and a box of Winchester cartridges."

"Coming right up," said the young man.

Moments later, Summers walked out of the store carrying a canvas sack filled with food supplies in his left hand. The two ten-pound sacks of feed for the horses hung over his shoulder by the short rope holding them tied together.

Out in front of the sheriff's office, he gathered his dapple gray and his three-horse string and led the animals around a corner of an alley and back to the town livery barn. It suited him when no hostler met him at the livery barn door. He preferred tending to his own horses.

He lit an oil lantern against the gloom of evening. He grained the horses and gave them each a handful of hay he pulled from a hay bin. As the hungry animals chewed hay, he set three oak buckets of water in front of them. As the horses drew water, he carved a slice of elk from the dried shank he took from the sack of supplies. He ate it and swallowed a mouthful of canteen water behind it. That would have to do for now, he told himself. It was time to go.

He laid two bits for the hay in a small wooden box beside the hay bin. Turning out the lantern, he gathered the string and his dapple gray and started toward the barn door. But before he and the animals reached the door, it swung open quickly and he stared down the barrel of a cocked Remington pointed straight at him. In reflex he grabbed the butt of his big Colt; then his hand stopped as he heard the sobbing and recognized the saloon girl he had seen earlier on the street.

"You—you killed him, you rotten son of a—" Her words stopped short as she pulled the Remington's trigger.

Summers braced for the shot, knowing there was no way for her to miss, not standing this close. He flinched when, instead of a hearing and seeing a blazing gunshot in the evening darkness, he heard the metal on metal click of a misfire.

"Damn this thing!" the girl cursed through a face full of tears. She struggled to recock the big revolver, but Summers wasn't giving her a second chance. In two steps he was upon her. Grabbing the gun barrel and shoving it away from him with one hand, he spun her around with his other hand, wrapped his arm around from behind and held her up on her tiptoes while she struggled against him. The dapple and the three-horse string shied back a step, away from the struggling humans.

"*Whoa.* Easy, ma'am," Summers said.

But she would have none of it. She sobbed, twisted and squirmed and kicked backward, battering his shins with the heels of her shoes. Summers ignored the kicking and concentrated on shaking the big Remington from her hand. When the weight of it finally broke free from her grip and fell to the floor, Summers let her down but kept his arm around her, his free hand clutching her wrist.

Her crying increased; her struggle stopped. He was too strong for her, and he wasn't turning her loose until she settled down.

"Go ahead, then, shoot me too!" she said, collapsing against him, sobbing uncontrollably. "You shot the man I love."

"Easy, ma'am," Summers said. "I'm going to turn you loose, but you've got to calm down."

She made no reply. She continued sobbing violently.

Jesus. . . . He'd never seen anyone cry with such total abandon.

He turned her loose anyway and stepped over quickly, picked up the Remington and looked at it closely. There were only three bullets in its cylinder, none of them close to the hammer. Still, he opened the cylinder and dropped each bullet onto the floor. He laid the gun over on a small table beside the hay bin.

"That was a fool thing to do, ma'am," he said. "You could have gotten yourself killed." He didn't mention that she could have very well also killed him had she checked the gun first.

She choked down the crying and let out a tight breath. "I don't care if I had gotten killed. I've got nothing to live for, not anymore."

"You and Jackie Warren . . . ?" He let his question trail.

"We were *in love,*" she said, finishing his words for him. "He was taking me away from Gunn Point." Her voice started to crack and tremble again.

Here we go . . . , Summers thought, seeing tears well in her eyes.

"I'm sorry for you, ma'am," he said, "and I'm sorry I had to kill your beau. But he shot at me . . . twice. I had no choice but to shoot back."

"Oh, you had a choice," she disputed him. Her crying stopped short. "You didn't have to shoot back. He would still be alive if you hadn't."

Summers didn't answer. He knew she was speaking in a state of mindless grief. It was the sort of thing he'd heard people say when they hoped for some mystical change in the face of unyielding reality.

"He's dead," Summers said with finality. "Killing me would not have brought him back. It would only make *you* a killer. Is that what you want?"

She didn't answer; she didn't have to. They stood in silence for a moment.

Good, he told himself, she was starting to settle down. She was no fool, he thought. She knew the kind of man Jackie Warren was. She had to let better reasoning set in.

After a pause, Summers looked her up and down in the shadowy evening light through the open barn door.

"You look familiar, ma'am," he said. "Have I seen you before?"

"No," she said bluntly, in a hoarse, grudging tone. She crossed her arms and stared down. But Summers could see she had settled a little.

"Did you ever work in Denton . . . a place called Dowdy's Fair Shake Saloon?"

She gave him a sullen look, turned her eyes up to him without raising her head.

"Maybe," she finally said. "Did you and me . . . ?"

"No," said Summers, "nothing like that. It's just that I recognize you from there . . . maybe three years ago?"

"Could be," she said, studying his face closely in the shadowy evening darkness. "That's where I started working."

Summers nodded, considering it. She couldn't have been more than fifteen or sixteen at that time—just a child.

She uncrossed her arms, reached a hand slowly inside her overcoat and took out a bag of chopped fixings.

"I was fifteen," she said, as if having read his mind. As she spoke she deftly filled a cigarette paper with fixings, rolled it into a smoke and ran it in and out of her mouth. She held it in the scissors of her fingers, produced a large match, struck it with her thumbnail and lit the cigarette. She let go a long stream of smoke. "It seems like a hundred years," she reflected.

Summers nodded, as if he understood. That was all she needed.

"Do I . . ." She hesitated, then said, "Do I look much different now?"

Summers knew the perils of answering such a question. He looked her up and down.

"Nothing's changed," he said tactfully. "You were a pretty woman then. You're a pretty woman now, Miss . . . ?" He let his words hang.

"Cherry," she said, "Cherry Atmore." She reflected for a second, then said, "I don't remember what my name was then, but it wasn't Cherry. . . . It might have been Lily." She gave a slight shrug. "Anyway, obliged." She drew a deep lungful of smoke, held it for a second and then blew it out. Summers smelled the musty sweet aroma of Indian tobacco—*setas de mayan,* he reminded himself, a powerful mix of chopped tobacco spiked with ceremonial mushrooms used by the Mayans.

"Well, Miss Atmore," Summers said, "my name is Will—"

"I don't know who you are. I don't care who you are," she said, cutting him off. Her voice took on its surly tone again. "I didn't come here to make friends. I came here to kill you, remember?"

Summers shut up as he stepped over to his three-horse string and picked up the lead rope.

"I'm glad you didn't," he said. "I mean it for both our sakes."

Cherry just looked at him, holding a breath of smoke for a second, then letting it drift out of her mouth. Her eyes shifted over to the big Remington revolver lying on the table, then back to him.

"Killing doesn't leave a good taste in the mouth," he said as he turned to his dapple gray and checked his saddle and tested it with both hands.

"How do you know I haven't already killed somebody? What makes you think you'd be my first?" she said.

"I can just tell, that's all," Summers said, looking back at her. "And I'd just as soon you not find out how it feels by killing me."

"The way you killed Little Jackie?" she said, still with a bitter twist to her words.

"Yeah, the way I killed Little Jackie," Summers said. He wouldn't tell her again that killing Jackie Warren was justified, self-defense. If she didn't know by now, she wasn't going to.

Through the open door, Summers heard a horse chuff quietly and stamp its hoof on the ground. He swung toward the door, his Colt out, up and cocked. Cherry noted the speed with which he'd made the move.

"Who's there?" Summer demanded. When no answer came, he gave Cherry a hard glance. "Who's with you?"

"Nobody's with me," Cherry replied calmly, letting out a languid stream of smoke. "It's my horse. Soon as I heard Jackie was the dead bank robber, I got my horse and went looking for you."

"How'd you hear it was Jackie Warren?" Summers asked, knowing the posse and Deputy Stiles were trying to keep the fact hidden for as long as they could.

"One of the posse men came in the saloon and told me," she said. "He knew about Jackie and me."

"Horace Dewitt . . . ," said Summers, having seen the engineer leaving the saloon.

"Yes," said Cherry.

"And you *rode* a horse here?" Summers said dubiously.

"That's right," Cherry said, holding a drawn breath of smoke. "See for yourself . . . if you don't believe me." She exhaled slowly and started to take a step forward.

"Stay right there," Summers ordered her, stopping her in her tracks.

He took a cautious step to the open door and looked out. A brown and white paint horse stood staring at him from five feet away. Seeing Summers, the horse sawed his head slightly and let out a low nicker.

"Easy, fellow," Summers said soothingly. He stepped forward and touched his hand to the horse's muzzle. He looked all around the evening gloom until satisfied there was no one there. Then he uncocked the Colt and slipped it into his holster. The horse blew out a breath and nudged his hand.

"See, I told you," said Cherry, having walked to the door behind him in spite of him telling her to stay were she was. "I'm alone."

Summers looked the paint horse over, seeing the carpetbag tied down behind its saddle. He got the picture; her plan had been to kill him and leave town. She had put some thought into it. She hadn't just grabbed a gun and come after him in a hysterical rage. It dawned on him, had she checked the gun first, odds were he would be lying dead in the livery barn.

"You were leaving town?" Summers said, not letting her know how much he read in all this.

"Were, and still *am*," Cherry replied, her voice sounding calmer now, a little bit dreamy from the effects of the strong smoke. "Jackie and I were leaving together. He was going to get lots of money and come by and take me way. I didn't realize the money was coming from robbing the bank."

Summer stood staring at her, his silence inducing her to keep talking.

"Look, mister," she said finally. "This was a mistake, coming here to kill you. I mean—I'm no murderer. I lost my head when I heard you killed Jackie Warren. I did love him. That is, I suppose I did, sort of." She took another draw from the cigarette, held the smoke for a second, then let it drift out of her mouth reflectively. Then she gave a short cough and shook her head. "Damn, I don't know. . . ."

Summers only stared, letting her get everything off her chest.

"I've got to get out of this life," she said. "It's killing me." She looked at the cigarette in her fingers; it was shorter now and she held it pinched between her thumb and fingertip.

Summer watched.

"Little Jackie was the only young man I ever met

who had money—I mean *real* money. It came from his pa, but still it was there *all the time*."

"All that money, yet he robs his own father's bank," Summer commented.

"Yeah, I know," Cherry said. "If you ever figure that out, tell me why." She paused, then said, "He was my ticket out of here—the life, I mean. He said he was coming to get me. We'd go see the world together." She shook her head. "Instead . . ." She left the word dangling.

Summers looked her up and down again. He saw the cigarette had burned down dangerously close to her fingertips. She didn't seem to notice. He took the small stub from her, dropped it and stepped on it.

"Where are you headed?" he asked, realizing she had no business on a dark trail, alone, half knocked out on Indian tobacco.

"Whiskey Flats," she said.

"So am I," said Summers. He paused, then asked, "Want to ride with me?"

"No strings?" she asked in reply. "Because I'm sick of men crawling up my belly every time I lie down."

"No strings," Summers said, and he meant it. Although he was interested in finding out whatever she might tell him about the Warrens—maybe give him an idea of what to expect.

Cherry considered it for moment, then let out a sigh that Summers was not able to read one way or the other.

"Sure," she said, "why not? It's probably safer."

Chapter 6

The three outlaws had slipped into an abandoned relay station on the edge of Gunn Point and walked their horses inside the debris-littered stone-and-timber building that had once accommodated stagecoach passengers on their way across the high plains headed for points north. The advantage of the dusty sun-bleached ruins was a rickety thirty-foot lookout tower that had been built up one side of the building and provided a good view of the flatlands. It also provided an even better view of the streets and storefronts of Gunn Point.

Less than an hour after the three had settled in and Cole Langler had built a small fire in a wide stone hearth, Lewis Fallon stepped down the tower ladder and though a trapdoor on the station roof.

"Summers just took on supplies," he said. "Now he's led horses around the corner of an alley, into the livery barn."

"Damn it," said Grayson, "looks like he's settling in for the night." He sat in a broken wooden chair with his elbow on top of a dusty desk, cupping his bandanna to the side of his head.

"Then so have we," Langler said. "If he was stupid enough to turn that money in, we're going to rob that damn bank all over again come morning, while they're not expecting it—get our money back."

"Our money?" Fallon said with short grin.

"As far as I'm concerned, it is," said Langler. "What do you say, Henry?"

"Yeah, I agree," Grayson said, clearly in misery. "But if we stay here I've got to have something for the pain in my head."

"It's not your head that got shot off, Henry. It's your ear," Langler said.

Grayson said testily, "I think I *know* it was my ear, Cole. But it's got my head pounding like a war drum. I've got to have something to relieve it."

"Ordinarily I carry a full supply of herbs, medicines, laudanum and whatnot, Henry," Langler said, taunting him, "but it appears you've caught me short."

"I need whiskey," Grayson said, ignoring Langler's remarks. "I can't go into town with an ear missing—"

"Forget it," Langler said, cutting him off. "I don't know about you two, but I'm busted belly up. I needed the money from this job."

Fallon put in, "I've got half a dollar."

"That's a *drink*, Lewis, Grayson said. "I need a *bottle*, at least. I am hurting something awful."

"Tough knuckles," said Langler. "Bite down on a stick."

A pause; then, "I've got some money," Grayson said hesitantly.

The other two noted something guarded in his tone of voice and looked at him.

"Oh, you do?" Fallon said. "Day before yesterday you didn't have a dime, I happen to know."

"I've got some money—a little," Grayson said, lowering his hand from the side of his head and examining the bloody bandanna idly as he spoke.

Fallon and Langler looked at each other, then back at Grayson.

"All right," said Fallon, "now tell us, how did you come by it?"

"Yeah," said Langler, half rising from a dusty wooden stool, "we'd both like to hear it."

"Okay," said Grayson with a sigh. "Don't judge me harshly, fellows. When we filled the bags with money, somehow one of the stacks got stuck inside my coat."

The two stared at him. He gave a slight shrug as if to play down the incident. But the two outlaws weren't going to let it go.

"*Somehow* got stuck?" said Fallon.

"See, I knew you'd take it this way," Grayson said. "That's why I hated telling you." He looked back and forth between them for understanding, but detected none. "I don't know how it happened, all right? I know it sounds suspect, but it's true."

"How much is it?" Fallon demanded.

"I believe it's a thousand dollars," Grayson said. "That's how it comes bound, you know . . . a hundred, a thousand and so on."

"We know how it comes," said Fallon.

"Get it out," said Langler.

"It's in my saddlebags," said Grayson.

"I'm going to get it," Fallon said. He started to take a step toward the door.

Grayson's big Dance Brothers revolver swung up

from atop the dusty desk, cocked and ready to fire. "Do *not* lay hands on my stuff," he warned.

Fallon froze, but Langler wasn't the least put off by the cocked pistol, since it wasn't pointed at him.

"To hell with *your stuff*," he said. "It's bank money. That means it's our money too."

Fallon just stood listening, waiting for the big Dance Brothers pistol to relax in Grayson's hand.

Finally Grayson relented, but the big revolver didn't. He kept it straight and ready to fire.

"All right," he said, "it is partly yours. I would have mentioned it anyway, sooner or later."

"No doubt," Langler said in a stiff, sarcastic tone.

"I'll get it," said Grayson. He stood up before lowering the gun. When he slipped it into his holster, Fallon decided not to go for his own gun. Instead he watched the wounded outlaw sidestep to the door and walk out to where they had hidden their horses from sight inside a half-fallen stock barn.

"A thousand dollars . . ." Langler considered it.

Both outlaws walked to the door themselves and stopped outside, staring toward the barn.

"You going for the whiskey, or am I?" Fallon said, their eyes toward the barn as he spoke.

"You go. I'll keep an eye on what the horse trader's up to," said Langler.

"We've got to kill Summers, after all he's done to ruin this job," said Fallon.

"I know it," said Langler. "We *will* kill him, you can count on it." He turned, walked back into the building, climbed the rickety ladder up to the lookout tower.

Fallon stood waiting, watching Grayson return from the barn carrying a bound stack of cash in one hand, his other hand holding the bloody bandanna to the side of his head. *This dirty son of a bitch . . .* , Fallon said to himself.

Grayson handed Fallon the stack of cash, saying, "Here, split it up. I was wrong about it being all hundreds. It's all twenties."

Fallon just stared at him for a second; then he jerked the bound cash from his blood-caked fingers. Breaking the band holding the stack, he spread the bills into a fan, counting them quickly.

"Yep, a thousand," he said. He estimated a third of the cash, folded it along with the broken paper band and shoved it down into his shirt pocket. He patted the pocket. "That clears me up." He handed the rest of the cash back and said, "You and Langler divide the rest between you." He grinned. "Now, if you still want some whiskey, I'll go get it for you."

"Oh yes, I still want it. Get four or even five bottles," Grayson advised him. "I'm hurting like hell." He held out an extra twenty. Fallon snatched it.

"I heard there's a doctor in Austin who can sew ears back on," Fallon said.

"That would be real good to know," Grayson said with sarcasm, "if I was in Austin."

"I'm just saying, if he can do it, so can most anybody else," Fallon offered.

"How's that whiskey run coming along?" Grayson asked dryly, his hand clasping the bandanna to his head.

"I'm gone," said Fallon, shoving the bill down into his trouser pocket. But before he could step away toward his horse, Langler stepped out of the building and walked right past them toward the horse barn, his rifle in hand.

"Forget the whiskey," he said. "Will Summers is leaving and Cherry Atmore is with him."

"Whoa!" said Fallon, falling in behind Langler, hurrying toward the barn. "Are you thinking what I'm thinking?"

"I'm thinking I smell a rat," said Langler without looking around. "I'm wondering if Summers coming along when he did was an *accident* or just *good planning.*"

"Damn it, what about my head, my ear?" Grayson said, hurrying along behind Fallon.

"Stick a rag in it," Langler said coldly. "We're getting to the bottom of this."

"What if you're wrong?" Grayson said pleadingly. "What if Summers had nothing to do with anything?"

"He still killed Little Jackie," said Langler without missing a step. "I'm betting it wouldn't break old man Warren's heart if we killed Will Summers for him."

"Yeah," said Lewis Fallon, "it might also keep Big Jack from wanting to shoot our eyes out once he hears what happened to his son."

Darkness had set by the time Summers and the woman rode up a hill trail and stopped atop a cliff overlooking a closed mining operation that belonged to a defunct French investment company. Twice in the past half hour, Summers had looked back over his shoulder with a feeling someone was following quietly on their back trail. Even as they sat on the cliff, he felt the dapple gray tense a little and turn an ear toward the trail. That was good enough for him.

"This is a good place to spend the night," he said to Cherry Atmore, who sat smoking her third cigarette since they'd left Gunn Point. "What do you think?"

"It's beautiful here," Cherry said dreamily, looking back and forth overhead across the deep starry sky.

"Yes, it is," Summers said.

"Me too," Cherry said quietly.

Summers just looked at her for a moment, realizing her mind had drifted off somewhere. Rather than disturb her right then, he nudged his horse forward down along a steep trail toward a line of shacks built into the side of the rocky cliff. When they reached the thin trail running out in front of the row of shacks, he looked each deserted building over until he found the one that best suited his purpose.

Every shack looked the same, battered tin roofs, no porch, weathered bare plank siding. A few had tin stovepipes still sticking upright from their roofs; some had pipes that had collapsed over onto their sides and hung on by guide-wires.

"This one will do," he said, veering over to a shack whose stovepipe still stood securely in place. On a peg beside the front door of the shack, a battered lantern hung by its wire handle. Summers stepped down from his saddle. He took the lantern from its peg, opened the front door and led the dapple gray and his three horses inside. Cherry stepped down, looked all around dreamily and, leading her paint horse, followed Summers into the shack.

She watched as he shook the lantern and found its oil tank half-full.

"Good deal," he murmured.

Lighting the lantern he walked over, opened the iron door of a short woodstove and looked around inside the stove's soot-covered firebox.

"Does it work?" Cherry asked.

"These things always work," Summers replied.

He left the stove door hanging open and walked to a pile of dried kindling wood still lying stacked in a dusty corner. When he'd walked back with a small pile of kindling and stuck it inside the stove, Cherry turned to her paint and started to untie her roll from behind her saddle. But Summers stopped her.

"Wait," he said. "We won't be sleeping here." He hung the glowing lantern on a wall peg. A soft circle light surrounded them.

"We won't?" she said.

"No," said Summers, "we'll boil some coffee and heat some food, but we'll sleep in one of the others."

"We will?" She looked confused.

Summers smiled to himself. "Take yourself a rest," he said. "I'll cook our dinner as soon as I take care of the horses."

Cherry looked around, found a short wooden stool and dragged it closer to the stove. She dusted it with her hand and sat down. She loosened a sash beneath her chin, took off her winter riding hat and held it on her crossed knees.

She said, "So, Will Summers, what takes you to Whiskey Flats . . . the horses?" She glanced at the three-horse string standing huddled in the far corner.

"Yep, it's always about horses with me," Summers said, striking a match he'd taken from his supplies and setting the kindling to blaze in the belly of the wood-stove. "I have these three sold to a freight company."

"They don't look like wagon horses," Cherry said, giving the horses another look.

"No, they're not wagon horses," Summers said. "The company buys them for other purposes, on-hand horses they call them."

"I see," said Cherry. She took out her bag of fixings while they talked and rolled herself a smoke.

Their conversation stopped as Cherry smoked and Summers poured water from his canteen into a small coffeepot. He set the pot atop the stove and took down his bag of supplies. He took out an air-tight of beans and the dried elk shank.

"I hope you like beans," he said.

Cherry just gazed at him and took a deep draw on her cigarette.

By the time the coffee had boiled and the aroma of it had mingled with the smell of the spiked tobacco, Summers had grained the horses. He'd loosened the cinch on his dapple gray and the paint horse, but he'd left their saddles on. Finished with the animals, he dusted the top of a battered table and dragged it over closer to the fire. He dragged two ladder-back wooden chairs and set them across from each other.

"There," he said, dusting his hands together, "just like being home."

The smell of the coffee and of beans heating in their open tin can caused Cherry to take an interest in getting the meal tabled and served. She had finished her cigarette; her face had taken on a satisfied glow.

"All right, what can I do to help?" she said, standing up from the stool and laying her hat on the corner of the table.

"There's a couple of tin plates, cups and spoons in my saddlebags," he said. "You can get them for us."

"Certainly," Cherry said.

Summers watched as she walked over to his dapple gray and lifted the flap on his saddlebags.

Cherry took out a small loaded revolver and turned it in her hands, examining it.

Summers continued preparing the meal. He'd known the gun was there. This was as good a time as any to see if she was still thirsting for vengeance. Besides, he had his big Colt holstered on his hip; his rifle leaned against the wall within arm's reach.

Still, he felt a little relieved when she stuck the gun back into his saddlebags. He watched her rummage around inside the leather bags until she found the small tin plates and cups and pulled them out. He looked away as she walked back to the table and laid the plates and cups out in front of the two chairs.

The area in front of the stove had warmed from the cook fire. Summers took off his coat and draped it on his chair back. He pulled his shirt cuff down over his hand and used it as a hot pad to pick up the can of beans from the top of the stove and stand it in the center of the table. He used his cuff in the same manner when he picked up the hot coffeepot and filled both of their tin cups.

Cherry sat down and pulled her chair to the table. He eyes were glassy and relaxed.

"Why is it we're not sleeping here where it's warm?" she asked.

In a far corner stood a dusty bed frame without a mattress, only a thick rope woven back and forth for support.

Summers stood beside her and carved slices of dried elk shank onto her plate.

"Because I think we're being followed," he said calmly.

Cherry stiffened and said in a hushed tone, "Followed? Why? By who?"

"I don't know," Summers said calmly, "but we're not going to let it spoil our dinner."

Chapter 7

An hour later, after lagging back to keep from being heard on the trail, the three outlaws arrived on the cliff above the dark, abandoned mining camp. Looking down, they saw the glow of lantern light through a single front window of one of a dozen otherwise darkened shacks.

"This is too damn good to be true," Langler whispered with a grin.

They backed their horses away a few steps, climbed down from their saddles and snuck forward in a crouch.

Grayson whispered, "Do you think he heard us coming up over that rocky stretch of trail earlier?"

"If his ears are that good," said Langler, "we've got no business fooling with him." He looked around Grayson at Fallon for agreement.

"You're a little fainthearted sometimes, Henry," Fallon said to Grayson, teasing him.

"Say it again, Lewis. I dare you," Grayson growled in reply, testy and cross from leaving town without any whiskey to ease his pain.

"Keep your damn voice down, Henry," Langler warned him harshly.

"Yeah, Henry, don't get so upset. I was just riling you some," said Fallon.

"*Riling* me is not a good idea right now, Lewis," Grayson said, rage swelling inside his head with each painful beat of his pulse. "A man hurts this bad, he don't mind killing a son of a bitch for goading him."

"All right, I take your point, Henry. No offense," Fallon whispered sincerely. "Speaking of ears, after we kill this horse trader, why don't you slice off one of his ears and sew it onto yours?"

"Are you being funny?" Grayson asked in an angry tone.

"No," said Fallon, "I'm dead serious. "I wasn't joking about doctors sewing ears back on."

"For God's sake," Langler said in disgust, "do you two rubes ever listen to yourselves?"

Grayson stared at him. "Do you suppose it's true, Cole, what he's saying?"

"Oh yeah," Langler said critically, "it's bound to work. Just make sure you don't sew it on upside down. Nothing you hear would make any sense."

Grayson looked puzzled, his hand still holding the wadded-up bandanna against the side of his blood-crusted head.

"Follow me," Langler said in disgust. He turned and walked back away from the edge of the cliff.

"If I thought it would work . . . ," Grayson whispered to Fallon as the two followed Langler.

"It's worth a try," said Fallon. "What's the worst can happen? You'd have to cut it off and you'd be without an ear, the same as you are now."

"That makes sense," said Grayson. "How bad is this anyway? I can't see nothing."

"Take your hand away," said Fallon.

Grayson lowered the wadded-up bandanna.

Fallon winced, examining the blue lower third of his ear still attached to the side of Grayson's head.

"Well?" said Grayson, expectantly.

"It's fierce looking," said Fallon. "You need to cut the rest of it off, or get another one sewed on. You can't go around looking like this. You'll be scaring the hell out of women and children."

Grayson nodded and said, "All right, I'm doing it."

"That's the spirit, Henry," Fallon said.

Back at their horses, Langler turned around to them and said, "Here's the deal. We give them another hour, make sure they're sound asleep, not expecting anything."

"What if they're not asleep?" Fallon said. "What if they're awake—"

"Yeah," said Grayson cutting him off, "if I was that horse trader, I wouldn't be asleep right now. I'd be going at it like a fiddler in a reel."

"I don't care what they're doing, awake or asleep," Langler said. "An hour from now we're going in. We're going to kill him—" He grinned and looked back and forth between the two of them. "And get Henry here a nice new ear for our trouble."

When Summers and the woman had finished eating, they left under the cover of darkness, leading the animals out through the side door and across fifteen feet of hard, loose shale that lay between each of the mining shacks. But instead of going inside the shack next door, they circled behind it and proceeded on to the next before going inside.

As Summers led the horses to a corner, Cherry stood looking around in the dark light of a half-moon through the single front window. Except for a fire in the stove and a glowing lantern, everything in the shack was the same as the other.

"Well, now, Will Summers," she said, "you sure know how to confuse a gal. If I had just finished a smoke, I'd swear we've walked in a full circle."

"I wish it were warmer for you," Summers said, "but it'll have to do."

"I'm not complaining," Cherry said. "I can stay warm in a blanket if it means not having somebody sneak in and kill us in our sleep." She paused and said, "I wish I could have a smoke before turning in, though. But no chance, huh?"

"Afraid not," said Summers. "We've gone to a lot of trouble to hide ourselves. It would be a shame to give our position away because of a cigarette burning." He stepped over to the dapple gray and loosened the cinch under its belly.

"I understand," she said with a sigh.

Summers smiled to himself and watched her take the rolled blanket down from behind her saddle and walk to an empty bed frame just like the one in the first shack.

"You can have my blanket too," he said. "I'm going to sit up near the window and keep an eye on things."

"You're not going to sleep?" said Cherry.

"I'll doze some, maybe," Summers said. "I've done it before. I can get by on two hours for a while if I have to."

"Just like a horse?" Cherry said, stepping over toward

him as he swung the saddle from the dapple gray's back onto the floor.

Summers loosened the rolled-up blanket from behind his saddle cantle.

"Oh. You know a lot about horses, do you?" he said, holding the rolled blanket out to her.

"Not a lot, but some," Cherry said. "I know most times they can sleep standing up. But they need two hours of lay-down sleep a night to keep healthy. Right?" She took the blanket from his hands.

"Close enough," Summers said quietly.

"What's wrong? Are you surprised I know something about horses?"

"A little," Summers said.

"I don't know why," she said. "I've been around horses all my life." She paused and said, "You're not one of those men who thinks saloon gals don't know anything, are you?"

"No, ma'am, I'm not," Summers replied. "In fact, I'm pleased to say that I know a woman who started out working as a saloon gal and became a doctor."

"A horse doctor?" Cherry asked.

"No," said Summers, "although that would have been good too. This woman became a regular medical doctor."

"Honest to God, you're not joking?" Cherry asked.

"I'm not joking," said Summers.

"And you knew her?" Cherry said.

"I still do," said Summers, "although I haven't seen her in a while."

Cherry cocked her head slightly and looked at him in the shadowy darkness.

"How well do you know this woman doctor?" she asked. "I mean, are you and her . . . ?"

"No, we're not," Summers said, catching her question. "We used to be, but we sort of went our own ways."

"A woman doctor, once a saloon gal . . ." Cherry considered the matter, then said, "A *dove*, like me?"

"Yep, a dove," Summers said. "She learned nursing from a town doctor. He saw promise in her and went on and taught her the profession."

"Look at me," Cherry said, studying his eyes in the darkness. "You're not one of those jakes who want to see a gal make something more of herself, are you? Because I hate those kind of do-gooders."

"No," said Summers. "I never try to tell anybody what to do with themselves. I'm just a plain ol' horse trader. I've got no right judging or advising . . . unless it's about horseflesh," he added.

She stood holding both rolled blankets in her arms. Seeing a wisp of steam in his breath, she looked at the bed frame in the corner, then back at him.

"You know what?" she said as if just stricken with a good idea. "There's nobody home here. We can do as we please."

She walked to the bed frame and tossed both blanket rolls onto the woven rope grid. Summers watched her raise the bed by its foot end and drag it toward the front window.

Summers just watched.

"There," she said, dropping the bed beneath the front window. "We'll both spend the night right here. You can look out the window as often as you want to. We'll wrap these blankets over both of us and keep each other warm." She looked at him. "Any objections?"

"No, ma'am," Summers replied without hesitation.

"And you promise to keep your hands to yourself?" she asked, her voice turning cautious.

"I do," Summers replied. "And so do you?" he asked.

"What's that supposed to mean?" Cherry said.

"Nothing," said Summers, dismissing the matter. "Make yourself comfortable. Let's talk about what we'll each do if I'm right about being followed. . . ."

Outside, at the bottom of the thin path leading down from atop the cliff, the three outlaws stepped down quietly from their horses. They stood in silence for a moment staring toward the glow of light and the wood smoke coming from above the shack.

"Damn, talk about waving a flag . . . ," Langler chuffed under his breath, seeing the rest of the mining camp wrapped in a blanket of purple darkness. "And this is the same man you're saying ruined the bank robbery for yas. You both ought to be ashamed."

"I don't trust it," Fallon whispered, his rifle at port arms across his chest. "People don't live long enough to get this stupid out here."

"Let's get this done," whispered Langler. "The thought of that warm stove is getting to me."

"Me too," said Grayson. "My head's killing me." He levered a round into his rifle, keeping as quiet as possible.

"I'll take the front door," said Langler. "You two cover the side door. "Be ready if they try to make a run for it. I'm kicking the door in and going in shooting."

"Got you," said Grayson. His rifle in one hand, his other hand against the side of his head, he and Fallon moved away in a crouch.

Langler waited until he saw the shadowy figures disappear around the corner of the mining shack. Then he moved toward the front door of the shack, rifle cocked and ready.

From the bottom edge of the dirty window, Summers had watched the three outlaws appear out of the greater darkness into the purple light of a half-moon. In the corner where the horses stood, Cherry's paint horse nickered slightly. Calmly, Summers reached down and shook Cherry gently but firmly by her shoulder.

"What?" she whispered with an awakening gasp.

"Company's here," Summers said. "Go over and keep the horses quiet, like we said." He looked at her in the grainy darkness. "Remember, sit tight until it's all over, one way or the other."

Cherry whispered, "I don't like that 'one way or the other' part."

"Neither do I," Summers said. "Now go."

Without further reply, Cherry rolled up quietly from the bed and slipped over among the animals, stroking the paint's muzzle, whispering in a soothing tone. With her free hand, she held the lead rope and the gray's reins firmly.

A moment later the sound of a door being kicked in resounded in the quiet night, followed by repeated rifle fire.

In the corner Summers heard the startled horses try to stir, but the woman held a firm grip and kept the animals from spooking.

Time to go, he told himself. He hurried to the side door and slipped out into the night.

Two shacks away, Langler stood inside the open

doorway in a cloud of rifle smoke, his ears ringing as he stared around the single empty room.

"Damn it to hell," he shouted, thinking Summers and the woman had heard them coming and made a run for it, "they're getting away!" He ran to the side door and threw it open. Realizing his mistake too late and not being able to change it, he flung himself to one side as Grayson's and Fallon's rifles exploded in the dark from their two separate positions. Bullets sliced past him. One clipped him in his forearm; another swiped his hat from his head.

"Don't shoot. It's me!" he bellowed between rifle shots.

"Cole?" Grayson shouted toward the open side door.

"Yes, *me*, damn it!" Langler replied.

"Where's Cherry and the horse trader?" Fallon shouted, looking all around in the dark.

"I'm right here," Will Summers said in a firm voice, less than ten feet behind him.

Fallon shrieked in surprise; he swung around with his smoking rifle cocked and ready. But all he saw was the blinding flash of Summers' shot as it hit him dead center. The impact flung him backward a complete flip and landed him facedown in the dirt. His cocked rifle hit the ground butt first and fired wild into the air.

"There he is!" shouted Grayson, having heard Fallon's shriek and looking around in time to see him fly backward with the gunshot. "He's shot Lewis!"

Langler and Grayson both fired toward the spot where they'd seen the muzzle flashes. But Summer had backed away twenty feet and taken cover behind a large stack of thick walk planks stacked alongside the next shack.

Bullets thumped into the stack of planks as the two outlaws fired steadily. Grayson belly-crawled to where Fallon lay in the dirt. He shook the downed outlaw by his shoulder. Fallon lay limp, dead. "Nothing I can do for you, Lewis," Grayson whispered. "I've got to look out for myself."

Summers waited for a lull, and when it came, he directed two rapid shots in the direction of the muzzle flash he'd seen coming from the shack's open side door.

Langler shouted loudly as one shot hit the edge of the doorframe and sent sharp splinters slicing into his cheek.

Hearing Langler cry out in pain, thinking he'd been shot, Grayson stood up from Fallon's body and backed away, trying to clear a jammed bullet from his rifle chamber. Seeing his dark figure, Summers fired, but without taking close aim. Grayson felt the bullet slice through the shoulder of his coat. Losing his nerve, he screamed, threw his jammed rifle away and raced away. He circled behind the shack and ran toward their waiting horses.

"You damned coward!" Langler shouted, seeing Grayson disappear around the rear of the shack. But before his words left his lips, two rapid-fire shots thumped against the doorframe and sent him running through the lighted shack, out the front door and toward the horses himself.

Summers waited until he heard the sound of horses' hooves beating a retreat up the narrow path. Then he stepped warily from behind and walked to where Fallon dead in the dirt. Seeing the outlaw was dead, he turned and started toward the shack. But seeing the dark figure step suddenly in front of him, he almost fired his rifle before realizing it was Cherry.

"Don't shoot!" she gasped.

Summers let out a tense breath and said, "I thought the plan was for you to sit tight 'one way or the other.'"

"I told you I didn't like that part," Cherry said shakily. "Anyway, it looks *over* to me."

"You got me there," Summers said. He took another deep breath and let it out. "Are you okay?" he asked.

"Yeah, I'm okay," Cherry said. "Are *you* okay?"

"I'm fine," Summers said, the two of them listening to the horses' hoofbeats move farther and farther away.

"What do we do now?" Cherry said, her hand trembling as she reached inside her coat and pulled out her bag of fixings.

Summers cradled his warm rifle in the crook of his arm. "Now that our *company's* gone, I say we go back to where it's warm and try to get some sleep." He nodded toward the shack with the stove and the lantern burning.

"Sleep? After all this?" Cherry said, struggling to roll herself a smoke. "I don't think so. Look at me, I'm a nervous wreck."

Summers looked down at Fallon's body, then back up at her.

"One of them called you by name," he said. "Do you know these men?"

She turned her eyes up to his as she ran the tip of her tongue back and forth along the edge of the cigarette paper.

"Most likely," she said. She ran the cigarette in and

out of her mouth, firming it up. "I think this one is
Lewis Fallon," she said, touching the toe of her shoe to
Fallon's side. She jerked her toe back and said, "Oh my
God! His ear is missing."

"What the—?" Summer stooped down and looked
at the clean cut along the side of Fallon's head. Blood
ran down the dead outlaw's cheek into the dirt. "It
wasn't shot off," he said. "It looks cut off." He stared off
in the direction the two fleeing outlaws had taken.
Then he turned Fallon onto his back and saw the wad
of money sticking up from his shirt pocket, the pocket
button having popped open. Summers fanned the
money in his hand and saw the broken paper band
that read *$1,000* in black ink across it.

Part of the stolen bank money, he reasoned. So not
all of the bank money was in the bags he'd taken
from behind Little Jackie's saddle. He thought about
it, hoping no one would think that he had taken some
of it.

He studied the money closely, took a single bill and
rubbed it back and forth between his finger and thumb,
knowing this was far less than the thousand dollars
that made up the stack. He needed to take this money
back. He wasn't comfortable even having it with him
long enough to return it, he told himself. But he had to
do it.

Something didn't feel right about the bill in his fingertips, but he needed a closer look.

"Yes, it *is* Lewis Fallon all right," Cherry said with
certainty, staring down at Fallon's dead face. She shud-
dered and added, "I can't take much of this."

She watched Summers fold the money, shove it

down into his shirt pocket and button the pocket flap. Seeing her questioning gaze, he said, "For safekeeping. We're going back to Gunn Point and turning this money in to the deputy."

"But what about Big Jack Warren, you shooting Jackie?"

"I'll have to risk it," Summers said. "How does it look, us having stolen bank money? It puts me right back into suspicion. Either I was in with the thieves or I took money from the bank bags when I took them off Jackie's horse. We're going back *tonight*," he said with finality.

She thought about it and said, "Okay by me, since you put it that way."

"What about the other two? Who are they?" Summers asked, prompting her back to their conversation.

"Oh." Cherry nodded and continued. "I'd guess one of the other two is Henry Grayson—they're always together lately." Getting a grip on herself, she held the cigarette between her scissored fingers and took out a long match. "The other one . . . I don't know who it might be."

Summers just looked at her. Something told him she had nothing to hide.

"Here," he said. He took the match from her shaky hand. He struck it and cupped his hands around the flame. "Why is Fallon's ear missing?" she asked.

"Beats me," Summers said. "I shot one ear off when they killed my string horse. But it wasn't this man."

"Ears. Jesus . . . ," she said, shaking her head.

"I know, it's peculiar," Summers said.

She looked at him in the small flicker of firelight.

"Does it bother you, me saying I know them?" she said. "I've been in Gunn Point for a while."

"It's okay," Summers said. He watched her bow her head over the match and light her cigarette. *It would bother me if you said you didn't,* he said to himself.

PART 2

Chapter 8

The Mexican cook, Juanita, looked up from the *chimnea* behind the large clapboard house, where she stood twisting dough into loaves and placing them on a tin baking tray. She saw the buggy circle into sight over a bare rise; a horse tagged along behind the swaying rig, its reins tied to a rear rail.

She studied the rig as it rolled closer. When she recognized both the deputy from Gunn Point and the bank manager, Bob Harper, she turned and hurried to the house, wiping her flour-streaked hands on her apron.

Seated in the rig beside Bob Harper, Deputy Stiles watched the woman run inside the rear door. He breathed deep, steadying himself, preparing to be the bearer of bad news. Idly his right hand fell across the butt of his holstered Colt. But he caught himself and moved it away as he stared ahead, seeing Big Jack Warren walk out into the yard.

Also watching, Bob Harper fidgeted in the driver's seat.

"I hope I'm doing the right thing, Deputy," he said, "bringing him such terrible news on the wake of his son Jackie's death."

"Bad news has no timing, Mr. Harper," Stiles said. "We have to deliver it when it falls to us to do so."

"Yes, you're right, of course, Deputy," Harper said. He gave a sidelong look. "Anyway, my task is light compared to the dark, terrible news you bring him."

"Neither task is pleasant," Stiles said, staring straight ahead. "But we do what we must."

"Sheriff Goss is fortunate to have such a man as you at his side, Deputy. If you don't mind me saying so."

Stiles only smiled modestly without reply. In the small seat behind him, Stiles heard the buzz of flies. He took off his hat, reached back and fanned the insects away from Little Jackie's blanket-wrapped body.

In the yard, a tall, rawboned gunman named Roe Pindigo stepped into sight from around the corner of the house and stood beside Jack Warren. He wore a black wool suit and a collarless boiled white shirt behind a long black riding duster. The ivory handles of a large Colt lay at the center of his belly, shoved sidelong into a dark leather slim-jim holster. He held a black derby hat in the crook of his left arm. In his right hand he carried a Winchester rifle.

Pindigo sidled closer to Jack Warren, who took out a long cigar, bit the tip off it and spit it to the ground.

"Something's wrong, I can feel it," Big Jack Warren said to his gunman without taking his eyes off the approaching buggy.

"Yeah, me too," said Pindigo.

When the buggy drew closer, Jack Warren and Pindigo spotted the wrapped body leaning in the small rear buggy seat. The short Mexican cook crossed herself and hurried back over to her baking.

"Here we go," Stiles whispered to himself as the buggy circled into the side yard and Warren and Pindigo walked around to meet them.

"Deputy," Warren said in greeting. "Bob." He nodded at Harper. "What brings you out here?" He noted Harper's swollen purple eye. "Everything all right at the bank?"

Harper turned nervously to the deputy, his derby hat in hand.

"I'm afraid it's not all right, Mr. Warren," Stiles said, grimly. "We're both bringing bad news."

"Oh?" Warren gave the wrapped body a troubled look. "Who is this?" he asked either of them.

As he spoke Pindigo walked around the buggy and slapped at flies with his black derby hat.

"It's Little Jackie, Mr. Warren," Stiles said somberly. "He was shot and killed after him and some other men robbed the bank."

"Robbed *my* bank?" Warren said in disbelief. His expression didn't change. But his knees appeared to go weak and almost drop him to the ground before he managed to catch himself.

"My God, Little Jackie," he murmured in a trembling voice. He gave Pindigo a somber look; the gunman reached out and peeled the top corner of the blanket away from Jackie Warren's dead blue face. Flies swirled.

"Get him out of there, Roe," Big Jack commanded Pindigo. Get him in the house. Take Juanita with you, tell her to clean him up." He turned to Deputy Stiles.

The gunman dragged the body from the buggy seat and rolled it up over his shoulder as flies careened and swirled around him.

"I'm awfully sorry, Mr. Warren," Stiles said, watching Pindigo walk away with Little Jackie's blanketed body.

"Which posse man shot my boy?" Warren said, anger boiling behind his voice.

"It wasn't a posse man," said Stiles. "It was a horse trader named Will Summers."

"Will Summers," said Big Jack. "I've heard of that son of a bitch. He comes through here peddling his horseflesh every year or so."

Harper put in timidly, "He said Little Jackie shot one of his horses. . . . I mean, not that is any comfort."

"You're right, it's no comfort at all," Warren said gruffly. "I don't give a damn if Little Jackie shot every one of his mangy horses. Summers had no business killing my son."

"We were right on their trail after the robbery," Stiles said, "but it was questionable whether or not we would have caught them. Hadn't been for Summers, they would have likely gotten away."

"Was anybody else shot?" Warren asked.

"Another robber was wounded," said Stiles. "Two others got away. Sheriff Goss got shot down in the street. But is looks like he might make it."

"Is the wounded man saying who was with him?" Warren asked.

"So far no," Stiles said, "but I haven't had a chance to question him yet. I wanted to get out here to you first."

"He—Summers that is—saved our money, Mr. Warren," Harper said.

"He did?" said Warren, staring at Deputy Stiles as he spoke.

"That's right, he did," said Stiles. He stepped back

over and took two carpetbags of the cash from the back floor of the buggy, carried them back and set them on ground at Warren's feet. "It's all there. But now I'm afraid Mr. Harper here has more bad news to tell you." He turned to Harper.

"Yes," said Harper, clearing his throat nervously. "I closed the bank and carefully counted all the money." He looked worried, and continued, saying, "It appears to all be counterfeit."

"What?" said Warren. "Counterfeit?"

"Yes, counterfeit," Harper said, looking more worried every time he said the word.

Warren stood with a curious look on his broad, rough face as he contemplated the news. He struck the toe of his boot against one of the carpetbags.

"How the living hell can it be counterfeit, Bob?" he said finally. "Are you saying the robbers switched the real money for counterfeit?"

"I don't see how there could possibly have been time for them to do that," Stiles cut in.

"Nor do I," said Harper. "But the fact remains, it is all counterfeit. You can check it yourself."

"If *you say* it's counterfeit, Bob, I don't need to check it. It has been checked by the best."

"Thank you, sir," said Harper. He continued, saying, "We'll be closed until Monday. But come Monday, the only money I have to issue is—well, it's phony," he said with a bewildered shrug.

"Good Lord," Warren said, looking baffled. "This makes no sense."

"I could not agree more," said Harper. "Either they switched the money, or else the money was counterfeit when they took it."

Both Warren and Stiles stared flatly at him until he grew uncomfortable.

"Which, of course, we all three know better than that," he said, feeling his forehead turning clammy with a sheen of cold sweat.

"Nobody is blaming you of anything, Bob," said Warren. "So put that thought out of your mind. I'll defend you to the gates of hell on this matter."

"Thank you, sir," Harper said, sounding relieved. "I stand prepared to follow any order you give regarding opening the bank Monday," he said, boldly. "That includes telling everyone the money is counterfeit, and that they will have to wait until we can recover their real money for them."

"That's most courageous of you, Bob," Warren said. He turned to Stiles and said, "You see, Deputy? This is the kind of man I have working for me. If it wasn't for Bob Harper, I don't know what I'd do in a time like this."

Harper gave a sharp yet modest little grin. "I am a banker, sir. This is what we prepare ourselves for when we run the garters up our sleeves."

"Who knows about this but us three?" Warren asked.

"Oh! No one," said Harper. "I would not dare break such news without first meeting in confidence with you. That would be unheard of in banking."

"Yes, of course, you're right," said Warren. He put a large hand on Harper's shoulder. "I should be ashamed, the way I sometimes fail to tell you what an asset you are to my business."

"Kind of you to say so, sir," Harper replied, a little misty-eyed.

"I want you to continue keeping this to yourself

until we figure out what we're going to do come Monday when the merchants will want some of their operating capital."

"You can count on it," said Harper. He produced a small receipt pad and a flat tin of pen and ink from inside his coat. He flipped the tin open and handed Warren the pen from inside. Warren took the pen, signed the receipt for the money and handed the pen back. Harper looked at the signature, put the pen in the tin case and snapped the case shut. He put the pad and the tin case back inside his coat.

"All right, then, Bob," said Warren, patting Harper's shoulder. "There's one problem we've got a little time to deal with. Now, if you'll excuse me, I need to deal with Little Jackie's burial arrangements."

"Yes, of course, sir," said Harper. He turned toward the buggy. Stiles walked beside him.

"Deputy, I see you brought your horse along," said Warren. "Let Bob start on back—you can catch up. I have a couple of questions I need to ask just to make all of this set right with me."

"Certainly," Stiles said. He walked past the buggy and unhitched his horse.

Warren pulled a big cigar from his coat pocket and slipped it into Harper's hand once the neatly dressed banker was in the driver's seat with the buggy reins in hand.

"Bob, thank you for coming out here and keeping me abreast of things," Warren said.

"Yes, sir, and *thank you*, sir," said Harper, holding the cigar. "I will keep the lid on it, as they say."

Warren and Stiles stood watching intently as Harper

swung the buggy around out of the yard and rolled away toward Gunn Point. Fine white powder wafted from the skiff of snow on the ground. Big Jack stood in silence for a moment until he saw Roe Pindigo walking back from the house toward them. Then he turned to Stiles and made a grab for the deputy's throat.

But Stiles had been prepared for such a move. And rightly so, he had calculated that it would not come until Roe Pindigo was close enough to back Warren's play. The deputy stepped back quickly away from Warren's big reaching hand; his Colt came out of his holster, cocked and ready.

"Don't pull your strong-arm abuse on me, Warren," Stiles said. "I won't tolerate it." His gun barrel stood only inches from the big man's chest.

"You son of a bitch!" said Warren, even as he stopped short with his big fists balled at his sides. "You've got to answer for this! What the hell went wrong out there?"

"I'll answer," said Stiles, standing his ground. He glanced at Roe Pindigo, then back to Warren. "First, you tell your trained ape to point that rifle away from me."

Warren cooled a little, realizing the deputy was not a man to take lightly.

"Roe, lower the rifle," he said to Pindigo. "I want to hear who's to blame for this mess."

The gunman Pindigo stared hard at Stiles, but he turned his rifle away and slid his gun hand farther up the stock away from the trigger.

"If I was to blame, Big Jack," said Stiles, "you can believe I wouldn't have come out here. I would have skinned out of the territory."

Warren settled a little more and let out a breath. Roe Pindigo relaxed a little himself, and stood listening.

"You might not want to hear this, but your son, Jackie, had a hard time listening to anybody," Stiles said.

"Don't speak ill of *my son*, Stiles," Warren growled. "He can't defend himself."

"I'm just being honest," Stiles said. "He shot Sheriff Goss down in the street. That was mistake *number one*." He paused, then said, "Even so, everything else was moving right along the way we had it set to. I held the posse back, not too much, but just enough to let Jackie and the others get away without it looking suspicious—"

"What, then?" Warren said impatiently, cutting him short.

"For no reason at all, he opened fire on Will Summers, who just happened to be on the trail. He killed one of his horses. Summers said for all he knew he would be next." Stiles paused again, then said, "So Summers returned fire. Jackie went down. So did Rochenbach. According to Summers, another one got his ear shot off."

"Damn, what a big mess," Warren said. "What about the money?"

"There was nothing I could do but take it back," Stiles said. "It was there when the posse and I showed up. I couldn't ignore it."

"My son is dead," said Warren. "Sheriff Goss is shot. Rochenbach is wounded."

"And I'm the one put Rochenbach onto this job," Roe Pindigo said.

"So Rochenbach knows it was a setup," said Stiles.

"No," Pindigo said to Stiles, "Rochenbach doesn't even know I work for Big Jack. I told him Langler and the others had a job coming up. Unless Jackie told him more, he doesn't know it was all a setup."

"I'm stuck with a bunch of counterfeit money," Warren said in contemplation.

"Be glad you took the real money out before we set all this up," said Stiles.

Warren nodded in contemplation. "But now I've got to figure how to keep the bank closed until I can slip some real money back inside."

"Yep, that's the problem," said Stiles, realizing the worst was over between him and Warren, for now at least. He nodded toward the buggy growing smaller in the distance, snow swirling behind its wheels. "How much do you trust Bob Harper to keep his mouth shut?" he asked.

"How much do *you*, Deputy?" Warren said with a flat, level stare.

Stiles looked back and forth between the two men.

"What about these other robbers?" Stiles asked.

Warren winced slightly.

"I told Jackie to keep his mouth shut," he said, looking down at the ground. He shook his head. "But whether or not he told Grayson and the others is anybody's guess now." He looked back up at Stiles and said, "Find out for me, Deputy. Be a good lawman and clean this mess up for me, whatever it takes."

"And . . . ?" said Stiles, staring at Warren.

"And you'll be taken care of for your efforts," Warren said.

"That's what I needed to hear from you," Stiles said. "For the right money, it'll all happen *just like magic*." He turned to his horse and swung up into his saddle.

Big Jack Warren and Pindigo watched him ride away. Warren looked off to the northwest at a low cloudy sky.

"I expect we best get Little Jackie buried while a grave can still be dug."

"Want me to ride out and round up your cowhands—send them in for the funeral?" Pindigo said quietly.

"Yes, you do that, Roe," said Warren. "While you're at it tell all of them that damned horse trader killed Little Jackie for no reason at all."

"Consider it done." Pindigo gave him a flat, tight grin, turned and walked away toward the horse barn.

Chapter 9

———————

Bob Harper thought about it as he rode along in the buggy. Something wasn't right, but he couldn't quite put his finger on it. He wondered for a moment if he should wire Leland Sutters, the other owner of Warren & Sutters Trust Bank. After all, Sutters had a right to know about the robbery and the counterfeit money. But would Sutters be as trusting as Jack Warren? He couldn't count on it, he decided.

He shook his head, considering everything. A bank owner's *son* involved in a robbery . . . The town sheriff shot down attempting to defend the bank . . . Now a large cache of counterfeit money . . . !

This wasn't banking as he'd always perceived it to be. This was not like banking in some civilized large city like, say, Chicago or Philadelphia. This was frontier banking, raw and rugged. This was lunacy! he told himself.

As he rode along he begin to consider any and all possible connections the phony money had to the robbery. When the truth begin to sink in, he whispered to himself, "Oh, Jesus," and slapped the reins to the horse's back. But just as he started to speed up the buggy horse, he heard Deputy Stiles call out to him. Looking back, he saw Stiles riding hard toward him from fifty yards behind. Stiles waved his hat back and forth in the air to get his attention.

"Jesus ... !" Harper whispered again. But then he quickly convinced himself that whatever was going on, Stiles was not a part of it. Stiles was the law, after all. If he couldn't trust the law, whom could he trust?

He took a deep, calming breath and slowed the buggy to a halt and waited until the deputy slid his horse to a stop alongside him.

"Couldn't you hear me calling out to you?" Stiles said. "I must have shouted three or four times." He looked Harper up and down. "Is everything all right? You look like you saw a ghost."

"Oh, I'm fine, Deputy," Harper said, feeling a clamminess beneath his hatband. He took a breath, then stopped himself and said, "No, that's not true. I'm not *fine* at all. I've given this matter some thought and I am most upset at what I fear is going on."

"Oh ... ?" Stiles stepped down from his saddle, let his reins drop and walked over to the side of the buggy and looked closely at Harper. "And what is it you think is going on?" he asked.

"I—I'm most hesitant to say," Harper stammered, looking away, out across the rugged snow-streaked land. "I'm not sure I can trust you, Deputy."

"Not *trust* me—?" Stiles cut himself short. "Look at me, Bob Harper," he said firmly, his words alone forcing the timid banker to turn his battered face back toward him. "What did you call me?" Stiles said.

"Call you?" Harper looked shaken, intimidated. "Well, I didn't—"

"No, you called me something," Stiles insisted, cutting him off. "What did you call me?"

"Deputy, I'm certain I—"

"That's right," said Stiles, "you called me *Deputy*, right?" Because that's what I am." He tapped his thumb against the badge on his chest. "Now say it again, with me . . . *Dep-uty*," he said distinctly, forcing Harper to recite along with him like some schoolboy.

"That's better," Stiles said with a smile. "I am *the law*, sir. There is nothing you can't tell *the law*. My job is to protect and defend innocent people like yourself."

"You're right, of course," said Harper.

"You better believe I'm right," Stiles said. "Now scoot over. Let me sit there beside you. Tell me whatever it is that's bothering you."

Harper watched the deputy spring up into the driver's seat and set the buggy's brake.

"I have a feeling Mr. Warren has tried to rob his own bank, Deputy," Harper said. Stiles sat turned toward him in the buggy seat.

Stiles gave him a strange look and smiled.

"Rob his *own* bank? Now, why on earth would a man like Jack Warren do a thing like that?" he asked.

"I don't know why, except that he has never been happy owning only half of the bank," said Harper. "He hates Leland Sutters, I can tell."

"He's told you this?" Stiles stared at him dubiously.

"Well . . . no, not in so many words," said Harper. "But *why* he would rob his bank is not my concern," he said, brushing that question aside. "I believe he needed big money, so he set up the bank for his son, Jackie, and some others to rob. He didn't trust them handling the money, so he planted counterfeit money in the bank."

Stiles continued to stare at him, appearing engrossed.

"Go on," he said.

"Big Jack already has the real money," said Harper. "He switched it the night before the robbery. He was there late, going over some records—something he seldom ever does," he pointed out. "His hope was for the robbers to get away. The counterfeit money would never be seen, and he'd have the real money. Sutters and the town would have to take half the loss." His eyes gleamed a little. "A fifty percent return on capital is quite enough reason for him to do it, wouldn't you say, Deputy?"

Stiles stared at him, considering it.

"*Deputy . . . ?*" Harper repeated, after a moment of blank silence.

"Yes, right. . . ." Stiles batted his eyes, coming out of deep thought.

"You do believe me, don't you?" Harper asked.

"It is a stretch, but yes, I believe you," said Stiles. He slipped a knife from his boot well.

Harper gasped. But then he settled when he saw Stiles take one of the buggy reins in hand and slice a three-foot length of leather from the end of it.

"Wha—what are you doing, Deputy?" Harper asked, his voice trembling.

"I'm going to choke you to death, Bob," Stiles said calmly, with the slight trace of a smile.

"You're . . . not *serious*?" Harper asked, almost smiling himself at such an improbable notion.

"Oh yes, I'm serious," Stiles said, wrapping one end of the leather reins around his left hand for a good grip.

Harper saw that he meant it; he reacted quickly. Snatching a small pepperbox derringer pistol from inside his black suit coat, he aimed it shakily at Stiles.

"Stay away from me!" he shouted.

But Stiles backhanded the small pistol away and sent it bouncing out across the buggy horse's back. The horse jerked once against the buggy brake, then settled.

"No, no!" Harper shouted. He turned to leap from the other side of the buggy. But Stiles slung the length of leather reins around his throat from behind him and jerked tightly, garrote-style.

"Why? Why?" Harper rasped just before his breath cut off.

"Because it's so much quieter this way, Bob," Stiles whispered close to his ear, his pleasant expression unchanged.

Harper's shoes dug and kicked against the wooden floor of the buggy. His arms flailed wildly. He reached back and clawed at Stiles' cheek, but the deputy quickly bowed his head, jammed it into the center of Harper's back between his shoulder blades and held tight. Harper bucked bounced and clawed at the leather buggy seat. But soon it was over.

Stiles sat in silence, staring out across the snow-dusted terrain. He put both ends of the leather rein in his right hand and continued holding on while he took a deep breath and let the banker's body roll down onto the buggy floor.

"All right," he murmured, "that's done." He unwrapped the length of leather rein and dropped it on the buggy floor. He stepped down from the buggy and straightened his clothes.

Looking over at the hills skirting the snowy flat-lands, he studied a high ridgeline where he'd seen a pack of animals move along at a low run while he'd sat listening to the banker's story and acting as he really gave a damn.

What were they? *Wolves? Coyotes? At this time of day, in broad daylight . . . ?*

It was one or the other, he'd decided, knowing how the changing weather had wildlife acting out of the ordinary. Whichever it was, he was sending it a feast, *still warm,* he told himself, stepping forward, taking the buggy horse and turning it toward the hills.

With a gloved right hand he gave the horse a sharp slap on its rump and sent it racing straight toward the hills.

"Enjoy . . . ," he said quietly toward the treed hill-side as he watched snow flair up from behind the bug-gy's spinning wheels.

This was good, he told himself. When the time was right he could ride out in a day or so and find the buggy easy enough. That would bode well for him, he thought, smiling.

He turned to his horse to step up into the saddle. When the horse nickered and shied a step, Stiles grabbed the saddle horn and shook it roughly before swinging up.

"Careful I don't send you to the hills too," he warned the horse under his breath, turning it, tapping his heels to its sides.

Late afternoon, inside the convalescence rear room of the doctor's office, Sheriff Goss sat propped up in bed against two feather pillows. On either side of the bed stood the druggist, Martin Heintz, and Richard Woods, the mercantile owner. At the foot of the bed stood Eric Holt, pad and pencil in hand, busily taking notes. When the doctor came in stirring a spoon around in a glass one-third full of a cloudy liquid, he gave the two men a stern look.

"I apologize for being here disturbing the sheriff, Dr. Meadows," said Woods. "But I'm going to have a problem keeping my doors open for business if I can't get in the bank and get some money. I've got goods being delivered. It has to be paid for."

"Yes," Heintz put in, "and I've got to make change for my customers."

"None of which the sheriff has anything to do with, gentlemen," said the young doctor. He held the glass to Goss' lips. "Drink this, Sheriff. It's three parts water, one part laudanum, just enough opium to make you sleep good."

"Careful, Doc, I don't want to sleep forever," the sheriff said.

"Nor do I want you to." The doctor smiled. "That's why even this small amount is three parts water. Any more than that would be lethal."

"There's nobody else to turn to," Woods continued, replying to the doctor as the sheriff drank the small amount of potent medication. "We've telegraphed Circuit Judge Louder, but so far we've received no reply."

"Be that as it may," said the doctor, "I won't allow you to kill my patient." He set the empty glass down on a stand beside the bed and looked closely at Goss, placing a hand on the sheriff's clammy forehead.

"*Kill* him?" Heintz said, giving Woods a concerned look, his hat hanging in his hand, chest level.

"A figure of speech," the sheriff replied, sounding tired.

Over his shoulder the doctor said in the same firm tone of voice, "Out of here, the three of you. I'll let you know when Sheriff Goss is well enough to be hounded by all your confounded questions."

"Please, Dr. Meadows," said Woods, "it's not only the two of us. Every merchant and business owner in town is growing concerned—"

"You heard the good doctor, gentlemen," said Deputy Stiles, stepping inside the room from the hallway, his rifle hanging in his hand. "Our sheriff needs bed rest."

"Deputy! Thank heavens you're back," said Woods, turning from the bed toward him.

Holt scribbled frantically on his notepad.

Heintz turned too, saying, "Yes, thank goodness! What did Jack Warren have to say? Where is Bob Harper? What the blazes is going on?"

"Listen to me," said Stiles. He spread his hands in a gesture of patience. "As soon as I talk with my boss here, I'll be around to answer whatever I can for you."

"But what about the bank?" said Heintz. "When is it going to open?"

"Right now I'm afraid Jack Warren has more on his mind than the bank," said Stiles. "He's so grief-stricken over Jackie's death, I don't think he realizes the bank is even closed."

"Where is Harper, then?" Woods asked, repeating Heintz's question.

"Now, that does have me curious," Stiles said, looking around as if the banker might suddenly appear. "He arrived at and left the Warren spread a full hour ahead of me. He should be here."

"But he's *not* here!" Woods said a little louder, starting to sound a little testy with the deputy.

Stiles gave him a strong look, took a step forward toward him and said, "I *see* that, Woods."

"Forgive me, Deputy," Woods said, taking a step back, picturing what Philbert Clancy looked like after his encounter with the deputy's rifle butt.

Sheriff Goss gave a half smile at the way his new deputy handled things.

"Everybody settle down," he said. "Let's not get overwrought. Deputy Stiles is doing a good job. Let him do it, until I get back on my feet."

"Obliged, Sheriff Goss," said Stiles. To all three he said, "I'm a little concerned about Harper myself. I saw a couple of Indians along the trail coming back from Warren's. If Harper's not back before long, I'll ride out and see if anything is wrong."

"Indians . . . ?" Holt asked, gazing up from his pad, looking both concerned and hopeful.

"It's probably nothing to worry about," said Stiles. "But it won't hurt to check." He wiggled his rifle barrel toward the door. "Now go on back to your stores. I'll be coming by there in a few minutes. We'll get this town settled and back to running the way it should, whatever it takes."

Sheriff Goss and Stiles both watched as the two merchant townsmen left the room. When they heard the front door of the doctor's office close, Stiles let out a breath of relief. Goss looked him up and down from his pillows.

"Being in charge is not the easiest job in the world, is it, Deputy?" he said with a bit of a slur in his speech.

Stiles could see the laudanum taking hold on the wounded sheriff.

"No, it's not," he said. "I'll gladly give it back to you, once you're on your feet."

Goss gave him a slight nod and said dreamily though half-closed eyes, "Tell me about Big Jack Warren. . . ."

"It's like I said, Sheriff." Stiles replied. "He's so broken up over Little Jackie he doesn't know either end from the middle."

"That doesn't sound . . . like Big Jack," Goss said, drifting away on the strong medication.

"It's him all right," said Stiles. "I'll be lucky to keep the prisoner alive until the circuit judge comes through here."

Stiles stopped talking and looked at the sheriff, watching his eyes fall shut. He didn't mention that Warren wasn't going to reopen the bank right away. *Let him sleep. . . .* Goss wouldn't remember if he'd mentioned it or not, he thought, smiling to himself.

"Well, you asked me. I told you, Sheriff," he said quietly just in case Goss was still able to hear him. "Now why don't you get some more rest and let me worry about how things are going here?" As he spoke, he reached down and picked up the empty water glass the doctor had used to administer the sheriff's laudanum. Stiles inspected the empty glass, then set it back down on the nightstand.

Powerful stuff . . . , he told himself, looking at the unconscious sheriff. He snapped his fingers close to the wounded lawman's ear; the sheriff didn't so much as flinch.

After a moment Stiles turned and walked out of the room to where Dr. Meadows sat in an office at an oak rolltop desk.

"He's asleep, Doctor," Stiles said when the doctor looked up at him.

"Good," said the young doctor. "Rest is what he needs most right now."

"Did you check on my prisoner while I was gone?" Stiles asked.

"I did," the doctor said, looking at Stiles above his reading spectacles. "He's doing well. He's afraid if something happens to Sheriff Goss, the townsmen will drag him out and hang him."

"Let him think it," Stiles said. As he spoke his eyes went to the tall blue bottle of laudanum standing on a shelf above the doctor's cluttered desk. "Maybe it'll give him pause to consider how he's wasted his life."

"Maybe," the young doctor said, turning back to a stack of paperwork on his desk. "At any rate, feel free to check back on Sheriff Goss anytime. If he is asleep, I will simply tell him you were here."

"Obliged, Doctor," Stiles said, turning, walking to the front door to let himself out.

Chapter 10

―――――

When Deputy Stiles walked into Woods' Mercantile Store, he found both Heintz and Woods eagerly awaiting him. Upon seeing him walk in, Holt, the newsman, jerked his pad and pencil from his inside coat pocket.

"Well, what about the bank?" Woods said, not even waiting until Stiles had crossed the plank floor to the counter where they stood.

Stiles took his time answering. He stopped, removed his hat and looked back and forth between the two of them.

"Sheriff Goss and I talked it over, gentlemen," Stiles lied. "Although I can't say I completely agree with him, he's decided it's best to keep the bank closed until Jack Warren gets to town and makes sure everything is on the up-and-up, moneywise."

The two townsmen gave each other a worried look.

"The *up-and-up*?" said Woods. "What the hell is that supposed to mean?"

Stiles raised a cautionary finger toward him and

gave him a strong gaze. "Before you make the mistake of using that kind of language with me again, I hope you'll *confer* with Philbert Clancy and ask him if wishes he'd chosen his words more carefully, our last conversation."

Holt stopped writing and stared, enthralled by the prospect of violence.

"I—I'm sorry, Deputy," Woods stammered, taken aback by the sudden look of fury in the young lawman's eyes. "It's just that I'm upset. I need my cash to keep this store running."

"I accept your apology this *one time*," Stiles said, his finger still raised. "But don't use that blackguarding language again," he warned.

Holt sighed and looked disappointed as he let his writing hand relax. Stiles looked at him.

"Get out of here, newspaperman," he said. "I want to talk to these two without your beak stuck in the pudding."

Holt offered no protest; he shot out of the store, pencil and pad still in hand.

"Deputy, please," Heintz asked Stiles in a most mild and civil tone, "what about our money?"

"You'll get your cash as soon as the bank reopens."

"But we have no idea when that will be, Deputy," Heintz persisted.

"That's why I'm asking you two, and everybody else in Gunn Point, to be patient for a little while longer. The bank will open when Jack Warren comes in and declares it open." He paused for a second, then said, "This is what Sheriff Goss said to tell you, and this is how it's going to be."

"Does this have anything to do with Harper being missing?" Woods asked.

"Nobody says he *is* missing," said Stiles. "But if he is missing, if he's run off with the bank money, I want you to know that Jack Warren and his partner, Leland Sutters, stand prepared to make good on your money."

"Oh my," said Woods. "Harper has taken off with the money."

"Stop it," said Stiles. "I won't have you spreading fear talk. Before we blame Harper of anything, I want to look him in the eye and hear what he has to say." He paused and looked back and forth between them again. "Meanwhile, before I go to search the trails for Bob Harper, I want both of you to give me your word that what I'm telling you will go no futher than this room."

The two townsmen looked stunned. This was why he'd gotten rid of Eric Holt.

"Do I have your word on it, both of you?" Stiles' hand rested on the butt of his Colt; his rifle hung from his other hand.

Both men nodded as one. "Yes, you have my word, Deputy," said Woods.

"Mine too," said Heintz. "What can we do to help?"

"Right now, nothing," said Stiles, "other than keep quiet and work with me."

"You've got it, Deputy," said Heintz, feeling relieved that Stiles didn't ask them to ride out and search the trails with him.

"Absolutely," Woods put in. "You have our support. We're behind you a hundred percent."

"Good, I appreciate it," said Stiles, knowing if these

two showed support for him, the rest of the merchants
and townsfolk would follow suit. "Now, if you'll both
excuse me, I need to check on my prisoner." He gave
them both a courteous nod, turned and left.

When he was out the door and out of sight, the two
merchants looked at each other in bewilderment.

Finally Heintz shrugged and said, "You heard him,
the bank will reopen soon."

"*Soon* is wide open to speculation," said Woods.
"How the blazes are we supposed to run our busi-
nesses *until* the bank comes through with our money?"

"Credit," Heintz said flatly.

"No business can run on credit," Woods said, "at
least not for very long."

"Let's hope we're not talking about *very long*,"
Heintz put in. "I'll feel better about everything once
Sheriff Goss is back on his feet."

The two gazed toward the door with equally concerned looks on their faces.

"Anyway," said Woods, "did you understand everything he said?"

"Sort of, I guess," said Heintz, scratching his head.

Leaving the mercantile store, Stiles walked to the sheriff's office, respectfully touching his hat brim to passing townsfolk along the way.

Inside the office, Jason Jones, the surveyor, stood up
from behind the battered desk when Stiles stepped in
from the street.

"I'm glad you're back, Deputy," Jones said. "I need
to get back to work."

"How's the prisoner?" Stiles asked.

"Seems all right to me," said Jones. He lowered his

voice a little. "He appears less nervous since the doctor told him Sheriff Goss is going to pull through." He looked at Stiles closely and asked, "How'd Big Jack take what happened?"

"He took it real hard, Jason," Stiles said with a grim expression.

"Damn—I mean, *dang*, that's terrible," said Jones, correcting himself quickly, seeing the look on Stiles' face turn severe. "Begging your pardon, Deputy," Jones added sincerely.

Stiles nodded. Changing the subject, he looked at a young livery hostler, Danny Kindrick, who stood sweeping a spot of plank floor in the hallway leading back to the jail cells. "How is Danny working out, helping you?"

"He's a good kid," said Jones. "I even let him take the prisoner to the privy—no problem at all."

"Good," said Stiles, "then I'll keep him here helping me for a couple of days." He looked at Jones. "You're free to go. Obliged for your help."

"Anytime, Deputy," Jones said. He picked his hat up off the desk, placed it atop his head and left.

When he'd left, Stiles looked back into the hall at Danny, who stood with a dustpan in one hand, a broom in the other.

"Danny, come here. I want to talk to you," he said.

The young man stepped lively to him and stood almost as if at attention.

"Yes, sir, Deputy," he said. "Is—is everything all right?"

"Yes, it is, Danny. Relax," Stiles said. "Jones was just telling me what a good, dependable hand you are."

"Thank you, Deputy," said the young man, looking a little relieved.

"How old are you now, Danny, fifteen, sixteen?"

"Sixteen, sir," said Danny, standing like a soldier, the broom hugged close to his side.

"That's old enough," Stiles said. "How would you like to keep working for me the rest of the week—keeping the place clean, looking after the prisoner?"

The young man's eyes lit up.

"I'd like that a lot, Deputy!" he said.

"Can you work here a few hours a day and still take care of the livery barn?" Stiles asked.

"Yes, sir, I sure can," said Danny.

"How does fifty cents a day sound?" Stiles asked.

"It sounds great, sir," said Danny. "I'd do it for free, you know . . . just to help you out."

"Obliged, Danny," said Stiles. "But a man needs to be paid for his efforts, wouldn't you agree?"

"I sure do, sir, if you say so," Danny said.

"All right, then, it's settled," Stiles said. "Go put your broom up. I want you to go to the restaurant and bring the prisoner back a dinner tray and some coffee—bring *me* some coffee too." He paused and then said, "Do *you* drink coffee, Danny?"

"Been drinking it for years, sir," Danny said eagerly. He gestured toward the wood stove where a battered coffeepot stood on a top burner plate. "I can fix some here, if you want."

"Not this time, Danny," said Stiles. "I'd like some coffee from the restaurant, wouldn't you?"

"Yes, sir," Danny said.

"Then get going," Stiles said. "And, Danny, stop calling me sir." He gave him a short smile. *"Deputy Stiles* will do just fine."

"You got it, *Deputy Stiles*," Danny said on his way out the door.

Avrial Rochenbach lay on his cot facing the wall, feigning sleep, listening for any scrap of information he might learn about the wounded sheriff's condition. He knew if Sheriff Goss died, his own death would soon follow. Even though he had nothing to do with pulling the trigger, the action of the wild-eyed idiot Jackie Warren had sealed all their fates. He would die on the end of a lynch mob's rope if the sheriff died. This was a tight spot, no doubt about it. . . .

"Listen up, Rochenbach," said Stiles from the other side of the barred cell door. "The doctor tells me you're doing pretty good."

Rochenbach rolled up onto the edge of the cot, his left arm in a sling. "I'm better," he said. But he didn't want to reveal how much better, not until he saw where this conversation with the lawman was headed.

"Good," said Stiles. "Get up and walk over here where I can see your face while I talk to you."

Rochenbach pushed himself up from the cot with his right hand and stepped out of the slanted barred shadows to the cell door. A length of shackle chain dragged the floor as he walked in short, halting steps in his stockinged feet.

"I'm not going to beat around the bush with you, Rochenbach," Stiles said. "Men like you make me see red. You were an honest lawman, but you disgraced the badge and brought shame to all of us who wear it."

Rochenbach stared at the floor.

"Look at me," Stiles demanded. As Rochenbach raised

his eyes and met the deputy's fierce gaze, Stiles said, "If there's anything you need to tell me that might save your life, now's the time to do it." He paused, then said in a lowered tone, "I'm talking about anything . . . *anything* at all."

Rochenbach saw the strange knowing look on Stiles' face. "You mean tell you about who the others were with me, that sort of thing?"

"I don't care who was with you. I already know," said Stiles. "I'm talking about who was behind the robbery. Who set it up." He searched Rochenbach's eyes for any sign that he knew the robbery had all been a setup. He saw nothing; Rochenbach only looked confused and shook his head as if trying to understand the deputy's questioning. "Keep in mind that I might even already know," Stiles added.

Rochenbach gave a slight shrug with his right shoulder.

"I have no idea what you're talking about, Deputy," he said. "A fellow I know told me if I needed work to look up Cole Langler, Henry Grayson and Lewis Fallon. I did, and this is where it led me. They led me to meet up with Little Jackie the day before we rode into town. Had I known the kind of fool he was, I never would have—"

"That's enough small talk," Stiles said, cutting him off. This man had no idea Big Jack Warren was robbing his own bank, Stiles was certain of it. If he did, he would have said so before now.

"You asked," said Rochenbach. "I'm just answering the best I can."

"It looks like you're coming to a terrible end," Stiles said. "The only thing keeping you from attending a hemp waltz has been the sheriff not dying. I just talked to the doctor and he says the sheriff has taken a bad turn. So the townsmen could be coming for you most anytime." He watched Rochenbach hang his head and shake it back and forth slowly.

"That stupid Little Jackie," he said under his breath. "I should have rode away the minute I laid eyes on him."

"Yep, you should have," said Stiles. "But it's too late now. What's done is done." He paused, then said, "I'm going to be honest with you. When the townsmen get fired up on whiskey and come for you, I'm not putting myself between them and you. I'll give you over without batting an eye."

Rochenbach raised his eyes from the floor and stared at him as if he had something to say. Then he appeared to have thought better of it, and remained silent.

"I don't owe you nothing," Stiles said. "That ol' sheriff has been like a father to me."

Rochenbach looked at him.

"I thought you hadn't been deputy here that long," he said.

"Been talking to Jones, have you?" Stiles gave him a short, flat smile.

"I just overheard it," Rochenbach said.

"It's true I haven't been here long," said Stiles. "But what time I've been here, Sheriff Goss has been like the pa I never had. Do you understand me?"

"Yeah, I understand," said Rochenbach, letting out a breath. "I meant nothing by it."

Stiles breathed easy.

"Of course you didn't," he said. He looked down at the shackle chain on Rochenbach's stockinged feet. "If

I take the chain from your ankles, will you give me your word not to try to make a break for it, first chance you get?"

"You'd take my word for something like that?" Rochenbach asked, studying Stiles' face curiously.

"If that's your answer, forget it," said Stiles. He started to turn and walk away.

"Wait! You've got my word, Deputy," Rochenbach said.

Stiles stopped in his tracks and smiled to himself. Then he got rid of the smile, turned and said, "Hold your feet over close to the bars. I'll take them off right here and now."

"Obliged, Deputy," said the prisoner, a little surprised by the deputy's sudden act of mercy. He held his feet over close to the bars as Stiles stooped down, taking a key from his vest pocket.

"Don't you go making a fool of me, Rochenbach," Stiles warned. "One false move and I'll clap these right back on you."

"I understand," Rochenbach said, staring down at him.

What was all this . . . ? Rochenbach asked himself. As he considered it, he opened and closed his left hand, testing his strength, his arm resting in the sling. He had no idea what the deputy meant by anything he'd said. But his shackles were coming off his ankles. That was a start, he thought. Now to figure out how to get out of here before the townsmen came calling, carrying a rope. He felt cool around his ankles when Stiles unlocked the shackle chain, lifted it through the bars and stood up and looked at him.

As Stiles studied his eyes, the door to the office

opened and Danny Kindrick walked in carrying a tray of food with a checkered cloth napkin covering it and a small pot of coffee.

"Looks like dinner is here, Rochenbach," Stiles said. He gave his short, flat smile. "Now mind your table manners."

Chapter 11

An hour before dawn, Rochenbach had been awakened by the smell of coffee boiling atop the woodstove. He rolled up onto the side of his cot and tested his left hand again, opening and closing his fingers. He could use his hand if he had to, he thought, assessing himself. He'd had enough rest; he was over his loss of blood. He had to keep his eyes open and be ready to make a move when the opportunity presented itself. There was no way he was going to wait until Sheriff Goss was dead.

Huh-uh. . . . First chance he got he was out of here. If they killed him while he tried to escape, so be it, he thought with resolve. It still beat sitting here waiting for someone to sling a rope around his neck. As he considered his situation, he saw his empty boots standing inside the cell where someone had set them through the bars. The sight of them gave him pause. He looked all around as if expecting someone to be watching to see his reaction.

His thoughts were interrupted by Danny Kindrick

walking in through the front door and down the hall toward the cells carrying a tray of food from the restaurant. Stepping in behind Danny, Deputy Stiles walked along carrying a steaming mug of coffee. Rochenbach stood and stepped forward.

"Feeling better this morning?" Stiles asked the prisoner. He waited until Danny pushed the tray through the open food slot onto a narrow iron shelf built into the barred door. Rochenbach's right hand came out and took the mug of coffee when Stiles passed it through to him.

"Some," Rochenbach said, not wanting to tip Stiles off that he was well enough to do whatever it took to get himself out of here ahead of a noose.

Stiles watched him take the coffee mug and raise it to his lips. He had no more questions for this man. Roe Pindigo had put him wise to the upcoming robbery and he'd looked up Grayson and the others and joined them. He'd had no idea what he was getting into. Avrial Rochenbach was just a loose end that needed tying down, Stiles decided, watching him sip the coffee. Not even an important end at that.

"When the prisoner is finished with his breakfast and gets his boots on," Stiles said to the young livery hostler, keeping his eyes on Rochenbach as he spoke, "handcuff him and escort him out to the privy." He reached over and dropped a handcuff key into Danny's shirt pocket.

Rochenbach watched every move closely, as closely as he listened to every word.

"Yes, sir," Danny said to Stiles. He glanced down at the shackle chain missing from Rochenbach's ankles. His eyes moved over to the boots.

"I set them in there," Stiles said. "There's no need in ruining a good pair of socks."

"Yes, sir," Danny said.

"I'll riding out of here shortly, Danny," Stiles said. "I'm leaving you in charge of the prisoner while I'm gone."

As Stiles spoke he watched Rochenbach set his coffee mug on the food tray and carry everything to the cot. He set the tray on the cot and sat down beside it.

"You mean *all the way* in charge?" Danny asked, sounding a little surprised.

"Yep," said Stiles, "unless you'd be more comfortable if I got one of the townsmen to come over—"

"No, sir," Danny said quickly, "I'm comfortable by myself. I've got the shotgun." He gave a jut of his chin. "He's not going to give me any trouble."

"That's the spirit, Danny," Stiles said, clasping a hand on the young hostler's shoulder. "But forget the shotgun. There's a Remington forty-five in a shoulder harness in the gun cabinet. You put it on and wear it, with my blessings. How does that sound?"

"I don't know what to say," Danny replied.

"No need to say anything, Danny," Stiles said. "It's a man-sized gun for a man-sized job. Don't be afraid to use it if this man steps out of line."

"I won't be, Deputy, I promise," the young hostler said.

"Good," said Stiles. "I won't be gone any longer than I have to be. The shape the sheriff's in, I want to be here if anything happens to him."

"Yeah," said Danny, "if that happened, things could get bad real quick."

"Well, let's hope that doesn't happen," said Stiles,

"for all our sakes." His gaze riveted on Rochenbach, then moved away. "Anybody asks, I'll be out checking the trail, seeing what become of the bank manager."

"Yes, sir, I'll say so if anybody asks," said Danny Kindrick

Stiles said to Rochenbach, "See to it you behave, Rochenbach, or else you'll find yourself back in socks and shackles."

"I understand, Deputy," Rochenbach said, not quite believing this opportunity, but not about to question it either. He wiggled his toes in his socks and looked at his boots. They stood as if waiting for him.

Outside, Deputy Stiles unhitched this horse and rode it to the doctor's office. He stepped down from his saddle, hitched his horse at the hitch rail and walked inside. Instead of being met by the young doctor, an elderly townswoman named Flora Ingrim waddled forward and stood before him inside the front door.

"Good morning, Deputy," she said. "The doctor had to leave in the night. Can I help you?"

"I'm checking on the sheriff," Stiles said. He sidestepped around her, taking his hat from atop his head. "I know where he is."

"Oh, all right," said Flora, "you go right on ahead. Dr. Meadows gave him something to make him sleep, but he said you'd most likely be by checking on him this morning."

"He did?" said Stiles, stopping, looking back over his shoulder at her.

"Well, yes," she said, "knowing how concerned you are about the sheriff—as are *we all.*"

"Right . . . ," said Stiles, walking on into the hall toward the convalescence room.

"While you're here, Deputy," she called out, "I'll just step across the street and let my cat out of the house, if you don't mind?"

"Of course not, go ahead," Stiles said. He smiled secretly to himself and stopped outside the door to the wounded sheriff's room and waited until he heard the front door close behind the woman.

Perfect. . . .

He turned away from the closed door and walked back along the hall and into the doctor's private office. Inside, he walked across the floor and took down the large blue bottle of laudanum.

Three parts water, one part laudanum . . . , he told himself, reaching over and picking up a drinking glass like the one he'd seen the doctor use. *Not this time. . . .* He smiled and filled the glass to the top, leaving the tall bottle empty. He recapped the empty blue bottle, placed it back up on the shelf and walked back to the sheriff's room.

Standing over the sleeping sheriff, Stiles shook his shoulder gently. "Wake up, Sheriff. "I've got something to make you feel better."

Sheriff Goss opened his eyes weakly and tried to focus up at Stiles.

"Wa—water?" he said thickly.

Stiles patted his shoulder and held the glass down to his lips and tipped it slightly.

"That's right, Sheriff, good cool, clean water," the deputy said. "You drink it all down—it's good for you." He smiled guardedly, watching the wounded man gulp down the water until the tall glass was empty.

"I—I was awfully . . . thirsty," the sheriff rasped. "I still am."

"You've had plenty, Sheriff," Stiles said, not wanting Flora to come in while he carryied out his terrible act. "More than enough," he added.

"Where is the doctor?" Sheriff Goss asked.

"He's off seeing a patient," Stiles said. "I just stopped in to see that you're all right."

"Help me . . . sit up so we can talk," the sheriff said, struggling a little but making no progress in rising.

"No, Sheriff," said Stiles, hearing the woman come back in the front door, "you lie still. I'm leaving anyway. We can talk another time. The main thing is that you're feeling better."

"I'm . . . so sleepy," the sheriff said, relaxing back onto the pillow.

Stiles smiled and patted his shoulder.

"Sleep tight," he said quietly. He turned and walked back through the hallway toward the front door.

Standing inside the door with a yellow cat in her arms, Flora Ingrim said, "There's so many dogs I couldn't turn her loose right now." She rocked the cat in her arms. "How is the sheriff . . . sleeping soundly, I bet?"

"Oh yes, very *soundly*," said Stiles. On his way out the door, he reached over and scratched the cat's head fondly. "Nice kitty," he said.

Only a few minutes after the deputy had left, Rochenbach finished his breakfast and stood up from the cot. He went to where his boots stood inside the bars, carried them over to the cot, sat down and pulled them on. He worked his left hand, testing it. After a moment, he walked to the barred door, took a few deep breaths to clear his mind and calm him.

Here goes. . . .

"Danny," he called out down the hallway.

In a second, Danny Kindrick came walking down the hall wearing a shoulder harness, the butt of a big Remington sticking up under his left arm.

"Yes, sir," Danny said, stopping and staring at Rochenbach through the bars.

"I need to go out back now, if it's all the same with you."

"Sure thing," Danny said. From his back pocket he pulled a brass ring with the cell key hanging on it. He reached out and started to unlock the cell door. But then he caught himself, stopped and said, "Just one minute."

Rochenbach watched him walk over to a pair of handcuffs hanging on a wall peg. He took the cuffs down, walked back to the cell and held them out on his fingertips.

"Turn around, I need to cuff your hands first," he said.

Rochenbach gave him a close and serious look.

"Behind me?" he said. "Are you sure you want them cuffed behind me? That means you'll have to unbutton my fly for me and all that. . . ." He let his words trail.

Danny winced at the thought of what "all that" meant. He looked a little embarrassed.

"I forgot about that," he said. "Just put your hands out in front of you."

Rochenbach did as he was told, lifting his sore left arm out of the sling. Danny reached the cuffs through the bars and cuffed his wrists in front of him.

"They're not too tight, are they?" Danny asked.

"No, they're okay," Rochenbach said. He wasn't sure

he trusted this. The deputy had to know that this young man lacked the experience needed to keep watch over a prisoner, especially one as desperate as he himself was. He looked all around, making certain this wasn't some made-up deal—the deputy looking for a reason to kill him while he tried to escape. It didn't matter; setup or no setup, he had to take the chance.

"All right, then, let's go," Danny said, reaching out, unlocking the cell door and swinging it open.

As Rochenbach stepped out of the cell past Danny, with one swift move he jerked the big Remington out of the shoulder harness with his cuffed hands, cocked it and jammed the tip of the barrel up under Danny's chin.

"Don't move!" he warned. "Don't make me kill you!"

Danny stood speechless, his hand instinctively rising chest high as Rochenbach shoved him into the cell and backward onto the cot.

"Get these off me," Rochenbach demanded, holding the gun and both wrists out in front of the frightened young man.

As soon as Danny fished out the small key and unlocked the cuffs, Rochenbach spun him around on the cot, cuffed his hands behind his back and stepped back. He looked all around, still leery of a trap.

"You won't get away with this, mister," Danny ventured.

"Keep quiet!" Rochenbach snapped. He pulled a faded bandanna from around Danny's neck and tied it tightly around Danny's head, between his parted lips.

Crossing the cell, he stepped out and closed the barred door. He turned the key in the lock, then took it out and pitched it and the handcuff key across the floor.

So far so good . . . , he told himself. Hurrying down the short hall to the dusty front window, he looked back and forth along the quiet street. Morning traffic; nothing out of the ordinary. All he had to do was slip out the door and cross the boardwalk to the hitch rail where three horses stood waiting at the rail. This was going to work!

Rochenbach hurried over to a coatrack, jerked a coat down and hurriedly put it on. He grabbed a battered black Stetson with a brim wide enough to hide his face. Pulling the hat down low onto his forehead, he uncocked the Remington and shoved it down into his belt.

Here goes . . . , he told himself. But to his stunned surprise, when he opened the front door he found himself staring right into Will Summers' eyes.

"Holy—!" He grabbed for the Remington, but before he got his hand around the gun handle, Summers' Winchester butt swung up and made a vicious jab into his forehead. He flew backward across the office and hit the floor, knocked cold.

Summers stepped inside. Cherry Atmore followed. She stared down, wide-eyed, at the knocked-out Rochenbach, who lay sprawled on his back, the battered Stetson lying on the floor behind him, rocking back and forth on its crown.

Summers stepped over Rochenbach and reached down and took the Remington from his waist. He took him by the coat collar and dragged the limp outlaw down the short hall to the cells where Danny Kindrick stood looking at him through the bars.

"There's the keys," Summers said to Cherry, nodding at both the large and small keys lying on the floor.

Cherry snatched both keys up and unlocked the cell door. While Summers wrestled the knocked-out Rochenbach onto the cot, Cherry quickly took the bandanna from across Danny's mouth and unlocked his handcuffs.

"Folks, I am so happy to see you," Danny said. "I have been made into a real rube here."

"Where's the deputy?" Summers asked.

"Our bank manager is missing," Danny said nervously. "Deputy Stiles left me in charge while he rides out to check the trail."

"I see," said Summers. He looked at the knocked-out Rochenbach, then back at the young livery hostler. "How is the sheriff doing?" As she spoke, he ushered Cherry and Danny out of the cell and swung the barred door shut.

"As well as he could be expected," Danny said, "for having a bullet through his chest."

Summers locked the cell door and turned and held out the key ring and the smaller key to the handcuffs.

"Can you hang on to these now?" he asked Danny.

Danny's face reddened. But he managed to look Summers in the eye and say, "Something like this will never happen to me again. You can lay wager on it."

"I believe you," said Summers. He dropped the keys into Danny's hand. "You're back in charge. We've got to go see the sheriff on a matter of importance." Noting the shoulder harness under Danny's arm, he handed him the Remington butt first and said, "You'd do well to take that rig off and get yourself a shotgun."

"Obliged," Danny said quietly, taking the Remington and looking it over as Summers and Cherry turned and headed for the front door.

Chapter 12

Stiles had ridden a half hour along a string of low hills east of Gunn Point before stopping and gazing back toward town. This spot would do, he told himself, stepping down from his saddle and shoving his horse's rump, sending it into the cover of rock and scrub cedar. From here he commanded a good view of the town from a distance far enough out that if anything went wrong he had time to fix it before anyone rode out from town to see what the shooting was all about.

He walked over, sat down behind a rock and laid his rifle atop it, its barrel pointed back toward town.

Besides, he thought with a short smile, this was on his way to where he would find what was left of Harper and the buggy. He played it out in his mind as he stared back at the roofline of Gunn Point, watching for any sign of flurrying snow along the trail.

All right, he'd ridden out to look for Harper when he saw the prisoner escaping, he told himself, rehearsing it, getting it all straight.

Bang, killed him, one shot. . . . Everybody loved a lawman who was deadly with a rifle. So, here he'd come, bringing the buggy and poor Bob Harper's chewed-over remains to town. *Saw the escaped prisoner flying along the trail. . . .*

Enough of that; he stopped himself. He knew how to tell what happened. Nobody would know which came first, killing Rochenbach or finding the buggy. It didn't matter. He could change it to however it best fit. The main thing would be to play it just right when he got to town and found out poor Sheriff Goss was dead—the chest wound had just been too much for him. Bless his heart, he'd gone to sleep and never wakened.

Stiles practiced shaking his head sadly. *How will I ever get by without that fine old lawman guiding me?* He would say. But there he would stand, the dead prisoner draped over a saddle, Harper's scraped-out skull lying on the buggy seat, eyeless sockets staring gaping up at the sky. He would shake his head gravely.

Gentlemen, I won't even consider taking over as sheriff unless I have the support of each and every one of you. . . .

Once he pinned Goss' badge on his chest, Big Jack Warren would realize what a job he'd done here, cleaning up the mess Little Jackie and his saddle tramp pals had made of things. *Just like magic,* Stiles told himself. He smiled. Just as he'd said it would be.

He waited; an hour passed.

Maybe he'd been wrong about this man, Rochenbach, he thought. Maybe Rochenbach was too afraid to make a move, even against a young whelp like Danny Kindrick. If that was the case, so be it. He wasn't going to spend the whole day waiting. His plan would work with or without him gunning down an escaped prisoner—he had other things to do. Still he sat watching the trail to Gunn Point, waiting.

Another ten minutes passed.

Forget Rochenbach. He stood up, slapped dust and snow from his duster tail and looked out across the flatlands toward the distant hill line. Then he walked to his horse and shoved his rifle into the saddle boot. Swinging up into the saddle, he turned the horse and put it forward across the snowy ground.

When he'd arrived at the place where he'd sent the horse racing away toward the hill line, he didn't even stop. He knew which way the horse had headed. The animal's hoofprints and the wheel marks of the buggy snaked away in front of him. He followed at an easy clip until he spotted the buggy turned half onto its side, against a split boulder at the foot of a rocky hillside.

"My, my . . . ," he murmured, seeing red and white bones and parts of Harper's horse lying strewn among the rocks and dried brush. "So this is as far as you made it." A strand of the horse's mane fluttered on a chilled breeze.

Looking all around, Stiles saw parts of Bob Harper strewn about as well. Harper's black suit coat lay in a ragged bloody pile. His shredded and chewed-up derby hat lay a few feet away. A few more feet away, he saw Harper's head and half of his upper rib cage lying in the rocks.

"Nice to know that Mother Nature always does her job," he said aloud with a thin smile. He pulled his bandanna up over the bridge of his nose against the raw smell of death in the air, and stepped down from his saddle. Drawing his rifle, in case he needed it, he walked first to the horse's stripped carcass and looked down at it and back at the overturned buggy.

He would have to turn the buggy upright and check the wheels and axles, but otherwise he couldn't complain. This had gone well—about the way he'd predicted it would. He glanced back across the flatlands toward the trail running from town. At least something had gone his way.

He went to work, setting the buggy upright and inspecting its wheels and axles. Finding everything to be in good enough working order, he gathered the reins and rigging from among the bloody scraps of horse and man on the ground. When he'd sorted the rigging and wiped everything down with a rag from his saddlebags, he took the saddle from his horse's back and laid it over the buggy seat.

In moments he'd hitched his horse to the buggy, dragged Haper's head and half a rib cage over and laid the grizzly remnants in the rear floor of the buggy. He covered the putrid remains with Harper's shredded suit coat and derby hat, and wiped his hands in the snow and dirt and dried them on his duster tails.

Big Jack did say he would be *taken care of* for cleaning up this mess, he reminded himself. Taking a deep breath, he stepped up into the buggy seat and turned his horse toward town.

It was afternoon when the townsmen of Gunn Point saw Stiles drive Harper's buggy onto the main street and veer toward the sheriff's office. All right, Stiles told himself, he had their attention. Men stopped and

turned from loading wagons out in front of Woods'
Mercantile. The barber, his razor in hand, and a man
wearing a bib, his face covered with foamy shaving
soap, stepped out of the barbershop and stood staring
as the buggy rolled past.

Out in front of Stems' Maplethorpe Saloon, drinkers
stepped out, beer mugs in hand, and stood on the
boardwalk craning their necks for a look at the deputy
and the missing banker's dusty, shredded buggy.

As the buggy continued toward the sheriff's office,
the teamster, Joe Leffert, appeared on Stiles' right and
swung up into the seat beside him.

"Dang, Deputy, I'm glad to see you roll in. Dr. Meadows said to tell you to come straight to his office as
soon as you get back."

Stiles saw the concerned look on the old teamster's
face. He knew it was about the sheriff, but he had to
play it out all the same.

"What's wrong, Joe?" he asked.

"I wasn't told what it's about, but it's bad news, I can
tell you that. I was told to keep quiet, and send you on
over first thing."

"Well, now," said Stiles, "I expect I best get on over
there. Are you going with me?"

"Are you inviting me?" Leffert asked.

Stiles thought about it. The fewer people around the
better, at first, he decided. After the doctor broke the
news to him, there'd be plenty of time to gather everybody in and deliver the sad news.

"No, you hop off here, Joe," Stiles said. "Whatever it
is, you'll know soon enough."

"All right, Deputy," Leffert said, not sounding too

disappointed. "Now that I've done my civic duty and found you, if anybody wants me I'll be at Stems' doing what I do best." He grinned, then said with a wrinkled nose, "What the hell—I mean *heck*—is that smell, Deputy?" He looked back in the rear seat but not down on the buggy's floor.

"I'll tell you later, Joe," Stiles said. "Hop off, let me get going."

"I'm gone," Lefferts said, swinging down easily onto the street and toward the gathered drinkers out in front of Stems' saloon.

Stiles drove the buggy over to the hitch rail in front of the doctor's office, climbed down and walked up onto the porch, preparing himself to look shocked and saddened. *Here goes. . . .*

Finding the door ajar, he opened it and walked inside, taking off his hat on his way down the hall. He stopped outside the door to the convalescence room and waited for a second before knocking softly on the closed door.

"Dr. Meadows?" he said quietly, already showing respect for the dead. "It's me, Deputy Stiles. You wanted to see me first thing?"

"Yes, Deputy," the young doctor said from inside. "Please, do come in."

Stiles opened the door and stepped inside. He stopped abruptly and felt his jaw drop a little when he saw Sheriff Goss staring at him from the bed, leaning back against a thick feather pillow. On the other side of the bed stood Will Summers, appearing to study him closely, he thought. At the foot of the bed stood Dr. Meadows, a tray of old bandages in his hands.

"I sent Leffert to find you as soon as you returned," the doctor said. "But it's Sheriff Goss here who needs to see you."

"Oh . . . ?" Stiles said, his own voice sounding strange and unprepared to him. When he'd seen Summers, his first thought was that his scheming had caught up to him. He'd come within a breath of pulling his Colt up from his holster and firing. But now that he saw the calm look on Summers' face, he was glad he'd kept himself in check. Maybe his game wasn't over after all.

"That's right . . . Deputy," Goss said in a weak, labored voice. "I've got some . . . bad news for you." He started to continue, but he broke into a deep painful-sounding cough.

"Easy, Sheriff," Dr. Meadows warned him, stepping around to the bed and picking up a glass of water. "Perhaps you'd better let Summers do the talking. You keep still. I've just changed those bandages. Let's not get them all bloodied up right away."

While the doctor settled the sheriff and gave him a drink from the water glass, Stiles looked at Summers across the sheriff's bed.

"I caught Avrial Rochenbach making a break from your jail," Summers said. Seeing Stiles' eyes flash with dark surprise, he added, "Don't worry, he's back behind bars now."

What was that look? Summers asked himself, thinking how stunned Stiles had been when he'd entered the room and seen Sheriff Goss looking at him from the bed.

"Obliged, Summers," said Stiles quietly, "but how did he manage to—?"

"The livery hostler, Danny Kindrick?" Summers said.

Stiles winced, looking a little embarrassed, and said, "I know that was a mistake, leaving Danny to guard Rochenbach. I take the full blame for that." He looked at the sheriff and said, "I'm sorry, Sheriff, I let you down."

"Forget . . . it," the sheriff whispered, waving the matter away. "We were lucky . . . Summers happened along." Talking was wearing the wounded sheriff down quickly. The doctor saw it and placed a hand on his shoulder.

"Yes, we were at that." Stiles nodded and turned back to Summers. "I have to say, I'm surprised to see you back in Gunn Point. I hope Big Jack Warren isn't going to find out you're here."

"I don't plan on being here that long, Deputy," Summers said. He looked at the sheriff for permission to continue.

Through his coughing, Sheriff Goss gestured with a weak hand.

"Tell him," the sheriff gasped.

Summers nodded and reached inside his coat. He took out the money and the broken paper band he'd taken off Lewis Fallon. Stiles watched him pitch it all on the foot of the sheriff's bed.

"Three of the men who robbed the bank tried to ambush me last night," he said. "I found this in one of their shirt pockets."

Stiles looked at the money, then back up at Summers.

"I take it the man is dead," he said, stalling for a few seconds of time while his brain worked on how to stay ahead of whatever this was leading to.

"Yep," said Summers, "he's dead. His body is lying over his horse in the alley beside the jail. The other two got away."

"I see," said Stiles. "If this is part of the stolen bank money, Bob Harper must not have counted as closely as he should have. He said it was all there." He reached over, picked up the paper band and read the amount written on it.

"One thousand dollars, eh?" he said. He looked at the money on the bed. "So, this is only part of what was in the band."

"If this was a full one-thousand-dollar stack," Summers said, "which I have to suppose it was. Your bank manager would know for certain."

The sheriff settled and lay watching the two.

Luckily he's dead, Stiles thought to himself.

"Our bank manager is dead, Summers," Stiles said. "I just brought what's left of him and his rig in from the hills. It looks likes wolves got him and his horse."

"Bob Harper . . . is *dead*?" the sheriff said in a weak, gravelly voice.

"I'm afraid so, Sheriff," said Stiles. He looked back at Summers and said, "So, I suppose we'll never know if all the money was there or not."

"Too bad," said Summers. "I got the money back here as fast as I could. I didn't want it on me."

"Good thinking," the deputy said. "You did the right thing." He pitched the broken paper band back onto the bed and picked up a bill and turned it in his hand. "I suppose the money will have to be counted again. That means the bank could be closed a little longer. I hate having to tell the merchants and townsfolk."

Summers studied his eyes closely as Stiles inspected the bill in his hand.

"There's more bad news," Summers said.

"And what's that?" Stiles said.

"The bill in your hand," said Summers, "it's fake." He studied Stiles' face for his reaction.

"A counterfeit?" Stiles said. "It looks real enough to me."

"Feel it without looking at it," Summers said.

Stiles looked away as he felt it between his thumb and fingertips.

"It doesn't feel right at all," he said, giving Summers a curious look.

"Now wet you thumb and rub a corner of it," Summers said.

Stiles touched his thumb to his tongue. He rubbed his thumb on the lower corner of the bill. He looked at both the bill and his greenish-blackened thumb.

"I feel like a fool," he said, shaking his head. He looked at Sheriff Goss. "I've failed you, Sheriff." He paused, then said, "I'll—I'll turn in my badge."

The wounded sheriff waved the idea away with his weakened hand. "You're . . . my deputy. . . ."

Summers stood watching closely, finding nothing out of the ordinary in Stiles' action or demeanor.

"Thank you, Sheriff," Stiles said humbly. He turned back to Summers and asked, "Are all the bills fake?"

"Every last one," said Summers. "It makes me wonder if all the stolen money was counterfeit."

"Yes, I'm wondering that myself," said Stiles. "The money should be at Warren's spread. I escorted Harper out there with it."

"You saw it?" Summers asked.

"I saw the bags it was in," Stiles said. "I didn't see the cash itself, come to think of it. I never saw the bags leave his rig."

"Then we can't check anything," said Summers.

"Too bad. We have to take Warren's word for everything now that the money is in his hands."

Yeah . . . , Stiles thought with relief. But he looked curiously at Summers.

"Are you thinking Warren had something to do with his own bank getting robbed?" he asked.

"No, but funny you should mention it," Summers said.

"I mention it because that's the first thing that comes to mind," said Stiles.

"Exactly," said Summers, "and that's why I brought it up. A man wants to rob his own bank, but he doesn't trust the men he has rob it. So he fills it with fake money."

"That's clever, if it's true," said Stiles. "Warren only owns half the bank, so he takes the money and replaces all of it with counterfeit. His partner and the town take the loss."

"Pretty sweet deal," Summers said, finishing the words for him.

Before Stiles could say anything else, Dr. Meadows cut in and asked him, "Where are Harper's remains? I'll need to go take a look—officially identify the remains."

"Right out front, Doc," said Stiles, "what little is left of him."

"Excuse me for a moment, Sheriff," Dr. Meadows said, turning toward the door. Stiles and Summers turned and followed him through the hallway and out the front door. On their way past the doctor's private office, they saw Flora Ingrim, a broom and dustpan in hand. She busily picked up pieces of the tall broken blue bottle and dropped them into a trash can.

"Flora's cat," the doctor said under his breath, walking

on. "It has to investigate every shelf in the place. When my medicine bottles are empty, I half-fill them with water until I get them refilled with laudanum—it makes them a little harder to turn over by wandering felines." He looked around at the two with a short smile. "I must've forgotten to fill this one. Too bad . . . those medicine bottles are *not* inexpensive."

"I bet," said Summers, following him out the front door.

Damn it! Damn it! Damn it to bloody hell! Stiles raged to himself, his lips clenched to keep from bellowing the words out loud.

Summers saw the look on Stiles' face.

What was that all about? he thought. *Something about the bottle, the cat . . . ?* Was he getting too suspicious of the deputy? Yes, he was, he told himself. But for good reason, he thought. Something wasn't right back there. He just couldn't put this finger on it.

Chapter 13

———

At the buggy, Stiles saw three men walking toward them from the direction of the saloon. Seeing foamy mugs of beer in their hands, he turned, facing them with a stern expression, his fists planted on his hips.

"I hope those beers are worth a night in a jail cell," he called out. "Because that's where you're going to be if you don't turn around and carry them back to the saloon."

Without missing a step, the three drinkers turned instantly on their heels and walked back toward the saloon. Other townsfolk stared curiously at the buggy, but they kept their distance.

Stiles reached down onto the rear floor and picked up Harper's derby hat enough for the doctor and Summers to see, without exposing it to the onlookers. He turned the hat upside down in his hand and showed the doctor Harper's name on the inside of the sweatband.

"Yes, I see," the doctor said quietly.

Summers watched in silence.

Stiles laid the battered hat on the rear seat. He took

a breath; then he took the shredded, bloodstained suit coat and flipped it back, revealing the banker's sparse remains.

"My goodness," the young doctor said. He shook his head and leaned in a little closer. "I don't see how I can *definitely* identify this as Bob Harper."

"It's his hat, his buggy," said Stiles. "It's Bob Harper all right, unless Harper comes walking down the street."

"Yes," the doctor agreed, "it's Harper. I'll send Flora to get someone to dig us a grave for him."

While the two had stood talking, Summers had drifted around the rig and picked up the reins. He noted one rein was shorter than the other. Examining the end, he saw where the leather recently been sliced through.

Stiles laid the suit coat back down over Harper's remains. He looked over and saw him lay the buggy reins down and walk back around the rig.

"What is it, Summers?" he asked.

"Nothing," Summers replied. He reached inside the buggy, raised the shredded suit coat and looked at the grizzly remains again, taking his time.

"Summers, *what is it*?" Stiles repeated. "What are you looking for?"

Summers gave him a questioning look for a second. Then his expression changed, relaxed.

"Wolves don't leave much, do they?" he commented, dropping the suit coat back on Harper's half-skinned head, neck and gnawed rib cage.

"No, I'm afraid they do not," the doctor said.

"Summers," Stiles said coolly, "I'm the law here. If you've seen something about Harper's remains that I need to know about, tell me."

"Believe me, Deputy," Summers said, swiping his fingers on his trousers, "if I saw something I thought you should know, *I would.*"

"Gentlemen, may I ask what's going on here?" the doctor said, seeing Stiles' demeanor change a little.

"Nothing," Summers said, his eyes on Stiles. "I came here to bring the money back. Even if it's fake, I didn't want anybody to get any wrong idea if they found some of it missing."

"Well, I think you're certainly clear in that regard," the doctor said, looking at Stiles for agreement.

Feeling their eyes on him, knowing he had flared a little for apparently no reason, Stiles relaxed.

"I've had a lot on my mind, Summers," he said. "I know you understand."

"I understand," Summers said.

"Now that we're clear on the money," Stiles asked, "what's your plans?"

"I'm leaving," Summers said. "I haven't forgot that Jack Warren will be coming to town."

"I didn't want to press the matter—make you feel unwelcome," said Stiles. He offered a slight smile. "But the less trouble, the better."

"Are we square, Deputy?" Summers asked.

"Yes, we are," Stiles said. "And I meant it when I said *obliged* for bringing my prisoner back, and for returning the bank money."

"You're welcome, Deputy," Summers said. "I'll just go say adios to Sheriff Goss, and I'll get myself out of here before night sets in." He turned and walked back inside, down the hall to the convalescence room. The doctor and Stiles lingered behind by the buggy for a moment longer, the doctor picking up the battered derby and the shredded suit coat.

Inside the room, Summers walked over to the bed and looked down at the sheriff's face.

"Are you asleep, Sheriff Goss?" he asked quietly.

The sheriff blinked and opened his eyes.

"No," he said weakly, "I'm just . . . lying here thinking, Will." He swallowed and said, "I've put a lot on Parley Stiles."

"He seems to handle it well," Summers replied.

"He's a good man . . . no question," Goss said. "But he needs help."

"You're going to be up and around before you know it, Sheriff," Summers said, seeing where the conversation was headed and hoping to cut it off first.

"I've got horses to deliver, Sheriff," Summers said. "I need to get in and out of Whiskey Flats before snow closes the high passes."

"I need your help, Will," Goss said. "So does Deputy Stiles." Goss stared at the ceiling in contemplation. Finally he said, "What is Whiskey Flats . . . three days up, three back?"

"About that," Summers said. "I figure a full week from here, round-trip."

"I'm going to be laid up . . . most of the winter," Goss said. "Think it over. When you get back . . . let me know."

"All right, I will, Sheriff," Summers said. He let out a breath. "What about Big Jack Warren?"

"You'll be . . . wearing a badge," Goss said.

"If I'm here there'll be trouble with him, badge or no badge," Summers said.

"Think it over . . . promise me you'll think it over,"

the sheriff said, ignoring the question of Jack Warren. His eyelids fell slowly shut as he spoke.

"I will, Sheriff," Summers replied. He backed a step away from the bed, turned and walked out of the room.

At the front door he met the doctor and Deputy Stiles on their way in.

"He's asleep, Doctor," Summers said.

"Good, that is what he needs most now, rest, with no aggravation."

"How long is he going to be off his feet, Dr. Meadows?" Summers asked.

"That's hard to say," the doctor replied. "But he's not a young man. Healing comes slower at his age."

"How long?" Summers repeated.

"Off his feet? I'd say most of the winter," the doctor answered. "Longer still until he's completely over it."

"Why are you asking, Summers?" Stiles cut in.

"He said he's worried about putting too much work on you, Deputy," Summers said straight out. "He asked me if I'd put on a deputy badge and work with you awhile."

"I see," Stiles said. Summers watched his expression. "Well, I'd be pleased and honored to work with you, Will Summers," he said. But something told Summers that wasn't really how he felt.

"I told him no," Summers said. "I've got horses to deliver in Whiskey Flats."

"Oh," said Stiles. "I'm disappointed."

"I'll collect my horses and be on my way," said Summers. "I left them in the alley beside the jail. I'll leave Fallon across his saddle. He's out of public sight," Summers added.

"Tell Danny Kindrick I'll be right along," said Stiles.

Summers nodded and left the doctor's big clapboard house.

From the dusty front window of the sheriff's office, Cherry Atmore watched Summers walk along the side of the street at the edge of the boardwalk. She stepped over and opened the front door just as he reached for the handle.

"How's the sheriff?" she asked, a stub of a cigarette between her fingers.

"He seems to be getting better," Summers said. "How's Rochenbach? Where's Danny Kindrick?"

"I got hungry," Cherry said. "I sent Danny to get us something to eat. The detective is okay." She shrugged and said, "His head hurts. I gave him a wet cloth. He's lying down with it over his face. Says he can't seem to make a move without you showing up and stopping him." She smiled. "I think it's got him spooked."

"Being spooked won't hurt him," Summers said. He walked past her, saying, "I'll just drop by and tell him hello before I leave."

Cherry only smiled and puffed her cigarette.

At Rochenbach's cell, Summers looked in and saw the detective turned outlaw lying sprawled on the cot, on his back, facing the ceiling, the wet cloth covering his forehead and most of his face.

"Avrial Rochenbach, are you all right?" Summers asked through the iron bars.

Rochenbach lifted the cloth from his brow and looked over. Recognizing Summers, he let out a resigned breath.

"Why do you even ask?" he said. "Are you going to hit me again?"

"You were breaking jail, Rochenbach," Summers said. "You had it coming."

"Please, call me *Rock*," the defeated prisoner said in a cynical tone. "We've gotten to know each other well enough."

"Why did you try it?" Summers said, not calling him by name. "Once you hit the street, you could have gotten yourself killed."

"Oh? Is death by bullet worse than hanging?" Rochenbach asked dryly.

"You're not going to hang," said Summers. "The doctor tells me Sheriff Goss is getting a little better every day."

"Really . . . ?" Rochenbach eased up on the side of his cot, the cloth hanging from his fingers. "I was told he'd be dead any minute. That I'd better be prepared to swing."

"That's not true," Summers said. "You need to get your news from a better source."

Rochenbach gestured a hand at his surroundings.

"As you can see," he said, "my pickings are a little slim at the moment." He stood up laboriously and walked over to the bars. "Should have known the escape looked too good to be true."

Summers saw the purple-red impression of his rifle butt lying oblong across his brow.

"Are you saying it was a setup?" Summers asked.

"Hell, I don't know." Rochenbach rubbed his temples against the pain in his head. "I thought it was at first, but as we know, I've been wrong before." He paused, then added, "I mean, you were a wild card in the deck, weren't you? You just happened to be stopping by, is what Cherry Atmore said."

"You and Cherry have been talking?" Summers asked.

"Some," Rochenbach said. "She gave me a few puffs on her cigarette—you know, for the pain." He gestured at his swollen forehead.

"Did it help?" Summers asked.

"It sure didn't hurt," Rochenbach replied, again rubbing his temples. "For a minute I thought I heard mice talking." He glanced toward a dark corner of the cell, then back to Summers.

Summers just stared at him for a moment.

"Let me ask you something, Rock," he finally said. "Back when you were a detective, how did you go about gathering proof that somebody was guilty, when all you had was a real strong suspicion?"

"You mean a gut instinct?" Rochenbach asked.

"Yes, something like that," Summers said.

"That's easy," Rochenbach said. "I'd just start asking questions. A man who's hiding something never wants to be asked questions."

"What kinds of questions?" Summers asked.

"Any kinds of questions," said Rochenbach. "When you don't even know what to ask him to find out what he's hiding, just ask any question that comes to mind. He'll think it's important how he answers it whether it is or not."

"Yeah . . . ?" Summers thought about it.

"You can ask a guilty man about the weather outside. He'll think you're putting him on the spot. The more pointless questions you ask, the more important he'll think the questions are. It makes him start running in circles—it drives him nuts." He laid the wet cloth back up on his uptilted forehead and closed his eyes. "Bear in mind, you're getting this information from a man standing in a jail cell."

"I understand," said Summers. "But sometimes good advice comes from the least likely places."

"That's true enough," said Rochenbach. "I don't know who it is you're suspecting, or what. But if I was out of here, where I could—"

"Forget it," said Summers. "You robbed a bank. You can't walk away from what you've done."

"In a more perfected civilized society, I think I could," Rochenbach said. He turned around, walked back to the cot and plopped down on it. "But like all of us, I'm stuck with what we've got." He lay back and draped the wet cloth back over his face. "If I can ever be of more assistance, don't hesitate to ask—I mean right up until they haul me to prison or hang me, that is."

Summers decided the former detective was still under the influence of Cherry Atmore's powerful cigarettes.

"Obliged," he said through the bars. "I'll keep that in mind."

When Summers walked back out to the front office, Cherry Atmore stood leaning against the closed door. But she straightened up and took a step to one side.

"Are you leaving now?" she asked.

"Yes, I've still got to deliver my string to Whiskey Flats," Summers said. "What are you going to do?"

"About what?" Cherry said.

"You were headed to Whiskey Flats, remember?" Summers said, trying to be patient. "Are you staying here now?"

"No, I'm still going," Cherry said. "Am I still welcome to ride with you?"

"Yes, you are," Summers said, not wanting to think

of her out on the trail alone. "I'll be ready to go as soon as Danny gets back."

"Me too," said Cherry. "Is the detective feeling any better?"

"You mean the *former* detective," said Summers.

Cherry gave him a crafty smile. "I say once a detective, always a detective." She tapped her finger to the side of her head.

"That's good, Cherry. I'll have to remember that," Summers said.

A moment later, Danny Kindrick walked inside carrying a woven basket of hot food.

Summers ate a fried chicken leg, a hot buttered biscuit and washed the food down with a cup of strong coffee from atop the woodstove. Cherry and the young livery hostler dug into the food as if it were their last meal.

From across the street, behind a stack of shipping crates, Deputy Stiles waited and watched. Finally Summers and the woman both walked out of the office and around the corner of the alley to where their horses stood. When they had mounted and ridden away along the main street, Stiles came out of hiding and walked over to the edge of the alley. He looked at the body and shook his head.

Walking inside the office, he motioned for Danny to stay seated and walked past him, down the hall to Rochenbach's cell.

"Hey, Rochenbach," he said gruffly, Rochenbach lying prone with the cloth over his face. "Did Will Summers talk to you?"

"Yes," said Rochenbach, "he came and said howdy. Said he was leaving town."

"Did he ask you anything, I mean about the robbery or anything?" said Stiles.

"No, nothing," Rochenbach said, tight-lipped. He took the cloth from his face and turned his head sidelong. "How's the sheriff? Is he *dead yet*?" he asked in a flat, sarcastic tone.

Damn it! Damn it to hell! Stiles said to himself. The two had talked. Something was said. He could tell by Rochenbach's attitude. *But what . . . ?*

All right, it didn't matter, he told himself. Summers didn't know anything. Neither did this has-been detective. Summers might have told Rochenbach that the sheriff was going to live. That didn't hurt anything. Rochenbach didn't know the jailbreak had been a setup, and if he had guessed it, so what? The man was his prisoner. Who was going to listen to him?

You're the law, he reminded himself. *You're still holding all the cards. . . .*

Chapter 14

———

It was late afternoon when Summers and Cherry Atmore reached the spot where Stiles said he had found the buggy and the remains of the deceased bank manager. The tracks of the buggy still stood out clearly in the dusting of snow all the way from the main trail to where the horse had flipped the rig over against a sunken boulder and failed to free it before the wolves closed in and made their kill. Bloody paw prints surrounded the scattered bones of the horse.

Cherry sat watching glassy-eyed from her saddle as Summers wrapped the lead rope to his three-horse string around his saddle horn, swung down and walked over and looked around in the dimming evening sunlight.

"I hate wolves," she said flatly. "All they do is kill and eat other animals."

Summers looked at the scraps of horse carcass.

"It's what they have to do to live, Cherry," Summers said quietly.

"I know, but I hate them anyway," she said.

Summers walked around looking down at the ground until he came up on a ripped and chewed-up shoe, a scrap of pin-striped trouser leg.

"Can we go build a fire?" Cherry asked from her saddle a few feet behind him.

"In a minute," Summers said. It was a long shot that he might find what he was looking for out here. But whatever his nagging hunch was, he had to start piecing it together somewhere. He moved the chewed-up shoe aside with the toe of his boot. Part of the buggy's leather rear upholstery lay fluttering on a chilly breeze.

"I could eat again, funny as it sounds," Cherry said.

Summers ignored her and flipped the piece of upholstery over with his boot. *There it is!*

He stooped and picked up a chewed length of bloodstained leather buggy rein lying on the ground. This was what he'd come looking for, but what were the odds of finding it?

Pretty good odds after all . . . , he thought, now that he *did* manage to find it.

He stooped and picked the leather rein up and held it out straight between his hands. It was about the same length that he'd noticed missing from Harper's buggy reins. All right, but now what? he wondered. But he only wondered for a second as he watched himself wrap the ends around each gloved hand and test it between them.

Stiles choked the banker to death . . . ?

As soon as the thought came to his mind, he stopped himself. A strip of leather didn't prove anything. Besides, even if somebody did choke the banker, that didn't mean it was Stiles. *Right . . .* , he thought, but it was something to keep in the back of his mind and see which way the thought led him.

"I could drink something too, Summers," Cherry called out to him. "Something hot, or even cold."

"I'm coming," Summers said absently. But before he walked away from the torn piece of upholstery, he spotted the tin case lying in the snowy dirt, and a few feet from it the open receipt pad fluttering in the breeze. Stooping again, he picked the items up and turned them both in his gloved hands. He flipped through singed receipts until he came to the last one and saw Jack Warren's signature on the bottom. He studied the name for a moment, running things through his mind.

This might be something worth keeping to himself, he decided. Closing the receipt pad, he shoved it inside his coat, into his breast pocket. The tin case he looked over good, then did the same thing with it. The length of leather he kept in his hand.

"What did you pick up?" Cherry asked as he walked toward back toward the horses.

"A leather strap," said Summers. He held it up across his palm. "Wolves have chewed it up. It looks about the same width as the buggy reins."

"What did you put in your coat?" Cherry asked, dismissing the length of leather rein.

"Nothing," Summers said.

"I saw you," Cherry said, her eyes glassy and shining in the dimming evening light.

"Sorry, Cherry, you're mistaken," Summers said, stepping up into his saddle and taking up the lead rope. "Maybe you're smoking too much."

"*Hmmph*, maybe," Cherry said. "But I saw something, I know I did."

"You need to leave the *secas de mayan* alone for a while, Cherry," Summers said. "It's making you stand a little off-center."

"I only smoke it to relax," she said. She looked down at her feet in the stirrups as if to see if she was off-center. Then she looked back up. "Anyway, I've cut back. . . . I'm almost out of it."

"I can't say I'm sorry to see it go," said Summers, turning his horse, leading his string beside him.

"Where are we making camp?" Cherry asked, turning her paint horse alongside him.

"Far enough from here to avoid any dinner guests returning for scraps." He gestured toward the horse carcass. "Wolves will come back several times to a kill, sometimes just to bring their young so they can roll in it."

"See? That's why I hate wolves," Cherry said.

They rode less than a mile from the horse's carcass. Higher up into the hills, they turned their animals onto a path that wound back into the shelter of pine, cedar and broken boulders and widened at the bottom of a narrow waterfall.

"This will do," Summers said. He swung down from his saddle and led his dapple gray and his three-horse string to the edge of the runoff water and let them drink. Beside him, Cherry stepped down from her paint horse and led it alongside him. As the horses drank, he walked around close by and began gathering twigs and dried downfall branches suitable for building a fire.

"Did you ever think of getting yourself a tent, Will

Summers?" Cherry asked, her eyes less shiny, her voice less dull, but sounding a little tense. She looked all around the clearing between two walls of rock.

"I think of it from time to time," Summers said. "But for the most part a tent is more trouble than it's worth."

"Oh? In what way?" Cherry asked, walking along with him, doing her share, gathering firewood.

"You have to put a tent up and take it down every morning when you're traveling," he said.

"But with a tent you wouldn't be sleeping outside," Cherry offered.

Summers looked around at her, noting how her voice sounded more tense.

"That's another drawback as far as I'm concerned," he said.

"Then you'd rather sleep outdoors than indoors?" she asked nervously.

Summers stopped and gave her a questioning look, his arms staring to fill with firewood.

"Are you all right, Cherry?" he asked.

"Yes—*yes*, I'm fine," she said, clearly sounding distressed. "Can you just answer the question?"

"Sure," Summers said, looking her up and down. "Given a choice, I sleep outdoors." As he spoke he walked over to a good spot for a campfire and dropped the wood at his feet. He turned to her as she walked over and dropped her wood in the same spot. "Now, what's got you so rattled?"

"Oh, I don't know," she said cynically. "How about last night, three men trying to kill us, remember?" She nodded back toward where the wolves had eaten Harper and his horse. "And of course that little dinner feast that went on back there—"

"If you're afraid, you should have stayed in Gunn Point," he said, cutting her off. "There's always a risk to being in the wild. I didn't ask to get put upon last night by those three."

"It happened because Little Jackie shot at you and killed one of your horses," said Cherry. "Then you killed him, remember?" Her voice rose; she stood trembling. She appeared ready to collapse.

Seeing her condition, Summers stepped over and took her in his arms before she fell.

"Hey, take it easy, Cherry," he said. She sobbed against his chest, almost as uncontrollably as when she'd tried to ambush him in the livery barn. He stroked her hair and comforted her as if she were some brokenhearted child. "It's all right. Nothing's going to hurt you. You're safe. . . ." He looked all around as he spoke.

"I'm sorry," Cherry said, toning the crying down. "I—I just get this way sometimes," she said shakily. "I think it is from smoking the *secas*. It's pretty powerful stuff." She wiped a hand across her forehead. "I—I really am trying to cut back."

"I understand," Summers said. He wasn't about to preach to her. He'd seen her resentment when he'd broached the matter earlier. "Let's get you seated. You can relax while I build us a fire and get some coffee boiling."

She allowed him to seat her on a rock beside the pile of firewood.

"I'm a mess . . . I know I am," she said.

"You're tired," Summers said. "You only dozed a little in your saddle on our way back last night."

"You're right," she said. "I am more tired than I realized. Last night *was* upsetting for a person unaccustomed to being shot at." She looked at him and gave him a reddened, tear-streaked smile. Steam wisped in her breath.

"I don't want you thinking I spend all my time going around getting myself shot at," Summers said. He paused as he broke a length of dried wood over his knee to lay in the fire bed. "Although it does occur to me that I seem to fall upon more than my share of trouble sometimes."

Cherry gave him another weak smile.

"In the barn," she said quietly, "when I told you I didn't know who you are? That wasn't true. I'd heard of you, Will Summers," she said.

"I figured you had," Summers said, banking some small twigs and dried leaves into the middle of the firewood pile.

"Oh, *really*?" Cherry said with a bemused look.

"I don't mean it boastfully," Summers said. "But in this part of the frontier, I've become used to people knowing what happened in Rileyville. How I rode with Abner Webb's posse and took down the Peltry Gang." He shrugged. "It just happened and people heard about it, that's all. Because of it, a lot of folks know me by name." He took out some long wooden matches from inside his coat.

Cherry watched him strike a match, stick it flaring inside the pile of wood and into the dried twigs and leaves.

"Folks I heard talk about you always say it was a brave thing you did—you and those others."

"*Brave* never feels like *brave* at the time," Summers said reflectively, fanning the fire a little to help it along.

"And afterward?" Cherry asked.

"Afterward feels more like foolish than brave," Summers said. "But by then you can't go back and change *foolish*, so *brave* comes into play."

Cherry smiled, this time more relaxed. She pulled her knees up, wrapped her arms around them and rested her chin on them.

"I do feel safe with you, Will Summers," she said. "Last night, even with all the shooting going on, I still felt safe for some reason—*scared* but safe. Does that make any sense?"

"Not at all," Summers said. They both laughed a little; then he said, "Yes, I think I know what you mean. Sometimes even though you're scared, you feel like you came in right and you'll leave the same way." He looked at her. "Is that what you mean?"

"Maybe," Cherry said, considering it. "I'm not used to being right, so it takes some getting used to."

Summers dusted his hands together and stood up.

"I'll get the coffee started," he said. "That'll make us both feel more *right* than we've felt all day."

"Do you think we've really seen the last of the other two?" Cherry said as Summers walked to the dapple gray, opened his saddlebags and reached inside.

"I hope so," Summer replied. "There's no reason why they should keep dogging us." He walked back with the small blackened coffeepot and a small canvas pouch with a handful of coffee beans in it. "But then, there was no reason for them to be dogging us anyway. Unless, the one is out to avenge his missing ear."

Cherry didn't reply. She watched Summers stoop down over a flat rock, take out his Colt and use the butt of it to break up the beans in the pouch.

"I lied," she said quietly. "I *did* know that Little Jackie was going to rob his father's bank."

Summers continued breaking up the coffee beans.

"Little Jackie told you?" he said, glancing up from his task.

"I—don't remember," Cherry said, seeming to have difficulty with her memory.

"He must've told you," said Summers. "How else would you have known?"

"I just knew," Cherry said. "I don't know how, all right?"

Summers heard her getting shaky on the subject and let it go. He shrugged.

"It doesn't matter," he said, "just making conversation."

When he'd put the pot on to boil, Summers stood up and walked to the horses. Cherry still sat with her arms wrapped around her knees, gazing into the fire, feeling the warm bite of it on her cheeks, the backs of her hands. She felt the urge to reach for her fixings, but she breathed deep and let the feeling pass. She felt good, calm. . . .

While Summers tended to the horses, he heard her call out to him.

"We could sleep together tonight," she said.

Summers smiled to himself and replied, "You mean keep each other warm?"

After a pause he heard Cherry say, "That too. . . ."

Moments later when he'd finished with the horses,

he turned and walked back to the fire carrying both of their saddles. He looked down and saw her sleeping soundly, her face resting sidelong on her knees.

Summers shook his head. He laid out the saddles and blankets and rolled her over into his arms. He carried her to her blanket and tucked her in, her saddle beneath her head.

"I don't . . . want to sleep yet," she whispered in a childlike tone.

"*Shhhh*, go ahead," Summers whispered, knowing she had been off smoking the Indian tobacco. "You're safe here. You'll wake up feeling better than you have in a long time."

She gave a thin, sleepy smile.

"You promise . . . ?" she whispered.

"You have my word," said Summers, brushing a strand of hair from her face.

"Your word . . . ," she said softly, drifting off to sleep, as if his word was good enough for her.

Chapter 15

Summers awakened early. He stood a pot of coffee to boil on a fiery bed of embers and sat watching the young woman sleep until daylight rose above the eastern horizon. A small pan sat to the side of the fire bed keeping jerked elk warm. An open air-tight of beans stood warm and waiting. When the aroma of food and coffee finally opened her eyes, he set a tip cup within her reach and sat back down with his Winchester across his lap. She blinked peacefully and lay staring at him for a moment from beneath her blanket.

"How did I sleep so long?" she said softly. "I don't remember eating, lying down or nothing else." She eased up and sat with the blanket around her. She looked over toward the horses. "Did I even tend to my poor horse?"

"Everything's fine, Cherry," Summers said. "Speaking of horses, I bet you're hungry enough to eat one."

"The wolves beat me to it," she said. She giggled, then chastised herself. "That was a terrible thing to say, wasn't it?"

"I've heard worse," Summers said. She'd awakened with her mind rested and clearer—a sense of humor. That was good, he told himself. "I fixed you some jerk and beans," he said.

"You are a dear. But first things first," she said. She picked up the tin cup and blew on the steaming coffee, using a corner of her blanket to hold the hot thin metal. Summers noted the bag of fixings lying beside her when she'd scooted forward and opened the blanket slightly in order to reach for her coffee. But she didn't reach for the bag *first thing*, he noted. That was good too.

"You're feeling good this morning, I can tell," Summers said.

"I'm feeling better than I have for a while," Cherry said. She cocked her head a little and looked at him curiously. "Last night. We didn't . . . you know, did we?"

Summers smiled slightly. He waited for a second before answering, sipping coffee and looking off along a ridge he'd been watching since daylight. He hadn't heard anything, or seen anything out of the ordinary. But the ridgeline was the only clear view of their camp from the surrounding hills. So it was worth his attention now and then, he'd decided.

"Well, did we?" Cherry repeated.

"No" He smiled, adjusting his rifle on his lap. "We didn't."

"But an invitation was given, wasn't it?" she said, trying to remember the preceding evening.

"Yes, but you needed your rest," said Summers.

"I'm sorry, Will Summers," she said. She scooted around in her blanket and sat beside him. They sipped their steaming coffee. "I'll make it up to you, I promise."

"Obliged, Cherry. But you don't need to promise me

anything," Summers said. "To tell you the truth, I was tired myself, after riding all night back to town."

"So, you're not *disappointed*?" Cherry said.

Another one of those perilous questions . . . , Summers told himself.

"Yes, I was disappointed," he said wisely. "But that's okay. Another place, another time."

She let her blanket down enough to hook her arm in his and draw closer.

"Tell me, Will Summers," she said, "do you not *like* me?"

"Don't be silly," Summers said. "Of course I like you." He reached a hand around and pushed a strand of hair from her face. "I like you very much."

"Very much . . . ?" She gave him a look.

"You do like women," she queried. "I mean, you're not . . ." She let her words trail

"I love women, Cherry," Summers said. "The fact is, any trouble I ever had, there's been women there— women or horses," he amended. "Most times, both."

"So . . . ," she pondered, "women and horses have always caused you trouble?"

"No, not at all," Summers, said. "It's just that any trouble I ever had, there's been women and horses in it."

Cherry said, "I suppose I could say the same thing about horses and men. I suppose anybody could, man or woman."

"I shouldn't have said that," Summers said.

"I shouldn't have asked what I asked," said Cherry. "I'll let you in on a secret. When a dove asks a man if he likes women, it's to make him start doing everything he can to prove to her that he does."

"That's no secret, Cherry," Summers said. "Everybody knows that."

"They do?" she asked.

"I think so," said Summers, "or else I know it and I figure if I know it everybody else knows it too."

"Oh . . . ," she said.

"Anyway, I like women," he said. "I *love* women!" He gave her a flat stare and added, "I particularly love women who happen to love me."

She considered his words and sipped her coffee.

"You don't have something against doves, do you?" she asked. "I mean, because we do it for money?"

"No," Summers said. "That has never bothered me. People *do* what they *do*, for whatever reasons." He looked off along the ridgeline again as he spoke. "I wouldn't make a very good judge."

"Okay, then!" Cherry laughed lightly. "Now we're getting somewhere."

He liked hearing her happy and bright for a change. She set the tin cup down and wiggled and squirmed out of her clothes beneath the blanket. Summers smiled and shook his head, studying the ridgeline.

"This beats everything," he murmured.

"Not yet, it doesn't," Cherry said. "You haven't seen anything yet." She laughed playfully, teasingly. "Will Summers, do you want to get inside this blanket with me, or not?"

Summers smiled, still scanning the ridgeline.

"Of course I want to get inside the blanket with you, Cherry," he said.

"Don't be bashful with me, Will Summers," she kidded. "Look at me when I'm talking to you." She stood in a crouch and moved around in front of him. She cupped his chin, making him face her. "You are going to have me for breakfast."

"Wait, Cherry," Summers said. "We need to get you fed and moving."

"*Huh-uh*, after a while," she said. "I've woke up with my mind sharp and my brain not swirling. Now come on. You can't turn a gal down when she's standing naked, waiting. I feel so good this morning, I don't want to smoke, I don't want to eat." She stood up quickly and spread her arms and opened the blanket wide. "All I want to do is get you in this blanket and—"

Her words stopped short as Summers saw the gaping red hole appear in the center of her chest, a split second ahead of the roar of a rifle shot. A red mist of warm blood flew out behind the bullet and streaked across the side of Summers' face. Cherry plunged forward across him, tipping him backward beneath her, dead as she hit the ground.

Summers knew she was dead; he didn't have to check, although he would, he told himself—but not now! Another bullet struck the ground beside his head, followed by the sound of the shot. Right now he had to get out from under the woman and target whoever was shooting at him.

Another shot hit the ground as he struggled free and crawled quickly away.

From atop their horses, three of Jack Warren's men sat watching as the fourth man did all the shooting.

"*Whoo-iee!* Look at him go," said a middle-aged cattle rustler and gunman named John Root.

"You hit the whore, Bert!" another rustler said, this one a younger gunman named Luther Passe.

"Couldn't help it, she jumped up at the wrong time," said the rifleman, Bert Phelps. "But it won't matter to Big Jack. He'd like to see her dead too."

"This is bad," a half-breed named Leonard Two Horse Tuell said. He shook his head and pulled his horse back a step, out of sight. "It's bad luck shooting a whore."

"He crawls faster than any man I've ever seen," said John Root. He heard Luther's rifle fire again and watched Summers duck away from the bullet when it hit the dirt. Root grinned and said, "Finish him off, stop fooling around."

"I've got him," Bert said confidently, staring down his rifle sights at the crawling figure two hundred yards away. He sighted the center of his target's back, then lifted his barrel a little, allowing for his target moving away from him.

But on the ground, Summers suddenly stopped crawling. He'd rolled onto his side, levering a round into his rifle chamber. He dropped, facing the direction of the shooting, and took aim as Bert Phelps started to squeeze the trigger again.

Summers' shot punched straight through the rifleman's face, lifted him from his saddle and flung him away like a dirty shirt.

"*Holy hell!*" Root shouted, turning his horse, wanting out of Summers' rifle sights. But before he turned the frightened animal, Summers' second shot hit him high in his left shoulder and knocked him from his saddle.

"Help him, Two Horse!" shouted Luther Passe, swinging his horse around as he jerked his rifle up to his shoulder and began firing back at Summers.

"Damn this," Leonard Tuell growled, even as he gigged his horse forward and rode into sight long enough to grab Root's reaching arm and help him swing up behind him.

"I'm hit bad, fellows!" Root said as Two Horse and Luther Passe reined their horses to a halt thirty yards away from the open ridgeline. He slid down from behind Two Horse and examined his bloody shoulder wound.

Two Horse stepped down from his saddle. Luther watched as the half-breed rummaged through his saddlebags and came up with a dusty cloth. Shaking the wadded cloth out, Two Horse handed it to Root.

"Hold this on it," he said.

Root looked at the cloth with disdain, but he took it and stuck it to his bleeding shoulder.

"I'll be lucky this don't kill me," he said.

"You're lucky the horse trader didn't kill you," Luther said from his saddle. "Now we'll all three be lucky if Big Jack doesn't kill us. What the hell were you thinking, you and Bert making a bet like that?"

"Bert was so damn cocksure he could hit something from up here," said Root, "I had to take him on." He frowned looking at his shoulder wound. "He hit something, but it was the wrong target. So I won," he concluded.

"Good luck collecting," Luther said.

"We didn't even know it was the right man," said Two Horse.

"The hell we didn't," said Root. "One man, traveling with a three-horse string? Cherry the whore riding with him? What else did you need to know? It's him all right."

"Yep, it's him," Luther agreed, "and we should have all opened fire at one time, not monkey around betting who can hit what."

"We need to go down and finish this thing," Two Horse said.

"I need to get back to the spread and get this shoulder looked at," said Root. "You go on down there if you feel like it."

"To hell with it," said Luther, nudging his horse away from them. "I'm going back to the spread. You two do what you think best."

"Come on, Two Horse," said Root, "let's go before he leaves us here. I'm not having him show up alone, telling Big Jack his side of the story."

"His side of the story?" Two Horse stared at him.

"Damn it, you know what I mean. Come on, help me up. Let's ride." He held out his hand for help.

Two Horse turned away from his hand and swung up into his saddle.

"Go catch your horse, Root," he said. "I'm not riding double. You smell like dirty long-johns."

"Damn you, half-breed!" Root slapped his bloody right hand to his holstered Colt.

But Two Horse's big Dance Brothers pistol came up fast and cocked toward Root's face.

"Huh-uh, Root, don't lose what little you have left," Two Horse said.

Root let his hand drop from his gun butt. He spit and wiped his hand across his lips and watched the half-breed ride away. Holding the wadded-up cloth to his shoulder, he turned and walked in the direction his spooked horse had taken.

On the ground below, Summers lay listening, watching. He had levered and fired one shot after another, the explosions echoing out across the hills like the well-spaced beat of a drum. Then, as suddenly as it had started, it was all over. The riders had disappeared out of sight.

He looked over at Cherry lying dead on the ground, a widening pool of blood still spreading beneath her. The blanket she'd held around herself—the warm blanket she had welcomed him into only a moment ago—now lay covering her from the waist down, a bullet hole in its center.

Summers walked over to her and stooped down and turned her onto her back. Her blank wide-eyed stare ignored him and gazed straight up into the morning sky. Her mouth was slightly agape in a surprised half smile.

"Jesus, Cherry . . . ," he whispered, cradling her in his arm, closing her eyes, her lips. He pulled the blanket up and around her, most of it wet with her blood. He swept her up and carried her over nearer to the horses and the pool of runoff water.

When Summers laid her down near the water's edge, Cherry's paint horse looked around at them and nickered low under its breath.

Had he failed her somehow? he asked himself, looking down at her dead yet still-warm body.

Stop it . . . , he told himself. There were many people who had failed her in her life, including herself, he thought. But he wasn't one of them, and he wasn't going to allow himself to think that way. He walked back to the fire and looked coldly off and up along the ridgeline.

The only person responsible for Cherry's death was the man who pulled the trigger—no one else. Summers had seen his own shot nail that man, and watched that man fly from his saddle. Was it the same two men who'd ambushed them the other night? He didn't think so. But he would find out.

He stooped and picked his Winchester up again and checked it, even though it had only been a moment ago when he'd levered a fresh round into its chamber. Looking back up at the ridgeline, he picked Cherry's discarded clothes from the ground and walked back to her and stooped down beside her.

"I'm going to dress you now, Cherry, and take you back to town," he said quietly as if asking her approval. He brushed dirt from the side of her face. "We'll get you buried, nicelike."

When he'd finished washing her face and rinsing the blood from her, front and back, he dressed her and rewrapped her in his clean blanket and rolled the bloody blanket up and left it beside the pool of runoff water.

He tended the horses and kept Cherry's paint horse beside him, her body lying across the saddle and tied in place. He led the string behind him on his other side, rode up the trail to the ridgeline and looked down at the body lying dead where it had landed, a large hole where its nose had been, the back of its head missing. A few yards away Phelps' blood-splattered horse stepped warily into sight and stood staring at him.

Stepping down from his saddle, Summers walked

over and led the shy horse closer and hefted Phelps' body over its back.

With five horses and two bodies in tow, he turned the animals and followed the others' hoofprints to the spot where Two Horse had abandoned the wounded John Root. Gazing far down along the trail, Summers saw a lone rider raising snow and dust across the flatlands. In the farther distance he saw the remnants of the other riders' flurry of dust and snow. He raised his Winchester from across his lap, steadied the dapple gray with his knees and raised the rifle to his shoulder.

He took close aim and said under his breath, "Here's another one for you, Cherry." Yet, as realization set in, he judged the shot and knew it was too far out of range. As unrealistic as speaking to the dead, he reminded himself. He lowered the rifle and let out a breath.

"Another time, Cherry, I promise," he whispered in spite of the futility of it. He uncocked the Winchester and shoved it down into its boot.

Back to Gunn Point, he thought with resolve—*be prepared for whatever comes.*

PART 3

Chapter 16

In the late evening light, Summers brought the horses to a halt out in front of the sheriff's office. He was thankful to find the street empty save for a skinny yellow hound that ventured from under a boardwalk and trotted alongside the string, its nose sniffing toward the scent of dried blood coming from the dead rifleman's horse.

Deputy Stiles looked out the dusty front window and saw the two bodies. As Summers turned the horses into the alley, Stiles hurried out, putting on his hat, and followed along the boardwalk.

"Every time I see you, you're hauling a body, Summers," he said, with dark, wry humor. "Ever think about buying yourself a hearse?"

Summers stepped down in the alley and gave him a grim look that offered no room for humor, dark or otherwise.

"One of them is Cherry Atmore," he said.

"Oh . . . ," said Stiles, turning serious, not because it was Cherry Atmore, but because the look on Summers' face demanded some show of respect. "What happened?" he asked solemnly.

"This man killed her," Summers said flatly, nodding toward Bert Phelps' body draped over the saddle, his limp arms swaying a little, his blue hands dangling toward the ground.

"*Whoa*," Stiles said, seeing the open cavity that had been the back of Phelps' head. "You—you shot him?"

"I shot him," Summers declared. "I don't suppose you can identify him."

"I'll try," Stiles said, with the gravity the situation called for, "but judging from the back of his head, I doubt his own mother could identify him."

Summers watched him step over and carefully find a way to grip the hair atop the dead man's head. As he lifted, a thick strand of black congealed blood fell from the corpse's mouth and bobbed toward the ground.

"No," said Stiles, dropping the head and stepping back as the thick blood broke free and plopped into the snowy dirt. "But I'm going to speculate it's one of Jack Warren's cowhands. His shirt looks familiar. So does the horse."

"Familiar from where?" Summers asked.

"Four of them rode through here last night," Stiles said. He paused, then said, "I'll be honest, they were asking about you."

"Asking who?" Summers persisted, his questions coming in rapid-fire fashion.

"Everybody," said Stiles.

"Including you?" Summers asked without a pause.

"Well . . . yes," Stiles said, "including me." He looked a little uncomfortable, but not too much. "I'm the deputy here. You might expect that they—"

"What did you tell them?" Summers continued without hesitating, cutting his reply short.

But Stiles saw what was going on. He would have none of it. He took a deep breath.

"I told them you left Gunn Point, Summers—you and Cherry Atmore. Anything wrong with that? I didn't tell them when you left or where you were headed." He gave a slight shrug. "I didn't rightly know where you were headed." He stared at Summers. "Any *more* questions?" he said, letting Summers know he didn't like the implication that he might have told the gunmen where to find him.

Summer didn't reply. He made no apology for his questions. He only stepped over to Phelps' horse and tied it and Cherry Atmore's paint horse a few feet away from each other.

"I'm taking my horses to the barn," he said.

"I'll take these two to the undertaker for you," said Stiles. "I'll have him prepare Cherry for a proper funeral."

"Obliged," Summers said, his voice turning almost friendly. "Do you have any hot coffee in there?"

"Yes, I do," said Stiles, a little surprised after the way Summers had questioned him so relentlessly. He stepped over to the two horses with the bodies over their saddles. "It's on the stove. If I'm not back yet, you help yourself." He watched Summers gather the reins to his dapple gray and the lead rope to the string. "Danny Kindrick is back there, if you want some help," he said as Summers walked away, the horses walking along behind him.

Before Summers reached the livery barn, the wide middle doors swung open and Danny Kindrick ran out carrying a lantern in the failing evening light.

"Soon as I saw it was you, I dropped what I was doing and come running," he said, reaching out and taking the lead rope from Summers' hand.

"Obliged, Danny," Summer said. The two walked on the last few yards and through the doors. "I see you gave up the shoulder harness."

"Yeah, I did," Danny said, patting the side of his shirt absently, looking a little embarrassed. "I said if it was all the same with Deputy Stiles, I'd just as soon not wear it anymore."

Summers nodded as they walked inside and Danny hung the lantern on a wall peg.

"Did he ask why?" he said.

"Yeah," said Danny, "I told him you said the shotgun might be better."

"What did he say?" Summers asked.

"He said he agreed, it might be. Said he should have thought of that to begin with. Said it was too easy for a man like Rochen—whatever his name is to snatch away from me and use to make a break for it. Said he was sorry that he might have gotten me killed."

"That's big of him to say so," Summers said dryly. He drew his Winchester from its boot and leaned it against a center post. He loosened the cinch under the dapple gray's belly and swung the saddle off onto a saddle rack.

"What brought you back this way, Mr. Summers?" he asked.

"Cherry Atmore got shot and killed," Summers said quietly, not liking the sound of his own words. "I brought her back to be buried."

"That's terrible," Danny said. "She was a nice woman. She said when I got a little older, she would take me to her room and, you know . . ."

"Yeah, I know," Summers said.

"She gave me some puffs on her Indian tobacco once when I was feeling bad. Told me to draw it down in my chest and hold it there, which I did. *Whooee!* I didn't feel bad for long. I kept crossing and uncrossing my eyes. Every time I did it, I could see farther on either side of my head. I could almost see behind me. I've always liked her for that."

"What a gal," Summers said, feeling sad for Cherry and what her short miserable life had been.

Danny said, "Does she have any family or anybody to come to a funeral if she has one?"

"I doubt it," said Summers. "Maybe some of the other girls from the saloon where she worked."

"I'd come to it," Danny offered.

"That would be real kind of you," Summers said. He changed the subject. "Speaking of Avrial Rochenbach, how is the prisoner doing?"

"He seems all right. Says his head is hurting less. He doesn't seem to carry a grudge for us sticking him back in jail."

"No reason he should carry one," said Summers. "He robbed a bank."

"I know," said Danny. "But as robbers go, he doesn't seem to be a bad fellow. He didn't shoot me, or knock me out. He could have. I wouldn't have been able to stop him."

"That's one way of looking at it," Summers said. He grained the dapple gray, watered it and wiped it down with straw while Danny attended the three-horse string.

"I know he's an outlaw now, but he once was a respectable lawman like Sheriff Goss and Deputy Stiles," Danny said.

"That he was, Danny," said Summers.

When he finished with the gray, Summers led the animal into a single-horse stall and flipped Danny a gold coin for tending to the three-horse string. "I'm going to the sheriff's office for coffee," he said. "Get those three in a stall when you're finished rubbing them down."

"Sure will, Mr. Summers," Danny said, looking favorably at the gold coin in his palm as Summers turned, picked up his rifle, walked out the door and headed back toward the sheriff's office.

In his cell, Avrial Rochenbach heard the front door open and close. A moment later he saw Summers walking back toward his cell with two mugs of coffee hooked on his fingers, his Winchester hanging from his right hand. Rochenbach looked him up and down warily.

"I thought you left town, Summers," he said.

"I did," Summer said. "I'm back."

"Is one of those for me?" Rochenbach asked, nodding at the mugs of coffee.

"Yep," said Summers. He reached inside the food slot and set one of the cups down in front of the prisoner. He noted the wide purple bruise on Rochenbach's forehead, the same slim oval shape of his Winchester's butt plate.

"Well, well," Rochenbach said dryly, "to what do I owe all this?" He picked up the steaming coffee mug and looked at Summers through the bars. "Feeling guilty about shooting me, punching me out or both?" His fingertips went idly to his swollen forehead.

"Neither," said Summers. "Just figured you might want some coffee. I can take it back if it's *unsettling* your mind."

"No, that's all right," Rochenbach said. He drew the mug away as if Summers might reach through the bars for it. "I'm obliged," he said. "I'm just surprised is all." He blew on the coffee and sipped it and made a coffee hiss.

"Tell me how you come upon this bank job, Avrial," Summers said bluntly.

Avrial . . . ? First names now. . . . Rochenbach looked at him curiously for a moment.

"If you're trying to pal up with me," he said, "it's not Avrial, it's *Rock*, or *Rocky*, either one. Nobody ever calls me Avrial—nobody who knows better."

"All right, Rock," said Summers, "what about the bank job?"

Rock, huh . . . ? He half smiled to himself.

"That's the price of the coffee?" he said.

"And maybe me getting the sheriff to talk to the circuit judge for you," Summer said. "See if we can get you out of jail before you're too old to know why you're there."

"If I thought you meant it . . . ," Rochenbach said, clearly tempted.

"I mean it," Summers said.

"Do you know the circuit judge?" Rochenbach asked.

"He's Judge Hugh Louder," Summers said. "I know him well enough. He'll listen to what I have to say."

Rochenbach sipped the coffee and considered it carefully for a moment. He finally let out a tight breath. "Like I told Stiles, a fellow I know told me about the job, had me meet up with Grayson and Fallon."

"Did you tell him who this fellow is?" Summers asked.

"He didn't ask," Rochenbach said.

Summers thought about it. Why would Stiles not ask, unless he already knew?

"I'm asking," Summers said.

Rochenbach considered it another moment.

"And you'll speak to the judge?" he said.

"What'd I say?" Summers replied in a firm tone.

The prisoner looked all around cautiously before offering the name.

"It was Roe Pindigo," he said barely above a whisper. "He works for Jack Warren—doesn't know I know it, though." He paused, then said, "Now my life is back in your hands, Will Summers."

"Roe Pindigo . . . ," Summers said. "I've heard of him. He calls himself a *personal detective*—he's really no more than a hired killer."

Rochenbach winced and said, "That's him. Maybe if you'll say his name a little louder, they can hear you across the street at the saloon."

Summers didn't think he'd spoken too loudly.

"You're that scared of him," he said, "even though you're going to prison?"

"Scared of him, *no*," said the prisoner. "Convinced he'll kill me, *yes*, to a certainty. If Pindigo wanted me dead, being in prison wouldn't protect me from him." Rochenbach gave him a serious stare. "Be sure and mention that to the judge," he added.

"You sure have come across some unsavory characters, Rock," said Summers.

"You don't know the half of it," Rock replied, holding on to a bar with his good hand. "Being an undercover detective put me in touch with more criminals than I care to think about." He pulled himself closer to the bars with his good hand. "I know the outlaw world down to their boot sizes. Tell that to the judge too. Maybe he can see a way to use me on the outside instead of me rotting in some—"

The two stopped talking when they heard the front door open and close.

"Keep everything between you and me, Rock," Summers whispered.

"You can count on it, Will Summers," he whispered in reply. "You're out to get the goods on Stiles, I can tell." He stared at Summers wisely.

"All the time I spent gathering information for Al Pinkerton's rogues' gallery? I can tell when a man has his nose to the ground trying to sniff something up." He gave him a faint, guarded smile. He stepped back from the bars toward the cot, his coffee mug in hand, as Deputy Stiles started down the hall toward them.

Summers just stood looking at Rochenbach, knowing the former detective's intuitions were right. His advice about asking pointless questions had been right too. He'd seen how jumpy it had made Stiles. This man could be of help, he told himself. He knew it.

"I hope I'm not interrupting anything back here," Stiles said, only half jokingly, looking back and forth between the two.

Summers only stared at Rochenbach, seeing how well he would handle answering the deputy.

"After *shooting me* and *cracking* my skull with a rifle butt, your horse trader pard here thinks a cup of coffee is all it takes to turn me into a lapdog." Staring coldly at Summers, he tipped his cup as if in toast. "Nice try, though."

"Settle down, Rochenbach," said Stiles, convinced by the prisoner's performance.

Summers turned on his heel without a word and walked down the hall to the sheriff's office.

Catching up and following him, Stiles said, "What was that all about?"

"You heard him," Summers said, tight-lipped. "I asked him some questions. . . . He didn't want to answer." He stopped by the desk and sipped his coffee, his rifle in hand.

"All right," said Stiles, as if to pacify him, "what kinds of questions? Maybe I already know the answer."

Summers turned to him and looked him up and down.

"I doubt it," he said craftily. "If you did you wouldn't want to tell me." He set the empty mug down, turned and walked out the door. "Obliged for the coffee," he said over his shoulder.

Stiles stood watching as Summers closed the door behind himself. "Damn it to hell . . . !" he cursed aloud to himself, the words sounding strange coming from his lips.

He turned and walked back to the cell and stared in at Rochenbach.

"What did he ask you?" he demanded.

The former detective gave a shrug and said, "He told me I better not tell if I know what's good for me."

"If you know what's *good for you*, Rochenbach, you *will* tell me," Stiles said in a threatening tone.

The prisoner stared at him intently from the striped darkness of his cell, his eyes above the coffee mug, his face feeling the heat of it.

Summers was right . . . , he told himself. Stiles was too jumpy and tight for a man *not* hiding something.

Chapter 17

———

Sheriff Goss lay propped up finishing a bowl of warm calf liver soup, an iron-rich substance for replenishing his weakened blood supply. When Summers walked into the room, the wounded sheriff looked past Flora's shoulder at him. Flora sat on the edge of Goss' bed spoon-feeding him. But the sheriff held up a hand, stopping her for a moment.

"I need to . . . talk to this fellow, Flora," he said, sounding only a little stronger to Summers than he had only the day before.

Flora stood from the bedside, touched a cloth napkin to the sheriff's lips and left the room, giving Summers a cordial nod.

"What brings you . . . back so soon?" Goss asked as Summers walked closer. Seeing the grim look on Summers' face, Goss said, "Something's wrong . . . I can tell."

Summers removed his hat and held it at his side.

"Cherry Atmore has been shot to death, Sheriff," he said quietly.

"That's terrible, Will," the sheriff said. "That poor dove never . . . harmed anybody. Didn't have . . . a mean bone in her body."

"I killed the man who shot her," Summers added. "Deputy Stiles says it's one of Warren's cowhands."

Sheriff Goss closed his eyes for a moment and shook his head slowly.

"This is all I need right now," he said.

"I'm sorry to have to tell you," Summers said, "but I figured you'd want to know right away."

"You're right . . . it's my job to know," Goss said. He opened his eyes and said with determination, "I've got to get up from here. . . ."

"No, you don't," said Summers holding a hand in front of him as if to block him.

The sheriff collapsed back against his pillows.

"Hell . . . who am I kidding?" he said. "I can't get up. I don't have the strength to . . . coil a short rope."

Summers leaned in close.

"You still want me to deputy for you, Sheriff?" he asked quietly.

Sheriff Goss studied his eyes closely for a moment.

"Not if you're doing it as a way for you to get vengeance for Cherry Atmore," he said.

"I think you know me better than that, Sheriff," Summers said. "You asked me to think about working for you, and I have. If the offer is still open, I'm accepting it."

The sheriff reached a weak hand over and laid it on his forearm.

"I'm obliged, Will," he said. "I'm afraid I'm . . . too weak to swear you in right now."

"Don't worry about it, Sheriff," Summers said. "Swear me in when you're feeling better."

"There's a spare badge in the desk . . . at my office," Goss said. "You get it . . . put it on. Anybody questions it . . . they know where to find me."

"You mean Stiles," Summers said.

"Yes . . . your fellow deputy." Goss gave him a weak smile.

"I need to know, Sheriff," Summers said. "Which of us has the most authority, him or me? He's been a deputy a short while."

"You're both the same, Will," the sheriff said.

"That could cause trouble, Sheriff," Summers said, cautioning him.

"You two . . . work it out," said Goss, his eyelids starting to droop. "Now get out of here . . . it's late. We'll talk more in the morning. . . ."

Summers backed a step away from the sheriff's bed. *Good enough . . . ,* he thought. He put his hat atop his head and adjusted its brim.

"Good night, Sheriff Goss," he said, knowing the sheriff had already drifted off to sleep. He turned and walked out, back along the boardwalk toward the sheriff's office. As he passed an alley, he looked down it, and in the dim light of an open side door, he saw two men taking Cherry's body down from across her paint horse and carrying it inside the town mortuary. Summers stopped for a second, seeing a hand reach out and draw the dim light into darkness behind the closing door.

He walked on.

Inside the sheriff's office, Deputy Stiles had walked

back out front, carrying the empty coffee mug Summers had given to the prisoner.

"I was just questioning Rochenbach about the robbery again," he said when Summers walked through the front door, stopped and stood staring at him.

"This is a good night for questioning," Summers said flatly.

"Oh?" Stiles looked him up and down. "What's on your mind, Summers?"

Summers took his time. He turned and closed the door behind himself, then turned back around facing Stiles, his hand inside his duster pocket.

"Take a look at this, Deputy," he said. He took his hand from his pocket and pitched the chewed-up length of rein on the battered oak desk.

"Yeah? What is it?" Stiles said, playing dumb, keeping his startled response from showing on his face.

Summers studied his eyes for a moment for any sign of recognition, seeing none.

"You tell me," he said. And he stood staring, waiting, watching the deputy closely.

Stiles spread his hands, apparently at a loss.

"I wouldn't have any idea," he replied. He offered a bemused smile as if Summers were kidding him.

Bad answer, Summers told himself. If the deputy hadn't recognized it, he would have looked closer, with more curiosity. Had he looked closer, he would have at least seen what it had been—a length of rein. Only someone had cut it.

"Sure you do." Summers said. He leaned his rifle against the desk, picked up the length and held it between his hands, holding it up for a closer look.

"Oh. Yes," said Stiles at last acknowledging the

item. "It's a piece of leather reins. Somebody cut it off. It must have been too long to suit its owner."

"It was cut from buggy reins," Summers said. As he spoke he wrapped it around his right palm, then his left.

"How can you tell?" said Stiles.

"I found it where you found Harper's remains," said Summers.

Stiles said, "But still—"

"Harper's buggy has a length of rein missing," Summers said.

"It does?" Stiles said, still plying dumb. "I hadn't noticed. I'll have to take a closer look."

Summers tightened the leather rein between his hands. "I can picture somebody choking the banker to death with this and setting his buggy out across the flatlands toward the hills, knowing he and his horse would be eaten."

Summers saw a nerve twitch in Stiles' jaw.

"Obliged for your help, Summers," he said, keeping himself cordial. "Like I said, I'll take a look at Harper's buggy."

"Or I can," Summers said. He loosened the leather rein from his hands, coiled it and stuck it back in his duster pocket.

"No, I'll do it," Stiles said. In spite of the tightness that had set into his jaw, he offered a thin, stiff smile. "It's my job."

"Mine too," said Summers. "I just agreed to be a deputy, help you out a little until the sheriff is back on his feet."

"Oh . . . ?" Stiles stood staring, not knowing what to say.

"I remember how disappointed you were when I turned him down before I left," Summers said.

Stiles caught himself. He wasn't going to play into Summers' hand. He was going to be his same helpful, accommodating self—for the time being anyway.

"Well, then," he said. "Of course I'll have to hear it from the sheriff himself, but I'm certain you're telling me the truth."

"Yep, you check with Sheriff Goss first thing in the morning," said Summers. "Meanwhile, I'm going to get a hot meal and a good night's sleep—get ready to pin on a badge in the morning. Maybe between you and me we can figure out what's going on with Jack Warren's bank."

Stiles looked tense, like a man trying his best *not* to look tense.

"I have to tell you, Summers," he said, "I think you're letting what happened to Cherry Atmore eat too hard at you. I think it's causing you some dark, distrustful thinking."

Summers stared at him blankly.

"Cherry Atmore was a harmless young woman who didn't deserve to die, Deputy," he said.

"Summers, I hate to say this, but Cherry was just a whore," said Stiles.

"Whores don't deserve to be shot down like animals, Deputy," Summers said, a rigid set to his jaw.

"I know that," Stiles said, "but you don't want to go making a bigger deal of it than it is, is all I'm trying to say."

"It is a *big deal*," Summers said. "Murder is always a big deal. I killed the man who shot her, but I want the others who were in on it too. Between you and me, we'll bring them all to justice." Summers knew the spot he was putting Stiles in.

"For God's sake, Summers," Stiles said, "Cherry was a low-down dope smoker! Didn't you even see that?"

"I saw it," Summers said. He wanted to keep the pressure on Stiles, knowing how greatly his presence here as a deputy was going to get under his skin. "That's one of the things I admired most about her," he lied.

From his cell at the end of the hall, Avrial Rochenbach listened intently, the side of his head pressed against the iron bars. When he heard the conversation stop beneath the closing of the front door, he walked back to his cot and sat down.

One of the things he admired most about her . . . ?

He smiled to himself. Whatever game this horse trader was playing, Rochenbach was betting on him to win it. He'd better be right, he reminded himself. His life depended on it.

Stiles had ridden hard through the middle of the night to get to the Warren spread. When he arrived, Roe Pindigo met him at the front door, a shotgun in one hand, an oil lamp in the other.

Behind Pindigo the big house stood dark and silent. Jack Warren had drunk himself to sleep in his large bedroom upstairs. Juanita, the cook, was asleep in her small room in the rear of the house.

"What are you doing out here this hour of the night, Stiles?" Pindigo asked.

"I need to talk to Jack Warren," Stiles said. "It's important."

"It's Mr. Warren to you, Stiles," Pindigo said, blocking the doorway.

"All right, then, *Mr. Warren!*" the deputy said, getting a little edgy.

Pindigo just stared at him, unmoved.

"I need to speak to Mr. Warren," Stiles said in a smoother, more civil tone.

"No," Pindigo said, "you need to speak to me. Then, if I decide it's important enough, I'll wake Mr. Warren and tell him you're here." He gave him a firm, unfriendly grin. "Now start talking before I change my mind."

Jesus . . . ! Stiles took a deep breath and calmed himself.

"Sheriff Goss has made Will Summers deputy, starting tomorrow," he said, "and he's already asking lots of questions."

"So?" said Pindigo. "What about all that *magic* you were going to put into play on everything?"

"It's not working the way I had it planned," Stiles said.

"So you come here for what, *sympathy*?" Pindigo asked. "You know this horse trader killed one of Big Jack's cowhands, wounded another one, all over that whore from Gunn Point."

"I know all about it," Stiles said.

"Then shoot him and be done with it, Deputy," Pindigo said. "Save these other cowhands from riding into Gunn Point and doing it for you." He started to close the door in Stiles' face.

"He knows about the money being counterfeit," Stiles said hurriedly.

"What?" Pindigo said, annoyed. He opened the door wider.

"Don't blame me," Stiles said. "One of the robbers

had some of the stolen money on him. Summers killed him and found the money—saw it was fake right off."

"Damn it," said Pindigo. "What about Harper, will he be opening his mouth if this horse trader starts pressing him hard enough?"

Stiles gave the gunman a sly grin. "If Summers talks to Harper, he'll be talking to wolves' asses." He gave a dark chuckle.

But Pindigo only stared coldly at him.

"Meaning what the hell, exactly?" he said dryly.

"Meaning I killed him and let the wolves eat him," Stiles said, his chuckle and sly grin both gone.

Pindigo's shotgun hammers cocked. The double barrel tipped up and pointed at Stiles' chest.

"From now on say what you mean the first time. I hate a turd who can't talk straight out."

"Sorry," said Stiles, staring at the cocked shotgun. "I won't do that again."

"That would be wise of you," Pindigo said. He stepped back and to the side, letting the shotgun barrel drop down from Stiles' chest. "Now come on in here. I'll go up and rouse Big Jack."

Deputy Stiles stood in the dark inside the door while Roe Pindigo climbed the stairs, holding the oil lamp up to light his way. Stiles heard Jack Warren's gruff voice cursing in his upstairs bedroom. Then he heard Warren's voice more clearly as the sound of footsteps started down the stairs.

"What kind of stupid son of a bitch is he?" Stiles heard Jack Warren growl.

"You'll have to decide that for yourself," Pindigo replied.

Stiles felt his face flush, hearing himself discussed

in such a manner and tone. He took a deep breath and
settled himself as the two came down into view in the
glow of the lamplight.

"Mr. Warren, sir, I hate waking you at this hour, but
I thought you'd better be made aware," he said as Big
Jack stepped off the bottom stair and stood in front of
him in the wavering lamplight.

"It better be a damned good reason," Warren said,
an unlit cigar hanging between his thick fingers.

"I was telling Pindigo here," Stiles said, "that Summers killed Lewis Fallon and found counterfeit money
on him."

"Damn it to hell," said Warren. He bit the end off his
cigar violently and spit it to the floor. He clamped it
between his teeth and stared angrily at Stiles. "Thought
you were *handling* everything for me in Gunn Point?"

"I am handling what I can," Stiles said. "This came
up out of the blue. Luckily I was there and found out,
else you would have rode in not knowing."

Warren thought about it and settled down. He
puffed on his cigar when Pindigo reached around with
a struck match to light it for him.

"All right, that's true," he said to Stiles. "What the
hell is Summers still doing in Gunn Point? You should
have gotten him to leave!"

"He did leave," said Stiles, "and he took that whore
with him. But four of your hands ambushed the whore.
Summers her brought her body back to—"

"I heard all about Cherry Atmore," Warren said,
cutting him off with an impatient wave of a hand.
"Who all has Summers told about the counterfeit
money?" he asked.

"The sheriff and me," said Stiles. "Nobody else that

I know of. Harper's dead. He can't tell anybody anything."

Warren puffed on the cigar and considered it for only a second. "But I did sign his receipt pad for him before he left here," he said. "If anybody sees that, I'm cooked."

"Those wolves didn't leave much of him," said Stiles. "I wouldn't worry about paperwork showing up. Even if it was lying out there, it won't last long—snow, rain."

"What about Summers having it?" Warren asked.

"Summers doesn't have it," Stiles said. "I know how he thinks. If he had it, he would have said so right off."

"That being the case, nobody can say I took the money from Harper. I never saw it after it was stolen." He looked at Pindigo as he spoke. "Harper stole it, far as anybody can ever say." He puffed on the cigar and blew out a stream. "I ride in tomorrow, open the bank with my own money, honorable man that I am." He grinned. The townsfolk should applaud me for it—making good on the stolen money, not even waiting for my partner, Leland Sutter, to come up with his share."

"But this isn't how you had it planned," Pindigo reminded him.

"No, I had it planned that I come out with all my money free and clear and some to boot. But that's not where it stands now. I'll sit on things until the circuit judge has come and gone, then start taking my money back out a little at a time." He looked at Stiles and said, "Maybe by then the poor sheriff will have gone on to a better place. . . . Maybe this horse trader will have gone along with him." He gave Stiles a knowing look.

"Goss has made Summers a deputy," Stiles said. "When you ride in you watch your step. He knows one of your cowhands killed the whore."

"Damn," said Warren. "He's the one supposed to be worried about *me*, for killing my son. Now you're telling me to *watch my step*?"

"I'm just saying—"

"Hold on, Big Jack," Pindigo said. "I think you should stay out of town. Let me ride in tomorrow. You need a new manager. I'm him. I can feel things out, make sure nobody is able to point a finger at you for anything. Like you said, once the circuit judge has come and gone, we'll clean this all up on our own terms."

Warren puffed on his cigar and nodded his head.

"Good thinking, Roe," he said. He looked at Stiles and said in a critical tone, "See why he *is* who he *is*?" He blew out a long stream of smoke and said confidently, "When this is all over, he'll serve me the horse trader's heart for breakfast." He looked at Pindigo. "Am I right, Roe?"

Pindigo gave an arrogant toss of his head.

"Would you like it medium or well done?" he asked.

Chapter 18

———

Summers spent the night at the Gunn Point Hotel, in a room that overlooked the main street and provided a good view of the surrounding land in every direction. At a corner table, his back to a wall, he had a hot breakfast of thick bacon, fried eggs and hot coffee. When he'd paid for his meal, he put on his coat and hat, picked up his rifle from against the wall and walked out onto street. He walked in the street alongside the boardwalk, his breath steaming in the crisp, cold air.

Before stepping onto the boardwalk out in front of the sheriff's office, he looked at Deputy Stiles' horse standing lathered and hard ridden at the hitch rail. As he walked up toward the front door, he saw Danny Kindrick come around the corner of the alley leading back to the livery barn.

"Morning, Will Summers," Danny said. "Or should I start calling you deputy now?"

"Whichever suits you, Danny," Summers said. He watched the young livery hostler take the reins to Stiles' horse and lead it toward the livery barn.

"Got to go," Danny said. "I have to get this horse grained and rubbed down before I go get the prisoner some breakfast this morning."

Summers had a pretty good idea where Stiles had been riding the horse to get the animal so lathered and worn. But he wasn't going to mention it. Neither would Stiles unless he'd been up to no good. Stiles didn't have to explain where he'd ridden his horse. But if he brought it up at all, it would be in an attempt to square himself.

As soon as Summers closed the door behind himself, Stiles stood up from behind the sheriff's desk and handed him the deputy's badge from inside the drawer.

"There you go," Stiles said. "I shined it up some for you. I know you were tired last night and been through a lot, Cherry's death and all. I hope you're feeling better this morning."

"Obliged," Summers said, taking the badge and looking it over as he turned it in his hand. "I'll pin it on later."

"Whatever you think is best," Stiles said. He gestured a nod toward the hitch rail out front. "You probably saw Danny leading my horse to the barn?"

Yep, here it comes . . . , Summers told himself. He didn't reply; he just stared at Stiles.

"Yeah," Stiles said, "I rode out late last night to see Big Jack Warren. I wanted to make sure I knew what to tell folks about him opening the bank today."

Summers only stared without comment.

"I figured it'd be best for your sake if I got an idea what you should expect when he gets here, eh?"

Summers made no response.

"Good news," Stiles said, "we won't have to worry

about it. He's not coming. He's sending his man, Roe Pindigo, to reopen the bank. Jack Warren is talking coolheaded about what happened. He said if the shooting was in self-defense, he has to abide by the same code as everybody else, like it or not. I think that's big of him, don't you?"

"Yeah, real big of him," said Summers, not buying a word of it. He noted the name *Roe Pindigo*, but he said nothing. The less he spoke, the more Stiles felt he needed too.

"I suspect that's why he's not coming to town anytime soon. He's so broken up and ashamed over what happened with Little Jackie, he doesn't want to show his face for a while."

No, not a word of it . . . , Summers told himself.

"What about the counterfeit money?" he said.

"What about it?" said Stiles.

"You told him about it, didn't you?" Summers said.

"No, I didn't," Stiles said. Then he followed up quickly, saying, "But he already knew about it." He looked amazed and said, "Don't ask me how."

Summers still just stared. He could tell the deputy was lying. But he would let it lie for the time being. He could tell Stiles was worried now, not at all calm and confident as he'd been before. Stiles was being just clear enough to try to save the situation, but not so clear that he couldn't jump back at any minute and let Warren take the blame for everything if it fell apart. The deputy was like a man who had stepped in manure and was trying to get it off his boots without it being seen.

"Anyway, here's some more good news," Stiles said. "Warren said he'd already made arrangements to replace the counterfeit money with his own money, just to keep the merchants from falling behind."

Summers stared at him for a moment longer, as if running it all through his mind. "So Harper did give him the money the day you and Harper were both out at his place?"

"No, he says Harper gave him nothing," said Stiles. "I believe him."

"What happened to the carpetbag you saw?" Summers said flatly. "Think the wolves ate it?"

"That's got me puzzled, I have to admit," Stiles said. "But with all the hard cases prowling around out there, who's to say? Could be, some of them found the money and lit out with it." He gave a casual shrug that Summers knew he didn't feel. "We might never know what become of it."

"No, we're going to know, Deputy," Summers said. "I'm going to find out. You can count on it."

Stiles just nodded and looked all around the dingy sheriff's office.

Changing the subject, he said, "Have you had breakfast yet?"

"Yep," said Summers.

"I haven't," said Stiles, anxious, like a man eager to get off the firing line. "Mind if I go get some grub?"

Did he mind . . . ? Summers noted to himself.

"Go help yourself," Summers said, nodding toward the front door. "I'll keep an eye on things here."

No sooner had Stiles gone out the front door and on his way along the boardwalk than Summers walked back to the cell and saw Rochenbach standing with his good hand gripping an iron bar. He chuckled as Summers walked closer.

"He *asked you* if he could go get breakfast?" he said with an incredulous look.

"You heard that?" Summers said.

"I did," said the prisoner.

"What do you think?" Summers asked.

"I think you've got him spooked, Will Summers," Rochenbach said. "He's on a hot spot and he doesn't know which way to jump to get himself off it."

"As a former detective yourself, how dirty would you say he is?" Summers asked, trusting Rochenbach's opinion for some reason.

"It doesn't matter how dirty I think he is," Rochenbach said. "You've got him pegged as a murderer, I can tell by the look in your eyes."

Summers just stared at him.

"All right," Rochenbach said, "I say whatever is going on, he's in it over his head. The trouble with a man like Stiles is that he'll never come out and admit to anything. He'll kill you when he figures his game is up."

"That's sort of what I've been wondering," Summers said quietly.

"No, it's not something you've been wondering, Summers," he said, gripping the iron bar. "It's something you've known and allowed for all along."

"You've got good instincts, Rock," Summers said. "It's a shame you're on that side of the bars."

"Thanks," said Rochenbach. "Be careful you don't get yourself killed. Jack Warren is the kind of man who has a way of doing any damn thing he pleases and never getting called down for it."

"I'll take it as far as I can," said Summers. "But I won't step outside the law, even to see justice done."

"If you want to bring these men to justice and stay within the law, you might as well stop now before you get your feelings hurt. If there's one thing I've learned, it's that law only works for them who live subject to it. The law means nothing to the likes of Jack Warren."

It was noon when a northbound stagecoach rolled into Gunn Point through a flurry of dust and snow, and Circuit Court Judge Hugh Louder stepped down onto the street. The tall, dapper man carried a dark leather-trimmed carpetbag in his hand and wore a tall stove-pipe hat above a long black overcoat, black gloves and a black and gray wool muffler.

Deputy Stiles spotted the judge from a block away, yet managed to be at his side almost before the man's high-top shoes touched the ground.

"Your Honor, Judge Louder," Stiles said, touching his fingers to his hat brim and reaching out to take the judge's travel bag from his hand. "Please, allow me," he said when the judge refused to turn the carpetbag loose.

"Do I know you, young man?" the judge said coldly, hanging on to the bag.

"Deputy Parley Stiles, Your Honor," Stiles said. "We met on your last trip through Gunn Point. I had just become Sheriff Goss's deputy."

"Yes, of course," the judge said, turning loose of the bag as he recognized Stiles. "To the hotel, Deputy." He nodded in the direction of the Gunn Point Hotel a half block away. "I mustn't tarry. The stage continues on to Whiskey Flats in three hours. I have time to eat, wash and rest at the hotel, then climb back inside that blasted rolling torture device. How is the sheriff?" he asked without pausing for a breath. "I received a wire that he had been shot in an attempted bank robbery?"

"Yes, that's true," Stiles said, stepping over toward the boardwalk, the judge right beside him. "It's a serious chest wound, Your Honor, but he appears to be holding up well so far."

The two walked along the boardwalk toward the hotel.

"I take it he's convalescing at Dr. Meadows'?" the judge asked sidelong, walking at a brisk pace.

"Yes, Your Honor, he is," said Stiles.

"Then I'll want to visit him first thing," said the judge. "Take my bag to the hotel. Tell the clerk I'll require my usual room for the next three hours."

"Yes, Your Honor," said Stiles. "I'll take care of all that. Once you've gotten settled into your room, you'll probably want to get with me and discuss how things are going here in Gunn Point."

The judge stopped in the middle of the boardwalk and stared at him.

"Is Sheriff Goss unable to speak, then?" he asked.

"No, Your Honor," said Stiles, "but he tires quickly and I'm the one who can tell you about the robbery incident and the prisoner I apprehended."

"Oh, you caught one of the felons?" the judge said, appearing impressed. "Good work, Deputy! Yes, perhaps I will want to talk to you. Please remain available until after I visit Sheriff Goss."

"Yes, Your Honor, I will," said Stiles. He left Judge Louder's side and walked into the lobby of the Gunn Point Hotel as the judge walked on toward the doctor's office.

Inside the convalescence room, Sheriff Goss and

Will Summers stopped talking and turned toward the door as Judge Louder and the doctor walked in.

"There he is, Your Honor," said Dr. Meadows. "Please don't wear him out."

"I'll try not to," said the judge, taking off his tall stovepipe hat. He gave the doctor a dismissing nod. The doctor took the hint and left the room as the judge walked over and stood looking down at the wounded sheriff.

"Howdy, Your Honor," said Goss, his voice still weak but improving, "I hope you haven't . . . cut something short."

"Nonsense, Turner," he said, calling his old friend by his first name. I was headed this way when I received the wire. I am en route to Whiskey Flats in three hours." He stooped down enough to put a hand on Goss' shoulder. "How are you, Sheriff?"

"I'm going to be all right, thanks," Goss said. "I'm glad you're here. We've had quite a stir of things." He shifted his eyes to Summers and asked the judge, "Do you know Will Summers, Your Honor?"

"The horse trader . . . ," the judge said. He looked Summers up and down appraisingly. "I'm familiar with the name, but I have not had the pleasure."

"Well, you have now," said Goss. He gestured a weak hand back and forth between the two. "Will here has agreed to be my deputy. He'll help Deputy Stiles until I . . . get back up and around."

The two exchanged a courteous nod.

"We're all obliged for your help, Will Summers," the judge said. "Were you here in Gunn Point when the bank robbery occurred?"

"No, Your Honor," Summers said. "I crossed paths

with the robbers while they were making their get-away. Their leader shot one of my horses."

"I see," the judge said.

"Will here foiled their plans," Goss said, all the talking starting to weaken him again. "He killed one, wounded another one—shot another one's ear off." He chuckled and coughed. "The one he wounded is in jail right now. I hope you'll try him right away, get him off my town's expenses."

"I'll try him as soon as I return here from Whiskey Flats," said the judge. Is he the one your other deputy captured?" he asked. "He was just telling me about it on the way to the hotel."

Summers and Goss looked at each other.

"Deputy Stiles didn't capture anybody, Your Honor," Goss said. "Will Summers did."

"Oh, then perhaps I misunderstood," the judge said, even though he knew better. He looked at Summers, wanting to hear what he had to say about Stiles claiming to have captured the prisoner.

But Summers made no comment on the matter. Instead he said quietly, "There's a lot to be talked about, Your Honor."

"Indeed . . . ?" The judge looked at Sheriff Goss.

"I'm going to let Summers talk to you about it, Your Honor," said Sheriff Goss. "Since he is the man responsible for catching the prisoner and stopping the town from losing its money."

"Very well, then," said the judge, looking back at Will Summers. "After I've visited with my friend here, I look forward to hearing everything over a nice hot bowl of stew."

Inside the abandoned relay station at the edge of Gunn Point, Henry Grayson lay propped against a wall in a corner, holding a blanket wrapped tightly around him in addition to his winter riding duster. Still, he shivered out of control, his teeth chattering so violently that the bandage on the side of his head pulled loose and hung down his jaw. His black swollen ear lay exposed, its stitches oozing a mixture of blood and greenish puss.

Cole Langler stepped down the ladder from the lookout post above the roof and walked over to him. Looking down at the swollen, blackened ear, he made a face of disgust.

"It's getting to where I can smell it across the room," he said.

"D-d-d-don't you worry about it," Grayson said, shaking all over.

Langler gave a dark chuff of a laugh and shook his head.

"Are you going to die on me, Henry?" he said.

"N-n-no," said Grayson, keeping the shaking under control just long enough to reply. "I'm g-g-going to be all right."

"Like hell," said Langler. "Look at you. Your hands are shaking so bad you can't take a piss without jerking yourself off."

Grayson just stared at him coldly, clasping his shaking hands together to keep them under control.

"Lewis Fallon's ear is not working out for you," Langler said. "It's blacker than a crow's ass. You need me to slice it off of there before it's too late."

"St-stay aw-way from me, Cole," Grayson side. "This sh-shaking just comes and g-goes. It'll p-pass."

"Only thing that's going pass is you, Henry," Langler said. "I never should have sewed it on for you. All that talk about sewing ears on is malarkey."

"Th-they do it all th-the time," Grayson said, picking up the bottle of rye standing on the floor beside him. He uncorked the bottle shakily and managed to raise the bottle to his trembling lips and take a long drink. In a few seconds the shaking subsided a little, as it had been doing for a time when the whiskey washed through his system.

He relaxed and took a breath, and raised his fingertips to the black throbbing ear.

"Hurts too, don't it?" said Langler, seeming to enjoy Grayson's pain and malady. "All those times they sewed somebody's ear on, it was that person's own ear. All you've done is turned yourself into Frankenstein's monster."

Grayson took another long drink and stared at him. "If you thought all this, why'd you sew the damn thing on for me?"

Langler shrugged, reached for the bottle, took it and rounded his palm over the top before taking a drink.

"I expect you never know until you try," he said. He took a long swig of the rye and wiped his hand across his lips. "But now it's time I slice that puppy off there and we go on and *rerob* this blasted bank." He paused, then said, "If they ever open the damn bank, that is."

"Frankenstein's monster . . . ," Grayson said under his breath, his brow lowered in a dark, menacing expression. "That is one hell of a thing to call me."

"You bring things on yourself, Henry, when you do stupid things." He shook his head. "Wearing another man's ear. Whoever heard of such a thing?"

Grayson just stared at him, unable to think clearly for a moment. A string of saliva spilled slowly from his lower lip. For a moment he thought he saw two Cole Langlers standing there pointing and laughing at him.

No-good son of a bitch . . . , he said to himself.

Chapter 19

Will Summers and Judge Louder sat in a small side room of Gramm's Restaurant, the judge eating and listening, Summer sipping coffee and telling the judge everything that had happened during and after the attempted bank robbery. He told him about Little Jackie Warren robbing his own father's bank; about the stolen money being counterfeit; about the death of the bank manager, Bob Harper; and about Stiles saying Warren denied ever receiving the stolen money before Harper died. When he had finished, he sipped his coffee and watched Judge Louder's face as the judge ran all the particulars back and forth in his mind.

"You have the length of rein?" He reiterated what Summers had mentioned early on in the conversation.

"Yes, I do," Summers said, realizing even as he did so that the length of cut leather rein meant nothing.

"And you have the receipt pad with Warren's signature on it even through Deputy Stiles says Warren denies having received the stolen counterfeit money?"

"Yes, I do," Summers said, but he had a feeling the

judge saw no evidence worth trying to bring a charge against Warren or Stiles, either one.

The judge fell silent for a moment.

"This is a very tricky legal situation, Deputy," he said at length. "You have a rich wealth of circumstantial evidence, but no hard proof that links anyone to anything that has happened." He shrugged. "The bank was robbed. But was Jack Warren involved in some conspiracy to rob his bank partner's share of their partnership?" He shook his head. "I'm afraid that would be most difficult to prove based on what you've told me. At best, I'm afraid all you have are suspicions. Accurate though they may be, they will not support bringing Jack Warren or his alleged accomplices before my bench."

"I see," Summers said. "So, even though everything points to Stiles and Warren being involved in robbery and murder, unless they decided to come out and admit to it, they'll never be brought to justice."

"Such is the world of courtroom law, Will Summers," the judge said. He sighed and added, "And I must tell you, I prefer this kind of law—that lets the guilty go free—to the risk of seeing the innocent punished."

"I have to agree, Your Honor," Summers said grudgingly. "It's just hard to swallow when you see this happen and know there'll never be anyone made to pay for this whole crooked incident."

The judge nodded and sipped the last of his coffee.

"What about Avrial Rochenbach?" Summers said. "I promised him I'd talk to you on his behalf. He gave me Roe Pindigo's name as the man who set him up with the bank robbers."

"Avrial Rochenbach is a sad case," said the judge. "The truth be known, he spent too much time living and working in the lairs of the criminal. I'm afraid it caused him to go wrong."

"Nothing you can do for him, then?" Summers asked.

"I'm afraid not," said the judge, "other than provide him a fair trail when I return. He *did* rob a bank. He shares responsibility for Sheriff Goss' injury even though he's not the one who pulled the trigger."

"I understand," said Summers in a resigned tone. "I told him I'd speak to you about him, and now I have." He sipped the last of his coffee.

The judge eyed him closely. "I have to say, Deputy, you're taking all of this very well. I've had men curse *me*, the court and God Almighty because the law doesn't view things the way they think it should. You appear to have given up far too easily." He grinned.

"I'm not a lawman, Your Honor. I'm nothing but a horse trader," said Summers. "I'm not familiar with the law or how these things are handled. If this is how the legal game is played, I'm not the one to try to change it." He stood up and laid a gold coin on the table for both their meals.

"Thank you for the food and the lively conversation," the judge said. "I wish more people looked at legal matters as philosophically as you do, Will Summers. It would make life easier for everyone concerned."

"I suppose I got caught up in wanting to see justice done," Summers said. "This is my first time ever carrying a badge." He patted his shirt pocket where he'd put the deputy badge.

"May I ask why you're *carrying* a badge and not *wearing* it?" the judge asked as he and Summers walked out onto the street in the chilled afternoon air.

"Sheriff Goss hasn't sworn me in yet, Your Honor,"

Summers said. "He said it was all right for now, but I still felt strange wearing it without being sworn in officially."

"How honorable of you, sir," the judge said. "It is important to keep with tradition in these matters. Be sure and have Sheriff Goss take care of it as soon as he's able. I would do it myself, but it is actually his responsibility, being the sheriff."

"Thanks, Your Honor. I'll see that he does it first thing," Summers said.

They walked on, Summers' Winchester hanging in his right hand. "Is Jack Warren going to try to kill you?" the judge asked.

"Yes, he will," Summers said. "It's just a matter of when. If it wasn't for staying and helping the sheriff, I would already be gone. I need to get my string to Whiskey Flats before the weather turns bad."

"What if I sent some territorial lawmen I trust to watch about Gunn Point? Would that free you up to leave and take care of your business?"

"Good men?" Summers asked.

"The best," the judge said. "I'll handpick them."

"How soon?" Summers asked.

"I'll wire them from Whiskey Flats tomorrow. They can be here tomorrow night, from Camp August."

"I'd be obliged, Your Honor," said Summers. "Why didn't the sheriff ask you to do that to begin with?"

"He's too weak to be thinking straight yet," said the judge, "else he would have." He adjusted the collar on his coat and said, "Consider it done."

"Do me a favor, Judge," Summers said. "Keep this between you and me?"

"Absolutely," the judge said.

They walked on.

But before they turned in to the front door of Gunn Point Hotel, a long, terrible yell resounded out along the nearly empty street as gunfire exploded from the edge of town.

"My *Lord*!" Judge Louder shouted, seeing a rider burst onto the street from the direction of the old relay station and come thundering down the street toward him firing a big Colt in every direction. Townsfolk flung themselves out of the rider's way. Buggies, wagons and saddle horses swerved off the street. Atop the charging horse sat Henry Grayson, wild-eyed, hatless, naked behind a flapping overcoat thrown open down the front.

"Get down, Your Honor!" Summers shouted, grabbing the judge with his left hand and pulling him behind the cover of a post as bullets sliced through the air past the judge's tall top hat.

As Summers stepped away from the judge and dropped onto one knee to take aim, he saw a large round object draw back in Grayson's hand as the gunman spun his horse and charged straight at the front of the bank building. With a loud scream, Grayson jerked his horse to a halt long enough to hurl Cole Langler's severed head through the large glass window, knocking out frame, curtains, flower pot and all.

"*I am the monster!*" Grayson bellowed and sobbed. "*I am the monster!*"

A woman screamed shrilly as Grayson turned his horse back to the street and charged on toward Summers.

Summers took his time as bullets whistled through the air. He placed his shot in the center of Grayson's naked, hairy chest and squeezed the trigger.

"I am the monster of Franken—" Grayson's voice stopped midscream.

From behind the thick post, Judge Louder stared in awe as the shot exploded from the Winchester and Henry Grayson rose into the air above his galloping horse like some large bird spread-winged, ready for flight. Only instead of flying upward, Grayson flew backward, turning a terrible naked somersault. His coat flared wide open; his horse stumbled in the commotion and bowed and fell and rolled in the middle of the street in a cloud of dust and snow.

From the sheriff's office Stiles came running, shotgun in hand. He slowed down as he approached the body lying naked in the street. Summers ran forward from the other direction and stopped and stood on the other side of the naked, bloody body, the overcoat twisted and bunched at Grayson's shoulders. A few yards away, Grayson's horse rolled itself upright and shook itself off.

"What happened, Summers?" Stiles asked, his finger on the shotgun's triggers, both hammers cocked and ready to fire.

"Turn that scattergun away from me, Stiles," Summers said firmly.

"For God's sake, Summers," Stiles said, "I'm not pointing it at you—" He heard the Winchester's hammer cock; quickly he turned the shotgun away from Summers. "All right, there, satisfied?"

Summers stepped forward and looked down at Grayson, seeing the gaping bullet hole in the dead man's chest. He saw the blackened stitched-on ear and remembered Lewis Fallon being short an ear the night the three had tried to ambush him and Cherry in the old mine camp.

"Jesus . . . ," Summers said. He shook his head in disbelief.

"What's wrong?" Stiles asked.

"It's one of the three men who tried to kill Cherry and me," Summers said to Stiles. "The one whose ear I shot off the day of the robbery."

Stiles stepped in closer and looked down at the naked, hairy body. The smell of whiskey and putrid flesh wafted upward to the two deputies.

"His name is Henry Grayson," he said. "What about that ear?"

"As crazy as this sounds, I believe he cut the ear off the other man I shot and had it sewn on him," Summers said.

Stiles looked stunned and amazed.

"Does something like that work?" he asked.

"I'm not the one to ask," said Summers, "but I don't think so. Look at it. No wonder he come charging up the street wild drunk and loco. He must've been out of his mind."

"He threw something through the bank window," Stiles said. "Did you see what it was?"

They looked over to where townsmen stood looking down inside the broken bank window.

"It looked like a head to me," Summers said as the judge walked up and stood beside him, staring down at the body and its black infected ear.

"My, my," the judge said, "I'm glad I'm only here for a stage stop, this trip. It looks like Gunn Point is going through some harsh and peculiar times." He gave Summers a look.

"Come along, Judge," Summers said, "I'll walk you to the hotel."

"I'll get some townsmen to drag Grayson out of the street," Stiles said.

On the way to the hotel, the judge swerved away from the front of the bank where a gathering of men still stood staring in at the floor through the broken window. Off to the side, Eric Holt stood scribbling away in his notepad. When he looked up and saw the judge with Summers, he stopped writing and walked toward them quickly. But the judge held a hand up, stopping him from even getting close.

"Summers, if there's going to be animosity between you and the other deputy," the judge said, "are you going to be all right here until help arrives?"

"I'll be all right, Your Honor," Summers replied. "I told the sheriff I would stay and help out for a while. That's what I'll do until your help arrives. If the law needs to question Jack Warren, Deputy Stiles or anybody else about the incident that happened here, I'll leave that to Sheriff Goss when he's feeling better."

"Good for you," the judge said. "Sometimes the law does not appear to be working, yet over time it always manages to sort itself out some way." He looked at Summers intently. "I hope you will take satisfaction in believing that."

"Yes, Your Honor, I will," Summers said. He wasn't going to say what he really thought about the law and how it always seemed to work best for men like Jack Warren who always had a way of breaking it without being seen or caught.

At the door to the hotel, Summers tipped his hat to the judge and watched him walk inside the door. When he turned to walk back toward the sheriff's office, he saw five horsemen riding slowly up the street toward the bank. This would be Roe Pindigo and some other Jack Warren gunmen, he thought. *Here we go. . . .*

By the time he'd walked to the front of the bank, the five men had stepped down from their horses at the hitch rail, walked up onto the boardwalk to the broken window and looked inside.

"Why is a head lying in the middle of the floor?" Roe Pindigo asked loudly enough for his men and the townsmen to hear him.

Stiles hurried up from the direction of the sheriff's office.

"There you are, Roe—I mean Mr. Pindigo," he said, correcting himself.

Pindigo turned a flat, curious look to him and asked again in a more demanding tone, "Why is there a head lying on the floor of Mr. Warren's bank, Deputy? Is there no law and order in this town?"

The four gunmen chuckled and watched.

"We had a shoot-out here just a little while ago," said Stiles. He gestured toward the blood lying in the middle of the street. "A fellow named Henry Grayson went loco, started shooting up the town. He ended up throwing the head through the window."

"Henry Grayson . . ." Pindigo feigned contemplation. "Now, where I do I know that name from?" He gave his men a knowing look. They chuckled and smiled and shared their private little joke.

Not only did they break the law, but now this one flaunted doing it, Summers told himself. *All right, take it easy . . .* , he warned himself. He'd done his duty; he'd reported everything to the law. *The law isn't going to do anything. . . .* He needed to get through one more day here until the judge's men arrived. Once he knew the sheriff was safe, he would take his horses and be away from here, he told himself.

"Who shot this Henry Grayson?" Pindigo asked.

"I did," Summers said, not wanting Stiles to speak for him. He took a step forward, his right hand wrapped around the small of the Winchester's stock for a fast upswing if he needed it.

"Well, well," said Pindigo, turning and looking him up and down, "Let me guess." He gave a flat, humorless smile. "You must be Will Summers."

"I am," Summers said. He glanced past Pindigo and inside the bank, seeing a large portrait of whom he could only surmise to be Jack Warren on the wall.

The gunmen bristled at the sound of Summers' name, at the sight of him. They stood facing him, their gun hands poised and ready. Townsmen spread in a wider circle and backed away. Some took cover; others ducked away into alleys and open doorways.

"Easy, boys," Roe Pindigo said under his breath. "If I wanted him dead, he'd be sucking dirt right now."

Summers stood returning Pindigo's hard stare.

Pindigo let out a breath and shook his head a little.

"You've got guts, horse trader, I'll give you that," he said. "I figured once you heard these boys and I were coming to reopen Jack Warren's bank, you'd skin on out of here."

Stiles cut in, saying, "I told you, he's a deputy, like me," he said.

"So you did," said Pindigo to Stiles without taking his eyes off Will Summers. "Let me ask you something, Summers. Does that mean you're bulletproof?"

Summer didn't wait for a second threat. Without

answering and without hesitation, his Winchester came up from his side, cocked, pointed at Pindigo's chest.

The gunmen tensed, but held themselves in check.

"Whoa! Hold on!" Pindigo's hand came away from his Colt and spread toward the men as if to hold them all in place.

Summers just stared and said nothing, his trigger finger ready to set things into action. What was there to say? Pindigo knew this same Winchester had killed Little Jackie, Lewis Fallon, Bert Phelps. . . . If Pindigo wasn't certain he would kill him by now, Summers thought, this was a good time to remove any doubt.

"What's gotten into him?" Pindigo asked Stiles, seeing there would be no talking to Summers.

"He didn't like that bulletproof remark," Stiles said in a low, even tone, worried himself about where he stood if Summers started dropping the hammer. "Right, Summers?" he ventured.

Summers still didn't answer. Both Pindigo and Stiles had shown there was room to defuse this situation. But Summers didn't jump at it right away.

"Judge Louder is in town," Stiles said to Pindigo, hoping to stop things from going any further. "He will be until this afternoon."

"Really, you say?" Pindigo kept his eyes on Summers as he grinned and spoke to Stiles, his hand still away from his Colt. "Well, we can't have His Honor thinking we're a bunch of pinch-necked gunslingers, now, can we?"

Summers offered nothing.

"Damn, what else can I say?" said Pindigo, starting to wonder himself if he would end the day with a big Winchester slug through his belly. "If you'll ease that hammer down, horse trader, I'm willing to start all over, like this never happened."

"Summers, let it go," Stiles said. "Either way it spins, you know you won't walk away. Think about Goss. He needs our help, both of us."

Summers waited for another tense moment; then he lowered the rifle and saw Roe Pindigo breathe a little easier.

"All right, now that that's over with, let me advise you of something, horse trader," Pindigo said, needing to save face with his men. "I'm going to be managing this bank until Jack Warren says otherwise." He looked at one of the men and said, "Dade, bring the money up here." He stood staring at Summers as a gunman named Dade Frawley walked to Pindigo's horse and came back carrying two large canvas bank bags.

"See?" Stiles said to Summers, but loud enough for the townsmen to hear him. "Mr. Warren is reopening the bank!" In a lower tone he said to Summers, "It's good U.S. currency. Check it for yourself."

Pindigo took both bags of money in one hand.

"Let's get this head cleaned up and this window fixed," he said to his men. "This bank is open for business."

Applause rippled along the street.

But before his men made a move, Pindigo pointed a gloved finger at Summers and said beneath a narrowed brow, "You ever point a gun at me or any of my men here again, you better use it right off."

Summers looked him up and down.

"I will," he said flatly. "You've got my word."

Chapter 20

Summers left Stiles, Pindigo and his gunmen at the bank and walked to the sheriff's office. Inside, Danny Kindrick stood up behind the battered desk with a cleaning rod in his hand and a rifle broken down on a cloth spread in front of him.

"I saw you shoot that man!" Danny said, having looked out at the first sound of gunfire. "I would have been there, except Deputy Stiles says this prisoner is not to be left alone again."

"I understand, Danny," said Summers. "If you need to visit the jake, go ahead. I'm going to talk to Rochenbach."

"Thank you, Deputy," Danny said, wasting no time coming around from behind the desk and heading out the door. "I won't be a minute."

"Take your time," Summers said.

As the door closed behind the young hostler, Summers walked back to Rochenbach's cell and found the prisoner standing at the bars waiting for him.

"What was all the shooting?" Rochenbach asked.

"Henry Grayson rode in shooting," said Summers. "Threw a head through the bank window and charged down the street at the judge and me."

"A *head*?" said Rochenbach.

"Yep," said Summers.

"And you stopped his clock?" Rochenbach said.

"On the hour," said Summers.

"Did you get to talk to the judge?" Rochenbach asked.

"I did," Summers said. "He says no deal."

Rochenbach hung his head and shook it slowly.

"Then I'm sunk," he said.

Summers gave him a moment of silence.

After that moment of pause, Rochenbach looked back up at Summers and said, "All the same, I'm obliged to you for trying."

"I wish I could have done you some good," Summers said, "even though you did rob a bank. This whole thing doesn't set well with me. Warren sets up his own bank to be robbed, and even double-crosses his robbers by sending them away with counterfeit money. Since it was his bank he had you robbing, it makes me wonder if you should even be in jail for it."

"It's always this way when a rich man like Warren breaks the law. They set it up in a way it's hard to tell the good guys from the bad," Rochenbach said. "If the law gets too close, his next step will be to stick a lawyer between himself and justice."

"I have to admit it makes me question the *right and wrong* of things," said Summers. "I'd have a hard time sending anybody to jail for it, except Warren himself."

"I like the way you're looking at it," Rochenbach said. "I just wish I could sell it to a jury."

"It appears the law works a lot different than I expected it would," Summers said.

Rochenbach said, "You're used to seeing how the law works among everyday folks like yourself. It works fast and simple. But this is law among the wealthy. The law gets more complicated, harder to understand when you throw money and influence into the mix. That's the main thing I learned in my line of work," he said bitterly.

"I hate disappointing you, Rock," Summers said.

"You didn't disappoint me too bad, Will Summers," he said. "I prepared myself for it when you said you wouldn't step outside the law even to seek justice. Folks like Jack Warren have moved up past *legal justice*. They own *legal justice*. It's what they use to protect themselves from the rest of us. Jack Warren can buy a bank. Think about that."

"I have," said Summers, "and it sticks in my craw. It sticks so bad, I have to step away from it. It's not something I want to think about too much. I don't like how it makes me feel."

Rochenbach took a breath and settled down.

"You're right not wanting to think too much about it," he said. "If you think on it too long and hard, it can turn you into an outlaw." He gave him a tired smile. "Sometimes I feel like that's what it's done to me."

"Are you and me square?" Summers asked, not even knowing why it mattered so much what this bank robber thought of him.

"We're as square as we can be," said Rochenbach. "I think you kept me from hanging. That has to be worth something. A man hates to think he spent his life working for the law and the thanks he gets is to end up swinging from a rope." He stared at Summers.

"Come on, Rock," Summers said, refusing to feel too sorry for him, "nobody made you throw in with these men and rob the bank. That was your choice."

Rochenbach let out a breath.

"Yes, you're right," he said. "I saw the trail I was taking before I started this journey."

"All right. It's best that you're able to look at it that way," Summers said.

"I have no choice," Rochenbach said. "Maybe I'll learn a new craft in prison, something besides working undercover," he added wryly.

Summers said, "I almost wish I had believed you when you told me you were working undercover."

"It's still not too late," Rochenbach said. "All you've got to do is unlock this cell and slip me out the back door."

"Nice try *again*," Summers said. "But I am working for the law."

"And we've both just discussed the kind of law it is," Rochenbach said.

"Yes, we did," Summers said, "but I can't turn away from it that easy. I gave my word. I'm Sheriff Goss' deputy."

"Yet I don't see a badge," Rochenbach said. "Have you taken your oath?"

"Stop it, Rock," Summers said. He turned to walk away.

"No, wait. Hear me out!" Rochenbach said, sounding desperate. He reached his good arm out through the bars as if to stop him.

"I'm through with it, Rock," Summers said, hearing Danny Kindrick walk back inside and close the front door behind himself.

Rochenbach slumped against the bars and watched Summers walk away.

In the afternoon shadows, Summers stood at Judge Louder's side and tossed his carpetbag up to the shot-gun rider who stood tying down cargo atop the big Studebaker coach. Down the street in front of the bank, Summers saw three of Pindigo's men lounging against the front of the bank building as if it were a saloon. The judge saw the look on Summers' face as he stared toward the men.

"It should console you to know that Sheriff Goss places great store in you as an honest, levelheaded man. And having met you and discussed the incident that occurred here, I must say, I agree with him." He smiled. "I have to say I'm surprised to know that you're a horse trader."

"Why is that, Your Honor?" Summers asked.

"Oh, you know, the way horse traders are publicly denounced and maligned." He smiled. "As outsiders we tend to only see the unsavory side of your occupation."

Summers nodded slightly.

"I suppose the same can be said of most any occupation, Your Honor," he said.

"Indeed it may," the judge replied, not catching any reference Summers implied. "At any rate, Sheriff Goss and I share a high opinion of you."

"Thank you, Your Honor," Summers said. "Good of you to say so."

"I hope at some time in the future, you'll consider pursuing a career in law enforcement. There's room for a man like you."

"I'm a horse trader, Your Honor," Summers said. "I doubt I'll ever be anything else." He wouldn't say what he felt like saying, that after hearing how difficult it was to bring felons like Warren to justice, he wanted nothing to do with it.

They stopped talking as Deputy Stiles walked up to them from the direction of the sheriff's office.

"Your Honor," he said, touching his fingers to his hat brim. "I'm sorry we never got the chance to talk while you were here."

"I'll be back in two weeks or less," the judge said curtly. "I'm sure we will find time then."

"Yes, I hope so," Stiles said, cutting Summers a glance, seeing the flat stare he received from him.

From atop the coach the shotgun rider stood among the secured cargo and looked down from above over his rounded belly.

"Judge, climb aboard and hold on to your teeth, we are *de-parting*," he said with a wide grin. He weaved through and over the cargo and plopped down in his seat beside the driver.

"God help me . . . ," Judge Louder murmured with a look of dread on his face.

Summers opened the stagecoach door and the judge stepped inside and plopped back into his seat. Dust puffed up around him. He fanned at it with a handkerchief.

He said with a cough, "You two take good care of the sheriff." He gave Summers a reassuring look. But the look was cut short as the driver slapped a whip above the horses and sent them forward with a hard jolt. The judge rocked forward like a limp scarecrow, almost leaving the dusty seat. His tall hat flew off his head.

"Hang on, Judge," the shotgun rider shouted down to him, a short-barreled shotgun wagging in his hand.

"Damn it to hell!" Judge Louder cursed as he slammed back into his seat and was gone in a rise of snow and dust.

Before the stage was even out of sight, Stiles looked up along the street at the men out in front of the bank. Then he turned to Summers.

"This will come as a surprise to you, Summers," he said, already sounding more sure of himself, "but I'm going to the town council when they meet in two days. I'm asking to be made sheriff until such time as the doctor says Sheriff Goss is able to handle his job."

"That comes as no surprise," Summers replied. "I'm only surprised that you've waited this long to do it."

Stiles ignored the remark.

"It needs to be done and we both know it," he said. "And if Sheriff Goss never gets better at all, Gunn Point still needs a sheriff."

"I understand," Summers said, knowing that in spite of the low opinion he had of Stiles, he was right about the town needing a sheriff.

"There's room for you too, Summers," Stiles said. "As sheriff I'll need myself a deputy. We both know you'd make a good one."

"What about when Warren and his men come to kill me, Deputy? Are you going to side with me, help me shoot it out with them?"

"I'm convinced that if you're my deputy, I can keep Warren from wanting to kill you," he said.

"You think so?" Summers said, just seeing how far Stiles wanted to go with this. Summers knew he was lying. When the time came to draw sides, Stiles would leap into Jack Warren's arms like a trained monkey.

"I don't *think* so, Summers. I *know* so," said Stiles.

"If I thought you were right . . . ," Summers said, wanting to sound a little swayed.

"I am right," Stiles said. He lowered his voice to a guarded tone. "Can you imagine how well two men like us could do running a place like Gunn Point? A year from now this town will be twice its size—three times more saloons, more gambling, more whoring. Somebody is going to run it. Why not me, who not you running it *with me*? You and I shouldn't be against each other. We should be working together."

Summers appeared to be considering it.

"I have heard worse ideas," he said. "This town could also be dried up and gone a year from now."

"All the more reason to take what's here while the taking's good," Stiles said.

"Give me a day to think it over?" Summers asked. He didn't trust a word Stiles had said. But he would buy whatever time he could to keep his word to Goss until the judge sent help. Once the territorial lawmen arrived, he would gather his horse and his string and ride away.

"Sure, think it over," said Stiles, "but let me know soon. It's time I move forward on this."

Summers touched his hat brim, turned and walked away.

Chapter 21

In the night, in the back room of the darkened bank, Roe Pindigo and two of his four gunmen sat drinking and dealing cards at a round wooden table. Dim light from an oil lamp flickered on their faces. The other two gunmen, Dade Frawley and a young Texan named Rudy Purser, had left through the rear door only a moment earlier.

Across the table from Pindigo, a gunman named Delbert Sweeney threw his cards onto the table in disgust.

"That's it for me," he said. "I've been throwing good money after bad all night." He looked all around the stockroom, at shelves stacked with flat folded bank bags, stacks of paperwork and a gem and gold scale. "I never figured I'd ever see myself in a bank, playing poker. I feel out of place here without a mask on my face and a gun in my hand."

"You can wear your mask, if it makes you happy," said a lanky gunman named Lyle Fisk, studying his cards. "We all have our peculiarities."

Pindigo chuckled.

"Stick with me, Delbert," he said. "Who knows? Someday I might own this bank instead of just managing it for Big Jack."

"I expect the only way you'd ever get this bank away from Big Jack is to kill him for it," said Fisk.

"So?" said Pindigo. "Nothing wrong with that." He grinned, with a shrug of his shoulders. "This is the land of *opportunity*—a man does what he has to do to get what he wants. If it takes a killing or two, that's just the cost of doing business." He laid his cards down faceup. "Three lovely ladies," he said.

"Damn it!" said Lyle Fisk. "I would've sworn you were bluffing." He threw his cards down and reached for the bottle of rye standing midtable.

Pindigo chuckled and raked a small pile of cash and coin to him.

"Speaking of killing," said Sweeney, "why didn't you send me along with Frawley instead of Rudy?"

"Rudy likes that kind of work," said Pindigo.

"So do I," said Sweeney.

"No," said Pindigo, "you *do it*. But you don't *enjoy* it. Leastwise not the way Rudy does." He grinned. "Besides, I wanted you here where I can take all your money."

"I've got five dollars says Rochenbach didn't tell the horse trader anything," said Sweeney.

"Why do you say that?" Pindigo asked.

"Rock ain't the kind of man who'll tell anybody a damn thing," said Sweeney. "He might have been a Pinkerton at one time. But he's a hard case now. He didn't say nothing about you. It ain't his nature."

"*Rock*, is it . . . ? I didn't know you admired the man so much, Sweeney," said Pindigo.

"'That's not it," said Sweeney. "Whether I like him or not has got nothing to do with it. I got to know him some last year. He's not the kind of man who would jackpot a fellow. That's all I'm saying."

"We'll know before long," said Pindigo. "If he did mention my name to the horse trader or anybody else, Rudy and Frawley will get it out of him."

"So, is it a bet?" Sweeney asked.

"No, it's not," said Pindigo. "That's me betting against my own interest. "I'm hoping he *didn't* tell anybody I put him in touch with the others on the bank job. Why would I bet good money that he did?"

"Just for sport," Sweeney said. He shrugged and reached for the bottle of rye.

"After tonight he's never going to tell anybody *anything* ever again," Pindigo said with a dark chuckle. "Now, there's something I'll bet on."

"No," said Sweeney, "I'm out of the notion now."

"That's what I figured," Pindigo said, shuffling the deck of cards in front of him. He looked back and forth between the two. "Either one care to double the ante?"

"Dang," said Fisk, "now you're out for blood."

"Have you ever seen me when I wasn't?" Pindigo spread a thin, sinister grin in the shadowy lamplight.

Inside his cell, Avrial Rochenbach's eyes jumped open at the sound of the key turning inside the iron door lock. He stared at the dusty back wall two feet in front of him. They were here, he told himself. The waiting and wondering was over. He knew what came next.

"Wake up, wake up, you sleepy boyo," Dade Frawley said in the mock voice of an Irish minstrel.

"On your feet, you son of a bitch," Rudy Purser said,

more direct and to the point. "We're going to take a little walk, the three of us."

Rochenbach rolled onto the edge of his cot and sat staring at him in the moonlight through the cell window. The welt across his forehead from Summers' rifle butt still throbbed when he first awakened. He cupped his good hand to it and squinted in the dim light.

"Where are we going?" he asked. But his question was a deft response, a learned skill from a lifetime of counter and query, all of it a means of staying alive—the odds of which looked awfully slim right now, he told himself.

"What do you care?" said Rudy Purser, a hard-boned gunman with thick red curly hair springing from beneath his hat brim. A bristly red beard covered his face to within an inch of his eyes. "You'll know when we get there."

"It's not far," said Frawley. He pitched a pair of handcuffs onto the cot beside Rochenbach. "Put these on one wrist," he instructed.

Rochenbach looked at the cuffs, then picked them up, turning his gaze back to Frawley as he clamped one loosely around his left wrist, keeping his right hand free should he see a chance to save himself.

Frawley grinned, reached down and pulled him to his feet by the dangling handcuff. He reached around Rochenbach's left wrist and clamped the cuff down tighter.

"You're not the only one reads *Police Gazette*," he said. Jerking Rochenbach's right hand out and clamping the other cuff around his wrist, he yanked him toward the open cell door.

"Can't blame me for trying," Rochenbach said. He

glanced back over his shoulder on the way out of his cell. "What about a coat? It's awfully cold out there."

"Don't trouble yourself," said Rudy Purser. "You won't need it."

"So, this is it for me, eh, fellows?" Rochenbach said.

"That all depends on you," said Frawley, nudging the prisoner forward with his rifle barrel. "Rudy here is busting to know who you told about Roe Pindigo sending you to Grayson and the others, to rob the bank."

Rochenbach stopped at the rear door while Rudy stepped in front and opened it, keeping a shotgun he'd taken from the sheriff's gun rack tipped against Rochenbach's chest. On Rudy's hip behind his open coat, the bone handle of a bowie-style knife stood in a leather sheath.

Rochenbach's eyes went first to the knife, then darted away. He weighed his chances of making a play for the knife with his cuffed hands, swinging it around fast enough to slice Frawley's throat and keep turning until he planted its blade deep in Rudy Purser's chest. The opportunity was there, but only a brief second, and then it was gone as Rudy stepped outside ahead of him and to the side, the knife handle getting farther from Rochenbach's reach.

Damn it, now what? Rochenbach kept searching, weighing odds, his chances growing slimmer with each passing second.

"What if I said I didn't tell anybody?" he said.

"You'd be lying, right off." Rudy Purser grinned, standing waiting until Rochenbach was outside and in front of him. He touched the tip of the shotgun barrel between Rochenbach's shoulder blades and nudged him along the alley toward the livery barn.

"Rudy hates a liar worse than anything," Frawley threw in with a dark chuckle.

"Of course, if you still say the same thing after I carve a few parts off of you," said Rudy, "I might gain a whole new respect for you, start thinking, 'Hey, ol' Rock here is telling the truth.'"

They walked on toward the barn.

"But I'm dead either way, is that it?" said Rochenbach, keeping them talking, knowing the more they talked, the more chance he would find to do something, *anything,* he thought.

"Depends on what you call *dead,*" said Rudy.

Frawley gave another dark chuckle.

"Or on what you call *living,*" he said grimly.

At the barn, Rudy stepped forward, opened the door and watched as Frawley shoved Rochenbach forward with the tip of his rifle barrel.

"Right there'll do," said Rudy, motioning in the darkness toward a thick center post.

Frawley raised his rifle butt and slammed it into the back of Rochenbach's head, hard enough to stun and send him falling forward against the post. Rochenbach felt the world swirl around him. He struggled to remain conscious. But by the time he regained a grip on himself, Rudy had loosened his cuffs and recuffed his hands around the post.

Frawley stood three feet away from the downed prisoner. He touched a match to the wick of an oil lamp and hung it on the post above Rochenbach.

"Let's commence," said Rudy, stooping down beside Rochenbach as he jerked the big bowie knife from its sheath. He grabbed a handful of Rochenbach's disheveled hair and laid the sharp edge of the blade along the side of his nose. "Who knows that Pindigo put you in with the robbers?"

"Nobody! You can ask me an hour from now, you'll get the same answer. Or you can kill me right now, save yourself the trouble," Rochenbach said, his head throbbing front and back, the front from Summers' rifle butt, now the back from Frawley's.

Rudy looked up at Frawley and grinned in the glow of the lamp overhead.

"Why, it's no trouble at all," he said in a tone of feigning cordiality. To Frawley he said, "I vote for an hour from now. What about you?"

"I don't really care," said Frawley, "but I could use some shut-eye."

"Don't be a wet blanket—" said Rudy, his words stopping short as they both heard a rustle of hay coming from an empty stall.

"Who's there?" shouted Frawley, swinging his rifle around toward the stall. Rudy dropped the big knife and snatched the shotgun up from against the post. He stood up, cocking both hammers toward the stall.

"D-don't shoot, *please*!" Danny Kindrick stammered, standing in the grainy darkness, his arms straight up above his head.

"That damn idiot hostler!" said Frawley.

"What are you doing here, boy?" Rudy demanded, the shotgun butt to his shoulder, his finger over the triggers ready to fire both barrels.

"I—I live here," Danny said in a shaky voice.

"Not from now on, you don't," Rudy Purser said menacingly.

At the shotgun in Rudy's hands, Danny's eyes widened in terror.

"Oh my God" he said. "Don't pull that trigger! I beg you!"

"There goes our plan, Rudy," said Frawley. He turned his rifle away from Danny and back to Rochenbach lying on the ground. "You kill him . . . I'll kill this one. Let's call it a night." He took aim down at Rochenbach's head, just as Rochenbach had managed to get his cuffed right hand around the handle of the big knife.

Before Frawley had time to pull the trigger, both he and Rudy froze, hearing another rifle cock, this one just inside the barn door.

"Pitch it away, mister," Summers said in a low, determined tone.

But Frawley held his ground. He slid a sidelong look at Summers.

"When I make my move, take him down with me, Rudy," he said.

Rudy turned slowly with the shotgun.

"My God, mister, *please don't shoot!*" Danny said again to Rudy.

"Shut up, idiot!" said Rudy. "It's not pointing at you!"

"But *still*—" Danny said.

"Drop down, Danny!" Summers demanded, cutting him off.

Danny dropped like a rock.

Frawley still had his rifle aimed down at Rochenbach. He studied Summers coolly with his sidelong stare.

"Well, horse trader, you must not have heard what Pindigo said about the next time you pointed a gun at any of us."

"I heard *him*," Summers said. "Did you *hear me*?"

The Winchester bucked in Summers' hands; Dade

Frawley's head jerked sideways with the bullet's impact. The other side of his face burst open like an overripe melon.

Frawley's rifle flew from his hands as he spun a full circle, slammed into the post above Rochenbach and collapsed on him. Rochenbach scrambled upward, knife in hand, spitting blood, brain and bone matter.

As soon as Summers had fired, he'd swung the rifle toward Rudy Purser, who had taken a step forward with the shotgun aimed straight at him. In that split second Summers realized he was too late. He saw both shotgun hammers drop. He pulled the trigger on the Winchester as he clenched his teeth against the bite of oncoming death.

Summers saw both barrels blossom in a blue-orange belch of smoke and lead pellets. But instead of the explosions coming at him, they blew upward into Rudy Purser's face, all but skinning his face, hands and shoulders to bare bone. The shotgun, minus its twisted scraps of wire twist barrels, fell to the floor as Rudy screamed loud and long through a bloody, lipless, toothless hole of a mouth and staggered to where Rochenbach stood with the knife in his cuffed hand. With all of his strength, Rochenbach swung himself around the post and plunged the blade into Rudy's throat, silencing him.

Summers stood stunned for a moment. In the darkened stall, Danny Kindrick stood up slowly. He stared in horror at the half bone, half shredded meat that had become Rudy Purser's face.

"That was . . . *strange*," Summers said quietly, stepping over to the post where Rochenbach stood trying to wipe the gore off his face.

"I—I've got a handcuff key," Danny said, badly shaken. He hurried out of the stall, taking the key from his trouser pocket.

Summers took the key, unlocked Rochenbach's handcuffs and let them fall to the ground.

"I cleaned that shotgun today, and I broke a cleaning rod and cloth wad off in the barrel!" Danny said shakily. "I—I meant to tell somebody, but I forgot." He looked pleadingly at Summers and said, "I begged this man not to shoot it—but he wouldn't listen." He shook his head, staring down at Rudy Purser's mangled face. "Is—is Deputy Stiles going to be mad at me?"

"It's possible, Danny," Summers said. "Do you have kin near here?"

"Yeah, my ma and pa," said Danny. "They live about thirty miles out."

"Why don't you go visit them a few days?" said Summers, knowing this was going to be no place for the young man until things settled down. "I'll see what I can do to get things cleared up around here."

"Thanks, Mr. Summers," Danny said, already backing away toward the rear door. Before he stepped outside, he picked up a saddle and a set of reins and stopped and looked back when Summers called out to him.

"Danny?" Summers said. "From now on be more careful with firearms."

"You can bet I will," Danny said.

Rochenbach stood wiping his face on his shirttails.

"What brought you here, Summers?" he asked as the rear door closed behind the livery hostler.

Summers stared at him and said, "You were telling me the truth, you *are* working undercover."

Rochenbach stared back at him and let out a breath of relief.

"Thank God," he said. "I was afraid I was going to die undercover—leave here with everybody thinking I was a thief, like the rest of Jack Warren's men." He continued wiping his face. "What *finally* made you believe that I'm a lawman?"

"I don't know," Summers said. "I might've thought so sooner had you tried a little harder to convince me."

"I couldn't risk it. I was in a tight spot," Rochenbach said. "What if I had tried harder? What if the others believed it and you didn't? If they wanted me dead because I might have mentioned Pindigo's name, imagine what they would've done had they known I was a detective."

"I take your point," Summers said.

"I took a big chance trusting you at all, Summers," the detective said. "A man has to walk a fine line in this game, be careful who he talks to." He paused, then said, "I've got to ask you still to keep it a secret."

Summers shook his head. "I'm not certain yet that you are what you say you are," he said. "But I knew these men would have killed you the way things were going. If I'm wrong about you, I can live with it easier than if I let you die—always wonder if you really were a Pinkerton agent working undercover."

"So, what the judge told you about the law makes more sense when you look at it close up and more personal?"

"Yes, I suppose that's it," said Summers. He glanced in the direction of the main street. "You best get going before they come to see what the shooting was about."

"Two shots?" said Rochenbach. "They'll take their time, figuring it was these two killing me."

Summers noted how cool and calm he seemed to be now that he was free.

"What about you, Summers?" Rochenbach asked, stooping to take Frawley's bloody coat from his back and throwing it around himself. He hurriedly yanked Frawley's boots off and stepped into them and pulled them into place.

"I'm here until tomorrow," Summers said.

"Why tomorrow? Why not right now?" Rochenbach said.

"I gave Sheriff Goss my word," said Summers. "I won't leave him alone with Stiles and these snakes. Stiles wants his job. I suspect he tried to kill him, but I just can't say for sure. The judge is sending men here from Camp August. They'll get here tomorrow. Then I'm gone."

"Whatever you think is best, then," Rochenbach said. He jerked a big revolver from a holster on Frawley's hip, the same model as the Remington he had carried on the bank robbery. He checked it, then took the dead man's gun belt from around his waist and slung it over his shoulder.

Summers looked him up and down.

Rochenbach saw a look of doubt come into his eyes.

"Go ahead and ask one last time if it makes you feel better," he said.

"All right, I'm asking," Summers said, but he asked with his rifle hanging loosely in his hand. At this point Rochenbach knew Summers only wanted reassurance.

Letting out a breath, Rochenbach said, "I worked undercover so long and so deep that everybody knew who I was. So my new cover had to be that I was an undercover agent gone bad." He gave a short, wry smile. "It worked so well, nobody knows what I am anymore—sometimes I have to stop and remind myself."

"Okay, you best leave now, *Rock*," said Summers, seeming again satisfied with his decision.

"I'm gone, Will Summers," the blood-smeared detective said. But he paused and said, "Let me ask you a question. If I wasn't a Pinkerton agent working undercover, do you think I would admit it to you right here, right now?"

Summers chuffed and shook his head. He walked away from Rochenbach to gather his dapple gray and the string of horses from the stalls where they stood intently. The gunfire had spooked them, but they were settled now.

"Get out of here, *Detective Avrial Rochenbach*," he said over his shoulder. "You're making my brain hurt."

Chapter 22

———

Summers heard Rochenbach's horse's hooves pounding away along a trail leading off from behind the barn. Looking through a crack in the front door, he saw two townsmen, one in a nightshirt and an overcoat, walking toward the barn. The other one held a lantern up to light their way. As the men drew nearer, Summers walked to the rear door, gathered the reins and the lead rope, led his horses out the rear door and closed the door quietly behind them.

He walked the animals away from the barn, deeper into the moonlight, sticking to the alleyways and shadows until he got to the rear porch of the doctor's large clapboard house. On the way past the rear of the bank, he saw a lamp glowing in the back room, and knew it had to be Roe Pindigo and his men. Their horses stood at the rear hitch rail behind the building.

He hitched his horse out of sight behind the doctor's house and stepped up onto the doctor's back porch. Finding the back door unlocked, he slipped inside quietly. Instead of calling out and announcing himself so late at night, he eased along the hallway to the convalescence room. Seeing a faint glow of lamplight beneath the door, he eased the door open and looked over at the bed and saw both the sheriff and Flora Ingrim lying asleep beneath a large patch quilt.

Summers smiled to himself, stepped back silently out the door, closed it and knocked on it softly.

On his second knock, he heard the soft pat of house slippers walk across the room.

"Who's there?" Flora's voice said on the other side of the door.

"It's Will Summers, ma'am," Summers said just above a whisper. "May I come in?"

The door opened a few inches and the little housekeeper looked up at him.

"Sheriff Goss is asleep," she said.

"Yes, ma'am," said Summers. "I just wanted to make sure he's all right."

Seeing the concerned look on his face in the glow of the lamp she'd carried with her from the nightstand, she opened the door a little wider.

"He's all right," she whispered. "But I don't think I should wake him."

Summers started to speak. "Ma'am, I came by to make sure everything—"

But Sheriff Goss' sleepy voice cut him off.

"Will, is that you?" the sheriff asked, looking over from the bed.

"Come on in, then," Flora said. She closed the door when Summers stepped inside, and she followed him to the bed and set the lamp back down on the nightstand.

"Thank you, ma'am," Summers said.

"Don't wear him out," she said, patting Summers on the forearm as she turned away. "I'll just go back to my knitting." She gestured toward a chair where beside it a knitting basket sat on the floor.

"Sheriff, I didn't want to wake you, but I need to keep you abreast of what's going on here," Summers said down to Goss' sleepy, drawn face.

"I heard two shots a while ago," Goss said. "Is that why you're here?"

"It is, Sheriff," Summers said. He eased down on the side of the bed and whispered, "Avrial Rochenbach has escaped. Two of Warren's men took him to the barn and tried to kill him, but he got away."

The sheriff stared at him for a moment.

"Why are we whispering?" he asked.

"Because I'm not supposed to know it happened yet, Sheriff," Summers said. "Folks are just now going inside the barn, seeing what happened there."

"You smell like burnt powder," Goss said. "Are you all right?" He looked Will Summers up and down, knowing that whatever happened in the barn, Summers was there.

"I'm all right, Sheriff," Summers assured him. "But things are going to get lively here. I want to get you somewhere safe beforehand."

"How *lively* are we talking about?" Goss asked, studying Summers' face in the soft flicker of lamplight.

"I can't say, Sheriff," Summers replied. "But I don't want Warren and his men coming for you, to get to me."

"My place is only a few miles out on the south trail," he said.

"No," Summers replied, "everybody knows about it.

We need somewhere nobody would think to look for you."

Goss' eyes moved sidelong to where Flora sat knitting, then back to Summers.

"Flora, come over here, please," the sheriff said.

The little housekeeper padded over in her slippers, her knitting in hand.

"Deputy Summers needs to hide me out for a while. Can he take me over to your place?"

Flora looked a little shocked.

"Sheriff Goss, is that going to appear untoward?" Flora said.

"It'll be all right, Flora," Sheriff Goss said. He looked back up at Summers and said, "She and I have been what you call 'close' for some time now."

"Why, *Sheriff*!" Flora said, shocked.

"Cut out the pretense, Flora," Goss said. "If I know Will Summers, he's already figured as much." He looked at Summers questioningly.

"Sort of," Summers said, picturing the two beneath the quilt only a moment earlier.

"There, you see?" he said to Flora. "Now, can I stay there awhile or not?"

"Of course you can," Flora said with a sigh. "You know you've been welcome there all along. You've just been too stubborn to ask." She turned and walked back and sat down to her knitting.

"She lives just across the street." Sheriff Goss whispered to Summers, "I hate her cats. She only has one, but there must be a dozen hanging around."

"But nobody would think to look for you there?" Summers asked.

"No," he said confidently. Summers noted his voice

sounded stronger than it had since the shooting. "We're the best-kept secret in Gunn Point since Latimer Gunn got drunk at a Chicago zoo . . . and shot a baboon for shaking its genitalia at him."

"I see. Then we need to tell the doctor and get you on over to Flora's while it's dark out," Summers said.

"Where does Deputy Stiles stand in all this, Will?" Goss asked. "Tell me straight out," he added.

"He's with Warren's men, Sheriff," Summers said.

"That's too bad," the sheriff said, shaking his head. "I had come to put a lot of faith in that man."

"He wants your job, Sheriff," Summers said.

"That's only natural," said Goss. "A *good* deputy always wants to be sheriff." He gave a weak smile. "Don't you?"

"No, Sheriff, I don't," said Summers. "But Stiles wants it bad enough, I believe he would kill you for it."

Goss stared at him for a moment.

"Have you any proof of that, Will?" he asked.

"No," Summers said, "it's just a suspicion I've had since the day Cherry and I came back here with the counterfeit money."

"I think you're wrong," said the sheriff. "Stiles come by here making sure I had water to drink . . . fluffed up my pillow."

Water to drink . . . Summers thought about Stiles, the doctor and himself walking past the office and seeing the broken laudanum bottle on the floor. *What was it about that broken bottle . . . ? The way Stiles acted, the way he looked . . . ?*

He didn't know, but whatever it was, he'd have to think about it another time. Summers turned to Flora and said, "I'll carry him. Make sure the way is clear and I'll follow you to your place."

"I can walk that far if I have to, Will," said Sheriff Goss.

"I know you could, Sheriff," Summers said. "But not as fast as I can carry you."

"What's going on in here?" Dr. Meadows asked, stepping inside the room in a long, wrinkled nightshirt. He saw Summers stoop to pick the sheriff up in his arms. "Where are you going with my patient?" he demanded.

"I'm moving him, Doctor," said Summers. "He'll be across the street at Flora's."

"Whoa, you can't move him. There's a good chance you'll kill him packing him like a sack of feed!"

"There's a better chance he'll die if I leave him here, Doctor," Summers said.

"The street's all clear," Flora called out in a hushed tone from the front porch.

"Come with us, Doctor," Summers said. "I'll explain everything once we get to Flora's."

When Roe Pindigo, Delbert Sweeney and Lyle Fisk had waited a few minutes longer, they got up from the table and walked to the livery stable, where Deputy Stiles stood inside the open door looking at the two bodies lying sprawled on the dirt floor. Four townsmen had arrived and stood gathered at the doorway looking in at the carnage, lanterns in hand.

"Everybody out of my way," said Pindigo, shoving the men aside and walking through the door. Expecting to see Avrial Rochenbach's body, he jolted to a sudden stop when he saw Dade Frawley and what he could only guess had been Rudy Purser.

"Damn . . . ," said Fisk right behind Pindigo. "Is that Rudy?"

"Beats me," said Sweeney. "That's Rudy's knife sticking in his throat, whoever it is."

"It's Rudy, you jackass," Pindigo said. He looked at the exploded shotgun lying on the floor. "It looks like a shotgun blew up on him." He stepped in closer to Stiles and said between the two of them, "What the hell happened here? Where's Rochenbach?"

"From what I make of it, he's gone," Stiles said, staring straight ahead as he spoke, seeing Frawley's stockinged feet, noting that his coat was missing. "He's dressed for the trail, not for sticking around Gunn Point."

Noting Dade Frawley's missing gun and gun belt, Pindigo said, "He's armed himself with Dade's Remington."

"It looks like he walked through these two like they were warm butter," said Stiles. He kicked the pair of loose handcuffs lying on the ground.

"Watch your mouth, Deputy," Pindigo warned. "These two were pals of mine." He turned to Fisk and Sweeney. "Get out back, see if you can find any tracks."

"Jesus, Roe," said Fisk. "It's a livery barn. It's nothing but tracks."

"*Fresh tracks*, damn it! *Rochenbach's tracks!*" Pindigo shouted. "See if there's fresh tracks on this cold ground! I want that man's head on a stick."

The two looked at each other, knowing how useless it was going to be searching for a man like Rochenbach; but they walked out the back door and walked back and forth looking on the ground for tracks leaving the corral behind the barn.

Sweeney stopped looking. He took a short, slim cigar from his shirt pocket, lit it and blew out a stream of smoke.

"Slow down," he said to Lyle Fisk. "If we find his tracks, the next thing you know he's going to want us to follow them."

"So?" said Fisk.

"So I don't want to go traipsing around in the dark on a cold night, trying to catch a man who just left two other men dead on the ground—him in handcuffs as far as we know. Do you?"

"No, come to think of it," said Fisk, "not when we've got Big Jack Warren and his gunmen riding in come morning."

"There you have it," said Sweeney, blowing smoke into the chilled air.

"Here's fresh tracks," Fisk said suddenly. "Two sets in fact! One set goes out that way. The other heads south."

"Damn it," said Sweeney, "you couldn't leave well enough alone."

Roe Pindigo and Deputy Stiles stepped out through the rear door and looked at the two.

"You found two sets?" Pindigo asked.

Damn it . . . , Sweeney cursed to himself, upset that Pindigo had heard them talking. "Yes, we did, Roe," he said, sounding enthusiastic. "Which one you want us to follow?"

"Split up, follow them both," said Pindigo.

"One of them is probably the hostler, Danny Kindrick," said Stiles. "He sleeps in an empty stall here some nights. If he was in here and woke up and heard your men questioning Rochenbach, he could be trouble too."

"All right, damn it," Pindigo said to the two gunmen. "Ride them both down and kill them if you can. It'll be daylight here in a couple more hours. If you haven't spotted them by then, turn around and get on back here. I want you both in town when Big Jack shows up."

The two stared as Pindigo said to Stiles, "That damn horse trader has a hand in this somehow. I'd bet my hat on it."

"So would I," Stiles said, looking all around. "His horses are gone, but he's still in town somewhere. When are you going take care of Will Summers once and for all?" he asked.

"Never," said Pindigo. "Big Jack made it clear, Summers is all his."

"Even if he's behind this?" said Stiles.

"That's right," said Pindigo. "I don't care if he pisses in your hat. Leave him be. Warren is going to kill him soon enough."

He turned and walked back inside the livery barn. Stiles followed closely.

"See?" said Sweeney as soon as Stiles and Pindigo were out of sight. "Now we're stuck with two hours or more in the saddle, cold as it is."

They walked away, back toward the rear of the bank building where they had left their horses.

Inside the livery barn, Pindigo looked down at the two bodies again and kicked Frawley in anger.

"Let yourself get taken down by some half-ass former detective," he murmured to the sprawled corpse. "Shame on you!" he raged.

Stiles and the gathered townsmen stared stunned as Pindigo's Colt streaked out of its holster and fired shot after shot in Frawley's limp, bloody body.

"Easy, Mr. Pindigo," said Stiles, for the sake of the townsmen staring wide-eyed.

"To hell with these flatheads," Pindigo said toward the four townsmen, staring at them angrily, his Colt smoking in his hand.

"Uh-oh, gentlemen," Richard Woods said under his breath to the other three townsmen. "We need to make ourselves scarce here."

He backed his way out the barn door, followed by the druggist, Martin Heintz, Jason Jones, the surveyor, and the telegraph clerk, Charlie Stuart. Once outside the livery barn, the four hurried farther away, then slowed to a walk and finally stopped twenty yards away.

"*Holy God!*" said Heintz, gasping to catch his breath. "What have we gotten ourselves into!"

"This man is dangerous," said Stuart. "Warren must have been out of his mind making him bank manager."

"Gentlemen, what are we going to do?" said Woods. "I depend on that bank to keep my business going. My money is in there. I'd be afraid to ask for my own money with a man like this sitting in the manager's chair."

Charlie Stuart said, "I'm wiring Leland Sutter, letting him know what kind of man Warren has put in charge here. I'll tell him I speak for all of us."

"You do that, Charlie," said Jones. "But for God's sake, keep quiet about it."

"What do we do until we hear something from Sutter?" Heintz asked.

"I don't know about the rest of you," said Woods. "I plan on just running my store, keeping my mouth shut and otherwise lying low and staying off the streets for a while."

"Good thinking," said Jones. "We need to spread the word, tell everyone to lie low as much as possible—stay away from the bank as long as this madman is running it."

"Where is Jack Warren anyway?" said Stuart. "He needs to show his face here."

Chapter 23

Delbert Sweeney had caught a glimpse of Avrial Rochenbach as Rochenbach left the flatlands and rode up into the hills in the gray morning light.

Yep, that was Rock all right, he told himself.

He had followed the set of tracks leading out across the flatlands all the way to the distant hill line. After spotting Rochenbach, he stayed on the tracks, seeing them run straight and long—a horse moving purposefully. But this last mile, the horse had slowed, its pace had broken and its direction swayed away toward a dry wash lined with dried wild grass.

You must be falling off your game, Rock, he thought.

Had he stopped to graze his horse? Sweeney asked himself, stepping down from his saddle fifty feet from the edge of the wash and sliding his Spencer rifle from its boot. Warily, he followed the stretch of hoofprints to the edge of the wash and looked down.

"I'll be damned," he murmured, seeing the horse standing alone, bareback in the wash, and instead of wearing a bridle, with a short lead rope circling its muzzle. The animal chewed on a mouthful of wild grass. Sweeney sighed in resignation and tossed his rifle over onto the ground. Raising his hands chest high, he said over his shoulder, "Don't shoot, Rock. I'm all in."

Behind him, Rochenbach reached out and slipped Sweeney's Colt Thunderer from its holster. Sweeney flinched each time he heard Rochenbach click the chamber in his free hand.

"Are you going to shoot me with my own gun?" he asked nervously.

Rochenbach uncocked the Colt and shoved it down behind his belt without answering. He took Sweeney's hat from atop his head and put it on, feeling the warm of it on his cold forehead.

"Let me ask you something, Del," he said amiably, stepping around in front of the gunman. "Did you ever find out the name for me?"

"Damn, Rock," said Sweeney, "that was over a year ago you asked me that."

"So?" said Rochenbach.

"So you show up behind me with a gun in my back and act like it's something we talked about ten minutes ago," Sweeney said. "Give a man a chance to collect himself."

"Sorry, Del, but time has been running tight for me lately," Rochenbach said. "Did you find out where Warren got the counterfeit money, or not?"

"Listen, Rock, I ain't even supposed to know about any counterfeit money," Sweeney said, sounding scared to even talk about it.

"Neither am I," said Rochenbach. "But what we know or don't know sometimes decides whether or not we live or die."

"Now you're threatening me?" Sweeney said. "If you're not a detective anymore, why do you even care?"

"I rode on a bank robbery, and then I find out I was being jackpotted by the father of the man I was riding with. Warren stuffed his bank with phony money. How would you feel?" He jammed the point of the Remington into Sweeney's back.

"Take it easy. I understand," Sweeney said. "All I can tell you is it wasn't the Canadians, like I thought it was. It was somebody close, maybe even in Gunn Point."

"You're not much help," Rochenbach said, believing the gunman had nothing more to tell him.

Sweeney half turned and looked at him over his shoulder, his hands still chest high.

"Hey, when you talk like that it makes me think you still are a damned Pinkerton agent."

"You don't want to know what I am," Rochenbach said. "But I promise you, I'm not a Pinkerton man—hell, I never was, not really." He grinned, knowing he was telling the truth for the first time in a long while.

Sweeney relaxed and lowered his hands an inch.

"All right, then, why are you holding a damn gun in my back?" he asked.

"How about this," said Rochenbach, "because you were trailing me? Because I know Roe Pindigo wants me dead."

"That's because he was afraid you'd jackpot his name to the law," said Sweeney. He shrugged. "Hell, you can't blame a man for getting a little concerned, can you?"

Rochenbach took a breath and let it out.

"I suppose not," said Rochenbach, steam wafting in his breath. "You can let your hands down."

"Damn, it's about time," said Sweeney, thinking, *That was easy enough.* . . . He lowered his hands and turned to face Rochenbach. "Can I have my hat back?"

"I hate to give it up," said Rochenbach. "Both Rudy's and Frawley's were too bloody to wear." As he spoke he reached up and took off the warm, battered Stetson and held it out.

"I bet they were," said Sweeney. "I saw those two poor bastards. Whooee! I hope you never get mad at me that way." He took the hat and put it back on.

"No reason I ever should, Del," Rochenbach said. He ran his fingers back through his tangled hair, already missing the wide-brimmed hat.

Sweeney adjusted his hat and gave him a steaming smile.

"You know, I could ride in ahead of you, talk to Roe Pindigo, soften him up some—tell him to get over his mad-on, stop wanting to kill you."

"Really?" said Rochenbach. "You'd do that for me?"

Sweeney shrugged and said, "Yeah . . . sure, why not?"

"Obliged," said Rochenbach, lowering the Remington, letting its hammer down.

"Consider it done," said Sweeney. He held his hand out and asked, "Can I have my Colt back? I just cleaned it last night."

Rochenbach gave him a thin smile.

"Yeah, sure, why not?" he said, repeating Sweeney's words. He pulled the Thunderer from his waist, flipped it around and handed it to Sweeney, butt first.

Sweeney took the gun with a grin. But the grin melted into a scowl as his hand closed around the gun butt and he jumped back a step.

"There, you son of a bitch!" he shouted, pulling the double-action Colt's trigger three times before realizing it wasn't firing. *Oh no!* Then he stared at Rochenbach with a strange look on his face.

Rochenbach raised his free hand and opened it, letting six bullets fall to the ground at his feet.

"Does this mean you're not going to soften Pindigo up for me?" he said quietly.

"Damn it! Damn it all! Damn it all to hell!" Sweeney bellowed. "Why would you unload my gun?"

"Because I figured you would ask for it back," Rochenbach said quietly.

Sweeney's eyes cut to his rifle lying five feet away, then back to Rochenbach.

"Dirty bastard!" he shrieked, throwing the Thunderer at the bareheaded Rochenbach.

Rochenbach ducked away from the flying Colt Thunderer and watched Sweeney leap toward the Spencer rifle. He reached out to arm's length, cocking the big Remington. It bucked once in his hand; Sweeney relaxed onto the snow, bits of his heart and muscle tissue lying in the dirt beneath him.

Rochenbach looked back and forth in the gray morning light as the shot echoed along the hills. He lowered the Remington into its holster, stooped down and gathered the Colt's bullets. He picked up the Colt Thunderer, wiped it off against his trouser leg and shoved it down into his waist. He stepped over, picked up Sweeney's Stetson and put it on again. He picked up the Spencer rifle, checked it and carried it with him into the dry wash where his bareback horse stood watching, a rope hanging from its muzzle.

Leading the horse from the dry wash to where

Sweeney's horse stood waiting, he swapped the saddle and bridle from Sweeney's horse onto his, then slapped Sweeney's horse on its rump and sent it trotting away.

He rummaged through Sweeney's saddlebags and pulled up a bottle of rye. He swirled it, pulled the cork, sniffed it, then took a long swig against the cold bite of morning. Recorking the bottle, he put it away and stood beside his horse for a minute taking quick stock of himself.

Two sidearms, a rifle . . . boots, coat, hat. All right. . . .

Not bad for his first night out of jail, he thought. He rounded his left shoulder, working some of the stiffness from it. It wasn't healed all the way, but it hadn't been that bad to start with—not enough to slow him down anyway. He stepped up into his saddle, turned the horse to the trail and rode away.

After helping Flora Ingrim safely tuck the sheriff away at her house, Summers had quietly gathered his horses from behind the doctor's house and led them all the way to the abandoned relay station at the far edge of town. Once he'd taken the horses inside and shut the door, he'd followed a terrible smell to a broken-down freight wagon where Grayson had dragged Langler's headless body. Summers looked in at the body lying in a dried circle of blood. He shook his head and walked back to the dusty building.

Inside the stone and timber ruins, he climbed through the trapdoor in the ceiling and to a platform thirty feet from the ground. After watching the streets, the doctor's house and the sheriff's office for a few minutes in the early morning light, he saw Lyle Fisk ride in from a back trail running northeast of town.

All right, he told himself, *let the day begin.* He climbed back down into the dusty building, checked his side-arm and his Winchester, walked out the front door and closed it behind himself. He'd decided he would lie low as much as he could, but otherwise treat this day like any other. With his rifle in hand, he pulled up his coat collar against the chilled morning air, circled wide away from the relay station, then walked toward Gramm's Restaurant from the opposite direction.

In the livery barn, Lyle Fisk stripped the saddle and bridle from his tired horse, led it into a stall and set a wooden bucket on the floor in front of the thirsty animal. He'd started toward the front barn door when it opened wide and Roe Pindigo stepped inside.

Fisk saw the angry look on Pindigo's face. He saw his big hand lying on his holstered Colt.

"I did like you said, Roe!" he said quickly. "We split up and took after each set of prints. I saw a man cutting across a ridgeline. It was still night, but when he sky-lined himself I could tell it wasn't Rochenbach!"

"Settle down, Fisk," Pindigo said, seeing fear in the gunman's eyes. He let his hand fall away from his gun butt. "Did you see any sign of Delbert on your way back?"

"I saw no sign of Sweeney or anybody else," said Fisk, calming down a little now that Pindigo's gun hand was down. "I can go look some more, if you want," he said, hoping Pindigo wouldn't say yes. "I'll need to saddle a fresh cayuse, though. Mine's done in."

"Forget it," Pindigo said. "It's just you and me left here until Big Jack arrives. It looks bad—two men dead, one still not back and Rochenbach running loose. Damn, what a mess," he added, shaking his head, looking down at the blood and matter on the straw-littered floor.

"Hell, Roe," said Fisk. "Don't count Delbert Sweeney out too quickly. He might just ride in any minute, Avrial Rochenbach's nuts hanging on a wire bracelet."

"Yeah . . . well, I just ain't looking for that to happen, Lyle," said Pindigo. "Go get yourself some breakfast. I'll be at the bank. "It looks like you and I will have to run the damn place until Big Jack gets here."

"Obliged," said Fisk.

The two turned and walked out of the barn and along the alleyway to the rear of the bank building.

"Bring me back some coffee," said Pindigo, pulling the bank door key from his trouser pocket as Fisk continued walking on toward the street.

When he got to Gramm's Restaurant, he swung the door open and walked in without seeing Summers at a rear table, his back to the wall, his rifle leaning beside him. But Summers saw him, and as he watched him cross the floor to a table along a wall, he eased his Colt from his holster, cocked it and laid it across his lap.

Fisk had started sitting down in his chair facing the door when he saw Summers and froze. Unsure of what to do, he cut a wary glance around the busy room, rose slowly, switched himself to the other side of the table and sat back down in the chair facing the rear wall, toward Summers.

Summers raised his coffee mug with his left hand and sipped from it. When he set the mug down, he scooted his empty plate away himself and sat staring straight at Fisk.

Fisk returned his stare, even as a young man in a

long apron carrying a coffeepot arrived and took his food order. But after the waiter had filled a mug with steaming coffee, Summers saw the gunman's expression soften a little. Eventually Fisk looked away, keeping Summers in his peripheral vision.

Good enough . . . , Summers thought. If the gunman didn't want to start a gunfight in a crowded restaurant, that suited him fine.

When the waiter left Fisk's table, Summers took the last drink of his coffee left-handed and slipped his Colt back into its holster. He took out a gold coin to pay for his meal and laid it beside his empty plate. Fisk watched intently, but he showed no signs of panicking and grabbing his gun.

Nice and easy . . . , Summers told himself, standing, reaching over and slowly raising his rifle from against the wall. As he closed a hand around the rifle stock, he saw Fisk grow more tense, but that was all right, he thought. As long as he made no sudden moves, everything was going to be just—

His thoughts were cut short by the loud crash of breaking dishes from the adjoining kitchen. The crash startled a woman sitting at a nearby table and she let out a short scream.

Uh-oh!

Seeing Fisk spring up from his chair, his Colt streaking up from its holster as he let out a short scream of his own, Summers had no choice. He swung the Winchester around at Fisk as the wild-eyed gunman fanned three shots at him. Two of the bullets streaked past Summers' head; the third bullet sliced across his left shoulder. Then the Winchester made its presence heard, and felt. The rifle bucked in Summers' hands; a blue-orange flame erupted from its barrel. The bullet nailed Fisk in the dead center of his chest and sent him spinning along the wall, blood flying as he toppled over an empty table to the floor.

Summers saw customers running out the front door. One heavyset man wearing striped trousers tried to jump through a partially opened window, but found himself stuck there, wiggling frantically. Dishes and cups fell from tables. A table overturned, spilling food, checkered tablecloth and all, to the floor.

Without a word, Summers walked through the kitchen, where he saw a cook drop down behind a freestanding shelf of dishes. He walked out the rear door, around the side of the building and took cover behind a stack of wooden shipping crates stacked at the front edge of an alleyway. He was a deputy. The shooting was in self-defense. He wasn't going to run, but he wasn't going to make himself an easy target either.

He untied a bandanna from around his neck and stuffed it under his shirt where the bullet had grazed his shoulder. He remained hidden from sight among the crates and watched the street between the bank and the sheriff's office.

Chapter 24

———

Within minutes of the shooting, Deputy Stiles showed up out in front of the restaurant, rifle in hand. Pindigo had joined him on the street after turning the sign on the bank's front door from open to closed. The two had walked the last fifteen yards together, looking back and forth as if leery of an ambush.

The restaurant owner, Denton Gramm, met the two at the open door of his restaurant. Morning customers shaken by the sudden burst of violence stood back in a half circle and stared. Eric Holt, the newsman, stood holding his pencil and pad, but not writing. A checkered cloth napkin hung as a bib from his shirt collar.

"Deputy Stiles, this is terrible!" Gramm said, wringing his thick hands. "This man opened fire on Will Summers for no reason at all." He gestured a hand toward the bloody corpse lying in a twisted heap on the floor.

"Where is Summers?" Stiles asked, looking around at the gathered townsfolk.

"Here I am, Deputy," said Summers, stepping out of

the alleyway, his Winchester in both hands, cocked and ready.

Pindigo turned quickly toward him, his hand going to the butt of his holstered Colt. Then he froze, seeing Summers' rife aimed at his belly.

"Take it easy, now, Deputy Summers," Stiles cautioned him, both him and Pindigo looking unnerved by Summers having walked up so close to them without their knowing it.

"Don't tell me," Summers said, stepping forward, "tell this man." He used the barrel of his rifle as a pointer.

For the sake of the townsfolk, Stiles half turned to Pindigo.

"Take it easy, Mr. Pindigo," he said. "We're all civilized people here."

Pindigo settled. He dropped his hand from his gun butt, yet kept a cold stare on Will Summers as Summers stepped closer to Stiles.

"What are you doing hiding back there in an alley, Deputy Summers?" Stiles asked.

"I wanted to make sure you two didn't come in shooting until you heard what happened here," Summers said. "It was self-defense, but I wanted to make sure you listened to how it happened."

"And how did it happen?" Stiles said.

"Ask those folks," Summers said.

"He's telling the truth, Deputy Stiles," said a dry goods drummer with a yellow streak of egg on his chin whiskers.

"We all saw it," a woman cut in. "This man was only protecting himself. The other man went crazy and just started shooting. Thank God for this man. Innocent people might have been killed."

"There you have it, Deputy," Summers said. "I wanted to make sure you got the story from eyewitnesses."

"Good enough, then," Stiles said, knowing there was nothing else he *could* say. He looked at a spot of blood that had seeped through Summers' coat before Summers had stuffed a bandanna against it. "Looks like you were hit. Come on, we'll take you to the doctor."

"I know the way," Summers said. He looked at Pindigo and said, "You best get back to the bank. It appears you've run out of help."

Pindigo gave him an icy stare, his jaw clenched tightly, fighting the urge to go for his gun.

"I've got more *help* coming," he said in a calm, civil tone.

"I look forward to meeting them," Summers replied in the same tone.

Pindigo started to say more on the matter, but Jason Jones, the surveyor, came running down the middle of street, his bowler hat having flown off his head.

"The newspaper's *on fire*! The *newspaper is on fire*!" he shouted as he ran. Seeing the crowd gathered out in front of the restaurant, he slid to a stop and waved them toward him. "For God's sake, come on! The newspaper is on fire!"

The crowd saw black oily smoke boiling upward from the clapboard building at the far end of the street. Orange flame licked and flickered within the smoke.

"Oh no!" shouted Eric Holt, snapping his writing pad shut. He sped toward the burning building. The onlookers raced along behind him, men stripping off their coats, knowing the hot, grueling job that lay before them.

"I have to get back to the bank," Pindigo said, as if

people would be coming to the bank while one of the town's larger buildings burned down. Yet no one questioned him as he turned and ran toward the bank.

"Here, we'll take my buggy!" the restaurant owner said to Stiles and Summers as he stripped off his long apron. He wadded it up and threw it into the backseat of a one-horse buggy standing at a hitch rail beside him. He stepped up into the driver's seat as the two deputies scrambled into the rig beside him.

Half standing, Winchester in hand, Summers stared ahead at the raging fire as the buggy rolled along the rutted street.

"Thank God the building stands off to itself a ways!" the restaurant owner shouted above the rumble of the buggy and cries of the townspeople as they ran along.

Ahead of the other townsfolk, Summers and Stiles both watched Holt, the newsman, running full speed, passing the others on his way to his newspaper. Then suddenly his feet left the ground and he flew even faster beneath the loud bark of a rifle shot.

"He's shot!" shouted the restaurant owner, seeing Holt slide a few feet on his face and come to a stop in a flurry of snow and dust.

"Let us off, Gramm!" said Summers, already searching the alleys and rooflines for any sign of a shooter, or smoke from his gun.

Gramm braked his buggy down hard, but Summers didn't wait for it to make a complete stop. He swung off the moving buggy at a run and headed for an alleyway. As he ran he called out to the townsfolk, "Get off the street!" as another shot exploded, this one only kicking up dirt in the middle of the street and sending the townsfolk scrambling for cover.

"What about the newspaper?" shouted a townsman who had stopped and stood looking all around with his arms spread.

"To hell with the newspaper. It's gone!" a running townsman cried out over his shoulder.

Another shot hit the dirt, this one five feet from the bewildered townsman's feet, yet close enough to cause him to panic and run shrieking for cover.

"Got it!" Summers said. He fired a quick return shot at a streak of smoke above the mercantile building. He heard his bullet ricochet off an iron support holding up a large sign.

He kept his Winchester raised to his shoulder, ready to take quick aim and fire again as soon as the shooter rose enough to make his next shot.

Down the street the clapboard-sided newspaper building stood totally consumed by smoke and tall, licking flames. There was no saving it, Summers thought, waiting, his finger on the trigger, his eyes on the roofline. In an alley across the street, Stiles stood watching him, his rifle also up, but appearing unsure of what he was going to aim at from his position.

After a moment, Summers lowered his rifle, realizing the ambusher must've moved after making the third shot, not wanting to reveal himself. At the far end of the street, the fire made quick work of the wooden structure while people remained behind cover and the newspaper owner lay dead in the street.

"Summers, I'm coming over there," Stiles called out, trying to keep his voice to a hushed tone.

Summers only nodded and scanned the roofline as Stiles ran in a crouch across the street and hurried into the alley beside him.

"What is all this?" he asked Summers, catching his breath, leaning back against a wall beside him.

"I don't know, maybe it's the Indians you saw the other day," Summers said wryly.

Stiles ignored the remark and said, "It looks like whoever it is didn't want the newspaper saved?"

"Then it looks like he got what he wanted," Summers said, cutting a glance toward the raging inferno. As he watched, a couple of bolder townsmen ventured out and hurried to the water trough with empty buckets in hand.

Summers and Stiles watched the roofline as more men appeared and formed a bucket brigade between the trough and the fire.

Stiles shook his head, his rifle lowering away from the roofline a little.

"Who would do something like this?" he said.

"Maybe it was your pal Jack Warren," Summers said dryly. "Maybe the newsman said something that upset him."

"Holt has never said a bad word about Jack Warren," said Stiles.

"First time for everything," said Summers. "Maybe Jack Warren was afraid he was getting ready to."

Stiles looked at him.

"You're suspicious of everybody, aren't you, Summers?" he said.

"I wasn't until I got here," Summers said, lowering his rifle, deciding that whoever had been up there shooting was long gone by now.

Before Stiles could comment, Dr. Meadows came running from his office, his black bag in one hand, his other hand holding his derby hat atop his head. From the alleyway, Summers waved the doctor toward him and Stiles in the alley.

"Get in here, Doctor," Summers called out. Meadows saw him and veered over to the alley. He came to a halt and stood next to Stiles against the wall.

"Whew!" he said. "I haven't run that fast since Gettysburg." He looked around Summers toward Holt lying in the street. "I shouldn't have stopped here. I need to see if he's still alive."

"Get on the boardwalk and follow it to him, Doctor," said Summers. "Get to him and drag him out of the street. We'll cover the roof for you." He felt sure the ambusher was gone, but he wouldn't bet the doctor's life on it.

"Thank you both," said Meadows, looking from one to the other. "Here I go."

"Wait, Doctor," said Stiles. "How is Sheriff Goss doing?"

"Much better," Meadows said, passing Summers a guarded glance.

"Who's with him?" he asked. "Because I can go stay with him until you get back, if he's there alone."

The doctor looked at Summers again.

"Go on, Doctor," said Summers, "while I cover you."

The doctor took off at a run and slid to a halt beside the newsman. He grabbed him by his coat collar and dragged him off the street. Two townsmen dropped their buckets and ran over and helped him heft Holt onto the boardwalk under an overhang. Summers and Stiles watched the doctor check the man's heart and shake his head; the newsman was dead.

"What was that look between you and the doctor?" Stiles asked.

"Nothing," Summers said, lowering his rifle but still watching the roof above the mercantile store.

"Don't tell me 'nothing,' " said Stiles. "I saw it. You're up to something with the sheriff. I want to know what's going on," he demanded.

Summers turned facing him in the narrow alleyway, his Winchester barrel positioned to swing up at his face if need be.

"I sent Sheriff Goss out of town, Stiles," he said, only telling him half the truth. "By now he's a long ways from here."

"Why'd you do that?" Stiles asked with a stunned look.

"To keep you from killing him," Summers said, "the way you killed Harper. You choked Harper to death with the length of cut rein. I *suspect* that you tried to kill Sheriff Goss the next day, and failed. I sent him away somewhere safe, in case you tried it again."

"You're loco! Plumb out of your mind, Summers!" Stiles said. He wanted to swing his rifle around at him, but he saw that Summers had already taken the upper hand on the situation. With a quick flick of his hand, Summers could put the tip of the barrel right into his face. He wasn't going to do anything to initiate it.

"I think you tried to load him up with straight laudanum while he was weak, so he'd go to sleep and never wake up," Summers said.

"Oh? How exactly did I do something like that?" Stiles said, managing a tight, nervous smile.

"I don't know," Summers said. "I haven't figured it out yet, but I could tell by the way you acted that day. The way you looked when Doc Meadows told us the cat had knocked over the empty laudanum bottle that he'd filled with water."

"Cats, laudanum bottles?" Stiles said. "The judge would laugh you out of court. You've got no proof of anything, just a head full of suspicions."

"You're right, Stiles, suspicions are all I have right now," Summers said. "But I've seen how you are. The more I look at it, the clearer the picture gets. It'll come to me soon enough."

"It better come quick, Summers," Stiles said. "Big Jack and his men are riding into town today. I've got news for you. He's going to kill you as soon as he gets here." He gave a dark grin. "I'm going to watch."

"No, you're not," Summers said confidently.

Stiles gave him a curious look.

"I've got news for *you*," Summers said. "Jack Warren and his men are already here, and you're not going anywhere."

Summers' rifle barrel swung up, struck Stiles' chin and set his head up perfectly. He jerked the rifle butt up and back and jammed it hard into the middle of Stiles' unsuspecting face.

Stiles slammed back against the wall and slid down.

Summers caught him before he fell over onto his side. He propped him back against the wall. Stiles sat there as limp as a scarecrow. His head lolled on his chest; blood ran freely from his shattered nose and his smashed lips.

Chapter 25

———

From the corner of the alley, Summers watched six horsemen ride into town from around the corner where the smoke and flames consuming the newspaper building had finally subsided under the relentless efforts of the bucket brigade. Steam and smoke still swirled and billowed above Gunn Point, but the flames inside the black smoke had lessened in wildly raging intensity and now appeared to struggle to cling to the edges of the charred framework.

The horsemen rode past the bucket brigade with hardly a sidelong glance and spread out abreast across the middle of the street. At the center of the riders, a few feet in front, leading them, rode Big Jack Warren. Summers recognized him from the portrait hanging inside the bank. Only, in the portrait Warren wore a black suit, a high white collar, a broad-striped tie and a wide smile.

Here on the dirt street Warren's tie and suit were gone. So was the smile. He wore a buckskin riding jacket, a tall Stetson and a bitter expression as his horse moved forward at a walk. The butt of a Winchester rested on his thigh. He kept his hand around the rifle, his finger inside the trigger guard.

Summers watched Roe Pindigo step out the door of the bank and lock it behind himself. Then Pindigo walked briskly up the middle of street, looked up at Jack Warren and pointed to where he'd last seen Summers and Stiles take shelter in the alley. Warren stopped his horse and gave a jerk of his head. Summers watched two of the men ride forward while the others stopped in line with Jack Warren.

One of the men, the half-breed, Two Horse Tuell, said to Luther Passe, "This feels as bad now as it did the other day. I wish to hell this horse trader had enough sense to get scared and get out of the territory."

"Maybe he's wishing the same thing about us," Passe replied, his eyes peeled on the alleyway Pindigo had pointed out to Jack Warren.

"Talk to me, Roe," Warren said, staring straight ahead as the two men rode their horses at a slow, cautious walk toward the alley. "I heard shooting the last mile."

"Somebody just shot Eric Holt from the rooftop," Pindigo said.

"I can't say that breaks me up any," Warren said with a private little smile.

"That's what I figured," said Pindigo. "I mentioned it in case whoever shot him is still up there." They both looked along the roofline.

"Where's the men who came here with you?" Warren asked.

"They're dead, Big Jack," Pindigo said flatly, both of them turning their eyes from the roofline to the alley.

"Summers killed them?" Warren asked.

"He killed Fisk just a short while ago," said Pindigo.

"Avrial Rochenbach killed Rudy and Frawley and escaped when they went to question him. Summers might have helped him, I don't know. Sweeney is missing. He went off trailing Rochenbach and never came back."

"So we still don't know if Rochenbach said anything to anybody?" Warren asked, shaking his head a little.

"Will it even matter after today?" Pindigo asked.

"No, I expect it won't," said Warren. "I'm killing Will Summers for shooting Little Jackie and messing up my whole deal. But this is as good a time as any to get rid of anybody else who's no more use to us."

"Including the sheriff?" Pindigo asked.

"Yeah, kill him," said Warren casually. "If the doctor is there and tries to stop you, kill him too."

"Suits me, Big Jack," said Pindigo. He looked at Dr. Meadows, who had turned and walked back along the boardwalk toward his office after checking on the dead newsman. "I'm on my way," he added. He walked hurriedly for a few yards and called out to Dr. Meadows, "Hey, Doc, wait up."

Big Jack nodded at his other three riders and they nudged their horses forward at a walk toward the alley Two Horse Tuell and Luther Passe had turned into.

As they rode forward, Warren saw Pindigo turn away from the doctor and come trotting back along the middle of the street.

"The doctor says the sheriff is gone, Big Jack," Pindigo said, sidling up to Warren.

Warren stopped his horse and stared down at him.

Pindigo said, "He told me Will Summers took him someplace out of town—*somewhere safe* is what Summers told him."

"Like hell," said Warren. "He's here somewhere. So is Summers. We'll have to search them out . . . door to door if we have to."

"Big Jack, over here," said Passe, backing his horse out of the alley, leading the half-breed's horse beside him. Two Horse walked out of the alley with Deputy Stiles wobbling along beside him, his face covered with blood, an arm looped over the half-breed's shoulder to keep him on his feet.

"What the bloody hell is going on here?" Jack Warren shouted, looking at Stiles, then all around the street. "All of you, get off your horses! Spread out and turn this town upside down! Find Will Summers and bring him to me! I'm going to quarter him like a beef right here in the street!"

The three mounted gunmen swung down from their saddles and slapped their horses' rumps, sending the animals bolting away. They hurried off in three different directions, while the townsmen in the bucket brigade watched as they continued passing buckets of water from one pair of hands to the other.

But just as the three men split up to begin searching, Will Summers stepped out from a narrow side street closer to the burning building and put a bullet through the chest of a gunman named Olsen Tillis.

Warren and the others turned toward the sound of the shot, but only in time to see Will Summers duck back out of sight and run away along the side street.

"Get that *son of a bitch*!" Warren shouted, firing his Winchester wildly, sending townsmen scrambling once again for cover.

Summers ran along the side street to an alley that led him back behind the row of buildings on the main street. He ducked down behind a stack of walk planks and watched until he saw two of the gunmen run to the end of the alley. They looked both ways, then turned and hurried back to the street.

As soon as they were out of sight, Summers ran in a crouch to the nearest alleyway between buildings, and ran back toward the main street.

"We're not going to play chase with this damned horse trader all day," Jack Warren said. He swung down from his saddle and slapped a hand to his horse's rump. Rifle in hand, he called out to the gunmen, "Be ready when he shows his face on the street again."

Pindigo walked over to where Two Horse stood leaning Stiles against the front of a building.

"You better show us something, Deputy," he said, threatening Stiles. "This is Mr. Warren's day for trimming back on what we don't need."

"I'm all right," Stiles said, shaking his bloody head. He jerked his rifle from Two Horse's hand when the half-breed held it out to him. "If I get him in my sights, *he's dead.*"

No sooner had Stiles spoken than Summers appeared at the edge of a building and fired a shot that lifted John Root off his feet and sent him slamming backward onto the ground. Root lay dead, his arm still in a sling from his last encounter with Will Summers the day Cherry had gotten shot.

As soon as Summers fired the shot, he ducked back out of sight. But this time before he had a chance to get away, a gunman named Buddy Moon fired three quick but accurate rounds from a big Colt. The bullets tore splinters from the edge of the building and caused

Summers to have to duck down in place instead of making a run for it. By the time Summers had collected himself and turned back to fire from cover, a steady barrage of bullets from the street kept him from taking aim.

"Keep him pinned there!" Warren shouted. To Pindigo and Stiles he said, "Get around the block, get in the alley behind him and push him onto the street. Let's have an end to this."

A long sliver of wood from the edge of the building had cut across Summers' brow. He wiped blood from his eyes and tried to get sighted on Buddy Moon, who stood half hidden behind a wagon out in front of the mercantile store. But Moon, Two Horse, Luther Passe and Jack Warren kept a steady barrage of gunfire on, keeping him pinned in place. Down the alley behind him, he saw Pindigo and Stiles; he turned and fired, sending them leaping for cover. They held their fire. But Summers knew the two wouldn't hold their fire long.

Warren knew he had him circled. He smiled to himself and raised a hand to get Moon and Two Horse to stop shooting. Down the street, the townspeople had abandoned the burning building and were watching the gun battle from behind whatever cover they could find.

"It's all over for you, *horse trader*," Warren called out. "We've got you surrounded front and rear. Now it's time you step out and face me for what you done to Little Jackie."

"This is not about me shooting Little Jackie," Summers said. "This is about me spoiling your attempt to rob your own bank."

Warren winced a little. He didn't need that kind of talk out here where the whole town could hear it.

"Call it what you will," he said. "But step out here and let's even up, just you and me."

"Fair enough," Summers said. But he knew it wasn't going to be a fair fight. Big Jack Warren wanted to put a bullet in his head. That much was true. But Summers knew that Warren would only do so after his men had first shot him full of holes.

"I don't believe you, Warren," Summers said. "If you had wanted a fair fight, you would have come here alone and called me out." As he spoke he looked back along the alley and saw where Pindigo and Stiles had hunkered down. It was going to get awfully bloody from here on, he told himself.

Warren gave a dark chuckle.

"Well, that's not how I did it," he said. "But you're coming out, else we'll shoot you into the ground where you stand."

"Tell your men to stay back out of it, Warren," Summers said, "and I will come out. If this is really about revenge for Little Jackie, you need to bring it down to just you and me."

To Warren's right, Moon said to Luther Passe and Two Horse under his breath, "The horse trader is right. Big Jack needs to chop him down himself."

"Are you going to start telling Big Jack how to do things?" Passe said to Buddy Moon.

Moon fell silent, his rifle resting over a hitch rail for support.

But Warren rose from behind the cover of a stack of nail kegs and stepped onto the dirt street. He stared toward the corner of the alley where Summers stood.

"Moon, Luther, Two Horse," he called back over his shoulder. Loud enough for Summers to hear him.

"Move down the street away from here. The horse trader and I are going to have our reckoning."

Moon and Luther looked at each other. Two Horse shook his head as if he knew better.

Warren said in a lowered tone of voice, "Be ready to kill this son of a bitch when I go for my gun."

Two Horse looked at Moon and Luther Passe with a faint, knowing grin.

"I don't like this," Moon grumbled. But he moved away along the street with the other two.

Summers stepped slowly out of the alley and side-stepped along the edge of the street. If Warren really wanted a fair fight, he would accommodate him, rightly enough, he thought. But even if it was a double cross, Summers knew he had to get out of the alley between Stiles and Pindigo and the men on the street.

So far, so good . . . , he told himself, not really believing it. If worse came to worst, he at least had a chance to duck and run.

"Tell Pindigo and Stiles to step out onto the street," he said. If he made a run, it would have to be down another alleyway. He didn't want those two already halfway down an alley with a head start.

Warren shrugged and said, "Roe, Stiles, both of you come on out. Watch the show."

The two moved out warily into the street, spreading out, half facing Warren, half facing Summers.

Warren and Summers moved around slowly until they faced each other down the middle of the street, twenty feet between them. Summers held his Winchester in his left hand, but his right hand poised at the Colt holstered on his hip.

He watched Warren pull his riding duster back

behind his holstered Colt and hold his hand poised near the gun butt. But as he reached for the Colt, he called out to the waiting gunmen, *"Kill him!"*

Not taken by surprise, Summers fell back along the street, firing as he went, toward the cover of a large freight wagon.

Even as bullets whistled past his head, he saw one of his shots nail Warren high in the chest and send him staggering about in place. Stiles and Pindigo were closest to him. He turned his shots toward them. But as he did so, he saw Stiles fall forward with a gaping bloody hole in his chest—hit from behind by a rifle shot from the roofline above the bank.

The roar of a rifle above them caused the gunmen to turn and look up just long enough to give Summers an edge. Instead of ducking behind the wagon, he dropped prone to the dirt, the butt of the Winchester coming to his shoulder. Here was his stand, he thought stubbornly, live or die.

His Winchester sent Pindigo flying backward into the dirt. As he turned to fire at the other gunmen, he saw another rifle shot from the roofline nail Luther Passe and send him flying brokenly to the dirt. Two Horse and Buddy Moon, seeing everyone falling around them, turned and ran without firing another shot. Big Jack Warren, staggering in the street, turned and raised his Colt toward them.

"You damned cowards!" he tried to shout in a broken, bloody voice.

"It's still you and me, Big Jack," Summers said, standing from the dirt, his Winchester smoking in his hand. He drew his Colt, raised it to arm's length and cocked it toward Warren.

"I don't . . . want no more," Warren said, almost in a pleading tone.

"I didn't figure you did," Summers said. "But I do." The Colt bucked once in his hand and Warren fell backward, dead on the ground. A puff of snow and dust rose around him.

Summers turned to face the roofline. He wasn't sure who was up there, but it was time he found out.

As townsfolk ventured out of hiding, Summers walked along the side of the bank building to the rear and ascended a set of wooden stairs to a platform where a ladder led ten feet up onto the tin roof.

As soon as he stepped onto the roof and looked across it toward the street, he saw Avrial Rochenbach lying hunched up against the front facade, a Spencer rifle lying across his lap.

"Jesus . . . ! So it was you," said Summers, seeing Rochenbach's bloody shoulder and left arm, the same shoulder he'd been wounded in the day of the bank robbery. As he walked toward the wounded man, he said, "Who shot you, Rock?"

"Take one guess," Rochenbach said flatly. "Who's shot me or cracked my head every time I turn around lately?"

Summers glanced around, then stooped down beside him.

"My shot hit you, earlier?" Summers said.

"Yep, a ricochet," said Rochenbach.

Summers shook his head and said, "I'm sorry, Rock. I had no idea you'd come back to help me."

"I didn't," Rochenbach said. "I came back to kill Holt and burn his newspaper to the ground. I saw what was going on. I couldn't leave you stuck in it, not after you saved my life."

"Obliged," said Summers. "But why'd you kill Holt and burn his newspaper down anyway?"

"Holt is the man who was running a counterfeit ring I've been investigating for a long time," Rochenbach said. "I came back, broke into his building and found the printing equipment he's been using. That's where Warren's phony money came from."

"So you were never out to nail Warren's men for bank robbery—?"

"No," said Rochenbach, "I just threw in with them to see what I could find out about the phony money that kept popping up across the territory. I'm not a Pinkerton, I work for the United States Secret Service—Treasury Department. Been there from the start, in 'sixty-five." He gave him a thin smile. "I'm the only agent who operates under the guise of being a Pinkerton gone bad."

"It seems to work for you," Summers said. "I'm baffled by it." He paused, then said, "But why'd you kill Holt? Why didn't you arrest him?"

"I seldom *arrest* anybody," Rochenbach said. "Word gets out. It makes it hard for me to keep doing my job among these hardcases. Besides, it was going to be hard to prove." He shrugged his good sholder.

"That's it?" Summers asked, sensing there was something more to it.

"No, there's more," Rochenbach admitted. "I wanted revenge. Holt got Cherry Atmore started on the dope. She had given me my first lead on Warren passing counterfeit money. She and I had gotten real close after that." He stared at Summers. "Do I need to say any more?"

"No, I suppose not," said Summers. "But the dope was her choice. Nobody made her smoke it."

"I know," said Rochenbach. "That's what everybody always says. But it's deeper than that. Anyway, he didn't start her on it because she was helping me. He didn't even know she was. He got her started on it because he was a sneaking, no-good turd. So I burned his building down for counterfeiting—I killed him for the grief he caused in Cherry's life. Hell of a strong position I'm in, being able to do something like that."

"Why are you telling me all this stuff, Rock?" said Summers. As he spoke he picked up the Spencer rifle from across Rochenbach's lap and helped him to his feet. "Aren't you afraid I'll tell?"

"Who are you going to tell, your horses?" Rochenbach smiled as they crossed the roof toward the ladder. "Anyway, who'd believe all this?"

"Beats me," said Summers, wiping blood from his forehead as they stopped and prepared to climb back down from the bank roof.

"All this will play down to a rich young man robbing his own father's bank. Everything else was just the aftermath of it." He grinned. "It's one more incident on this wild frontier that's best forgotten over time."

Summers shook his head and said, "The judge's men will be here sometime today. The less said about any of this, the better, as far as I'm concerned."

"That's the spirit," said Rochenbach. "Keep it simple."

"Yeah, simple . . . ," said Summers. He looked him up and down appraisingly. "Let's climb on down from here, get you over to the doctor." He added, "I've still got horses to deliver."

Avrial Rochenbach's story continues with
the first book in a brand-new series!
Don't miss a page of action from America's
most exciting Western author, Ralph Cotton.

MIDNIGHT RIDER

Coming from Signet April 2012.

Denver City, Colorado Territory

In the silvery light of dawn, U.S. Secret Service Agent Avrial Rochenbach stepped down from his big dun out in front of the seedy Great Westerner Hotel, located on the outskirts of Denver City. He unwrapped a wool muffler from around his bare head and left it hanging from his shoulders. He looked back and forth along the street, which had just started to come to life for the day. A curl of steam wafted in his breath.

Scabbed onto the right side of the hotel stood Andrew Grolin's Lucky Nut Saloon. On a faded, hand-painted sign above the saloon, a large nut—of a variety Rochenbach was unfamiliar with—stood upright between a large frothy mug of beer and two large tumbling dice.

Rochenbach spun his reins around an iron hitch rail, stepped onto the boardwalk and inside the Lucky Nut. Before he'd made three steps across the stone-tiled floor, two gunmen at the bar turned toward him quickly.

"Whoa! Stop yourself right there," one called out, a Henry rifle in his hand, leveled at Rochenbach. "Did you hear anybody say we're open for business yet?"

Rochenbach made no reply; he didn't stop either. He continued across the floor, his forearm carelessly shoving back the right side of his long wool coat, where a black-handled Remington stood across his lower belly.

On the other side of the bar, Andrew Grolin looked up from counting a thick stack of money, a big black cigar in his teeth. He stalled for a second before saying anything, observing how everyone handled themselves.

"Hey, sumbitch! Are you deaf or something?" the same gunman called out to Rochenbach, he and the other gunman spreading a few feet apart, ready for whatever came next.

Grolin already saw what was coming if he didn't do something to stop it. A belly rig like this? The slightest move of either of his men, this newcomer would pivot left a half turn. The big Remington would slip out of its holster as if his body had moved away from it and left it hanging midair. It would come up to arm's length, slick and fast—*bang, you're dead!* Grolin thought.

"It's all right, Spiller, I've been expecting this man," he said at the last second, before the scene he'd played out in his head began acting itself out on the floor.

"Whatever you say, boss," said Denton Spiller.

The two men backed a step; Spiller eyed the bareheaded newcomer up and down as Rochenbach stopped and returned his stare, his long wool coat still pushed back out of the way on his right side. The wool muffler hung from his shoulders.

"You need to be more careful how you enter a room,

mister," the gunman cautioned him, lowering his rifle barrel almost grudgingly.

"Obliged," Rochenbach said flatly, "I've been working on it." He let his coat fall back into place now that the rifle barrel wasn't pointed at him.

Rochenbach held the gunman's stare until Andrew Grolin took his cigar from his mouth and looked back and forth between the two, still appraising, still gauging the tensile of each man's will.

"Spiller," he said, "you and Pres meet Avrial Rochenbach." He turned his eyes to Rochenbach. "Rock, this is Denton Spiller and Preston Casings. Two of my best damn men."

Rochenbach nodded; the two nodded in return. None of the men raised their hands from gun level.

"I heard of you, Rochenbach," said Casings. "You're the Midnight Rider, the fellow who prefers working in the dark of night." He looked Rock up and down. "Also the fellow who got himself chased out of the Pinkertons."

"Really . . . ?" said Spiller to Rochenbach with a cold stare. "How does that feel, getting chased out?"

"I can show you," Rochenbach said.

Spiller started to bristle.

"Easy, men," Andrew Grolin said with a short, dark chuckle. He gestured to Spiller and said, "You and Pres take a walk. I want to talk to Rock here in private. He's going to be riding with us."

"Come on, Dent," said Pres, half turning toward the front door.

"*Rock*, huh? That's the name you go by?" Spiller asked, not giving it up yet.

Rock stared at him. So did Andrew Grolin. Ordinarily

Grolin would have had none of this—a man not doing what he was told right away. But he knew this was good. It showed him who he could count on when the going got tight.

"*Friends* call me that," Rochenbach said.

"Yeah? What do them who are *not your friends* call you?" Spiller asked, his contempt for this newcomer showing clearly in his eyes, his voice.

"Nothing, for long," said Rochenbach.

The threat was there, but it took a second for Denton Spiller to catch it, and that second was all Grolin needed to decide the better of the two—at least when it came to showing their fangs. It might be a different story when it came to hard testing. But for now, he'd seen enough. So far Rochenbach was living up to everything Grolin had heard about him.

"How's that walk coming along?" he asked Spiller in a stronger tone.

Spiller didn't answer. He jerked a nod toward the front door.

Grolin and Rochenbach watched as Casings followed Spiller out of the saloon.

After the two had moved along the street and out of sight, beyond reach of the large front window, Rock turned to face Grolin behind the bar.

"*Cowboy* Pres Casings . . . ," he said.

"Yep," said Grolin. He eyed Rochenbach. "Used to be a man who called him *Cowboy* would be warming his feet in hell before he got the words out of his mouth."

"I didn't name him," said Rock.

"I know," said Grolin, sweeping up the cash from atop the bar. "Call it friendly advice."

"Taken as such," Rock said.

"I was surprised you heard of him at first," Grolin said, eying Rochenbach. "Then I remembered you must know lots about us ol' boys who drop gun hammers for a living."

"I do," said Rock. "Does it bother you, my having worked for the law?" he asked.

"I don't *bother* easily," said Grolin. "Not to piss on your hoecake, but I don't figure you worked for the rightful law. You worked for the *Allen Pinkerton law.* I see a vast difference between the two."

"See it how it suits you," said Rock. "It makes me no difference. Whatever I was, I'm a long rider now." He gave a slight shrug. "I figure Juan Sodorez and some of his *pistoleros* must've vouched for me, else we wouldn't be standing here talking all tough and friendly to each other."

Grolin chuckled under his breath and seemed to relax a little.

"I expected you three weeks ago," he said. "Wondered if I ought to come looking for you."

"You wouldn't have wanted to be where I was three weeks ago," Rochenbach said.

"Oh . . . ?" Grolin said. "Is that where your forehead ran into a rifle butt?"

Rochenbach touched his fingers deftly to his forehead, his dark-circled eyes and mending nose.

"It's a long story," said Rock. "But yes, I did stop a rifle butt up at Gunn Point."

"I see," said Grolin. "Was it over a whore, or over a card game?"

"Does it matter?" Rock asked.

Grolin grinned. "I'd like to think you were late for a good reason."

Rochenbach could tell by the look in his eyes that he had already heard what had happened in Gunn Point. He wasn't going to offer any more than he had to on the matter.

"I don't remember," he said. "It might have been both."

"But nothing you want to talk about," Grolin concluded.

"Right," Rochenbach said, "nothing *worth* talking about, that is." He nodded at a coffeepot sitting on a tray behind the polished bar. "Not as important as a hot mug of coffee—hearing what you've got in mind for us." He kept his gaze on Grolin.

Outside on the street, Denton Spiller and Preston Casings walked along in the grainy dawn light and stopped at a public fire burning out in front of a blacksmith and ironmongering shop. They stared at a ragged old man until he stopped warming his rough, calloused hands and walked away from the fire. They stood in his place and warmed their hands as a two-pound forging hammer rang against an anvil in the background.

Spiller rolled himself a smoke and lit it carefully on a licking flame. Behind them on the street, steam wafted in the breath of passing wagon horses, pulling their loads.

"What do you think?" he asked Pres Casings. He blew out a stream of gray smoke.

"About what?" Casings replied, wringing his gloved hands near the flames.

Spiller stared at him with a no-nonsense look and took another draw.

"Oh, you mean Rochenbach," Casings said.

"Yeah, I mean Rochenbach," Spiller said in a short tone. "What the hell else would I be talking about?"

"How would I know?" said Casings, his voice equally testy. "Any number of things, I reckon."

Spiller shook his head and stared back toward the Lucky Nut. He drew on the thin cigarette between his lips.

"Anyway, I don't trust the sumbitch. I don't trust any man who once wore a badge," he added.

"You can't hold it against a man," said Casings. "A lot of lawmen get tangled up in things and go afoul of the law."

Spiller took a breath and let it out, considering Casings' words.

"Yeah," he said, "that's true enough. Still, I can't trust one. I believe there's a peculiar, gnawing little animal lives inside a man that makes him want to work for the law."

"I can see that," said Casings, nodding, warming his hands. "But a man can change his mind, decide to hell with the law and go his own way."

"Yeah," said Spiller, looking back from the saloon and into the fire. "But once he turns outlaw, I wonder what's become of that gnawing little animal. It still has to be fed, don't it?"

Casings didn't try to answer. He shook his head slowly and stared into the fire.

"I expect if Grolin wants Rochenbach with us, he's *with us*, like it or not," he said. He paused reflectively. Then he added, "Everything I've heard of him, he's a straight-up outlaw, no doubt about it. Maybe you just worry too much."

"Get this straight, Pres," Spiller said in a strong tone. "I don't worry about a *damn thing*." He coughed and blew smoke around the cigarette in his lips. "The only thing that worries me about hanging is that they tie the knot wrong."

"That would worry me too," said Casings. "Maybe they'd let me tie it myself."

"Naw, they won't let you do it," said Spiller. "I asked around."

The two chuckled darkly and warmed their hands.

"Still, I'm going to watch this Rochenbach sumbitch like a hawk," Spiller said, staring back toward the saloon in dawn's light.

No other series packs this much heat!

THE TRAILSMAN

Follow the trail of Penguin's Action Westerns at
penguin.com/actionwesterns

"A writer in the tradition of Louis L'Amour and
Zane Grey!" —*Huntsville Times*

National Bestselling Author

RALPH COMPTON

**Available wherever books are sold or at
penguin.com**

Charles G. West

"RARELY HAS AN AUTHOR PAINTED THE
GREAT AMERICAN WEST IN STROKES SO
BOLD, VIVID AND TRUE."
—RALPH COMPTON

Outlaw Pass

When impetuous Jake Blaine doesn't return home
from a prospecting trip in the gold-rich gulches of
Montana, his staid older brother Adam sets out to
find him. But his investigation draws unwanted
attention from some very dangerous men—who are
more than happy to bury Adam to keep their secrets.

Also Available
Left Hand of the Law
Thunder Over Lolo Pass
Ride the High Range
War Cry
Storm in Paradise Valley
Shoot-out at Broken Bow
The Blackfoot Trail
Lawless Prairie

**Available wherever books are sold or at
penguin.com**

GRITTY WESTERN ACTION FROM
USA Today BESTSELLING AUTHOR

RALPH COTTON

NIGHTFALL AT LITTLE ACES

AMBUSH AT SHADOW VALLEY

RIDE TO HELL'S GATE

GUNMEN OF THE DESERT SANDS

SHOWDOWN AT HOLE-IN-THE-WALL

RIDERS FROM LONG PINES

CROSSING FIRE RIVER

ESCAPE FROM FIRE RIVER

GUN COUNTRY

FIGHTING MEN

HANGING IN WILD WIND

BLACK VALLEY RIDERS

JUSTICE

CITY OF BAD MEN

GUN LAW

SUMMERS' HORSES

JACKPOT RIDGE

LAWMAN FROM NOGALES

SABRE'S EDGE

Available wherever books are sold or at
penguin.com